GW01086530

Trial of Thorns

Wicked Fae, Volume 1

Stacey Trombley

Published by Stacey Trombley, 2020.

TRIAL OF THORNS

First edition. March 4, 2020.

Written by Stacey Trombley.

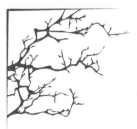

Caelynn

My bunkbed rattles beneath me and I sit up straight, hair grazing the uneven ceiling. I wince as bits of dried paint rain down on my lap.

My plain bedroom is dark and still. Shadows shift and pull, causing my stomach to flip pleasantly. Humans dislike the dark.

I love it.

I've always loved it. Unfortunately, there are some very bad creatures who also enjoy the magic of darkness. I blink the sleep from my eyes and immediately feel the swirl of magic in the air. Magic that doesn't belong in this place.

I swear under my breath as anxiety shoots through me. Though the top bunk is rickety and the mattress too hard, I'm warm and comfortable in my plush blanket—a gift from Raven this past Christmas. I'm going to have to leave it behind.

I'm going to have to leave *her* behind.

There is very little in my life that makes me happy. She is one of them. I shouldn't be surprised even that will be ripped from me now—my past mistakes are relentless in their haunting. *Who is hunting me today?* I wonder.

The house is quiet. The tremor is subtle enough it doesn't seem to have woken the others in the house, but I can feel the dark power coiling. Building. Rushing like a coming storm just on the horizon.

I've played this game many times before. Run, hide, and pretend to be a normal teenaged human *not* being hunted by fae royalty and evil monsters alike.

I brush the paint flecks from my hands and hop down from the bunk, pushing away every doubt. I have no time for feelings right now. There is only one option for me if they're coming.

Run. It's the only way to keep her safe.

The room is pitch dark, but I don't miss a beat, strolling out the door with sure steps and no hesitation.

"Caelynn!" a voice whisper yells just before I shut the door behind me. *Dammit, Raven.*

I pause and shake my head. The lovely human teenager from the bunk below me scrambles to follow me into the hall, brushing her wild black hair from her eyes.

"Go back to bed, Raven."

She crosses her arms. "Stop treating me like a child."

In the human world, she's almost an adult—she just turned seventeen. I get it. But she's not ready for the horrors outside these walls. So yes, I'm going to protect her whether she likes it or not.

"If you're sneaking out, so am I. You promised you'd take me to your next party." The floor trembles beneath our feet. "What is that?" she whispers.

I heave a dramatic sigh. Of course that's the only thing a human teenager would have on her mind. Parties. Boys. Girls. Fun.

"I'm not sneaking out for a party, Ray," I say, continue down the hall speaking under my breath. "I don't *want* to leave, but I—"

"You're leaving?" Raven is the second oldest of all the foster kids living in this home. Unlike me, she has two parents hoping to regain custody. If only they could kick the drug habit. They've tried. Her mother has almost made it work several times—only to let it slip through her fingers and Raven along with it.

My frame is slight, my eyes large and in the human-world, hazel. I look like a sixteen-year-old human, so that's what I pretend to be.

Everyone seems determined to protect me, despite the fact that I could crush them easier than blinking. It's tedious, being treated like a child, but it does have its perks. I am given a home—good or bad—without even having to ask for one. I have a place.

"I have to." I've told her entirely too much—about my life, my world, the magic in my blood. All things humans aren't supposed to know, but there's something about Raven that makes me feel—at home. Comfortable. I want her to know me. The real me. Because I'm fairly certain she's the only person in either world that could know everything and still love me.

She's the only person in the last decade to look at me like *this*. Her big eyes full of adoration and other emotions I don't dare name. My fingertips rest on her cheek and my stomach squeezes as she closes her eyes. "I always told you they'd come for me."

She knows I'm not human. And my enemies aren't either.

Her eyes pop open, apparently just now realizing what's really happening. "You didn't say they'd come in the form of a small earthquake."

"It'll get bigger." It'll most likely come in the form of something not-unlike a hurricane, but there's no need to elaborate. "I'll find you again, okay? I promise."

It's a stupid promise. It'll only put us both in danger, but I can't bear to abandon her like everyone else in her life.

She doesn't stop me as I pull away, and I skip down the stairs quietly. I almost make it to the front door without incident when someone grabs my wrist just inches shy of the door knob clenching tightly.

"Where do you think you're going?" Mrs. Collins, our foster mom stares at me with sharp angry eyes.

I swallow and take in a long calming breath, summoning my magic. It's annoying, but glamouring her won't be overly difficult. The darkness outside is closing in, and I only have moments before it could blow this place to bits, with me inside it.

"Oh!" I tilt my head innocently and breathe out long and slow, magic shimmering through the air. She sucks it in, chest heaving and then blinks rapidly. "You told me I could go out for a breath of fresh air—don't you remember?"

She blinks, eyes glossy. "No." Her voice is sharp. Firm.

I narrow my eyes and then swallow. *That can't be good.* "What?" I can see the magic at work in her so why didn't she—

"You have somewhere to be, Caelynn." I recognize the strange echo layered behind each word, and I suck in a breath.

I rip my arm from her grasp and leap for the door, realizing a beat too late why my magic didn't take effect.

Because Mrs. Collins has already been glamoured.

I RUN OUT INTO THE night. Dark tentacles wrap around my soul like an old friend. It feels so good it sends a shiver down my spine, overcoming the panic. *Dammit do I miss the night.* I miss the magic.

I don't have time to appreciate the welcoming because I am not alone in the darkness.

Caelynn, a hissing voice wisps through the wind, but it's not the inhuman sound that scares me the most. It's the soft—human—footsteps following behind me.

I whip around and grab Raven by the upper arms and drag her into the brush beside the road. "Ow!" she squeals.

My heart clenches. "God dammit, I don't care if I die," I say aloud in my anger. It would be an escape, in a way. "But I won't allow you to die because of me."

"If you're running away, I want to come." Her voice quivers.

"If I die, do you want to die too?"

"You promised you wouldn't leave me!" she says desperately, tears welling in her eyes. "Don't leave me, *please.*"

I suck in a breath, ignoring the pit in my stomach. That was another stupid promise. I don't want to leave her, but I'll break any promise to save her life.

"*We have business to attend to, Caelynn,*" the voice slithers from the inky blackness on the open street. The dark spirit is waiting for me. It wants me out in the open.

I press my forehead to Raven's, my eyes closed, trying desperately to remain calm. "Stay here," I hiss. "No matter what you hear. No matter what happens to me. Don't move until the sun rises—then go back into the house."

"What?" Her voice trembles.

"Trust me, okay?"

My heart slams into my chest, and I leave the coverage of the trees.

I could run. The creature even knows I could. He can track me when I'm sleeping and my guard is down. But if I veil myself, I can hide from anyone and anything.

Only problem is—I can't hide Raven. Not now.

I step out into the streetlight and take in long breaths, my head held high.

"Ahh, you are ready to face me, are you? Because of the human. Interesting."

My stomach clenches, and I summon every ounce of energy I have into my act. "You said you had business. I'm intrigued." I place my hand on my hip. I don't want his thoughts anywhere close to that girl.

Black smoke swirls in front of me, forming the silhouette of a man. I know better. This is not a man. This is the spirit of an evil fae. It's the form I'll take one day, when my time comes. Which very well may be today.

"What kind of business is it?" I ask. "My execution, perhaps?"

The glinting blackness explodes, rushing at me. I wince, but pain never comes. Only the tickling of a whisper in my ear. *Do you wish for death*? it asks, before curling back around and forming the silhouette again.

"Was banishment not punishment enough?" The creature's voice echoes through the streets. "You are a hero in our court, my lady."

I groan. "Don't call me that. I am no hero, nor a lady."

"Many in our world would disagree, did you not know that? The brave countess, willing to do anything to increase her court's status. You are quite respectable in many circles. Beloved in some."

I roll my eyes. "I murdered a fae prince and was banished from my own world. If that's what you find respectable—then you're all insane."

"A fae prince that just so happened to be next in line to rule over High Court? A right unfairly stripped from the Shadow Court over a hundred years ago? Yes, we know exactly what you did, my lady."

I grit my teeth, knowing I could never admit to being proud of my crime. Even though, in the darkest of moments—I am. That's what scares me most. That's what most assures me that I will become a wraith when I die.

"And if I told you my actions were not even remotely motived by anything political? I just killed a boy. That's it. I am deserving of my punishment."

"To be frank, my dear, your motives are meaningless. Your action spurred a worthy rebellion. You should be proud of that. You should own it."

"I should be proud of the worst thing I've ever done, just because you all took it and used it for your own gains?"

"Indeed."

I wince. The thought of being praised for something I still hate myself for is soul-crushing. "Why are you here?" I ask the wraith, my patience running thin. If he's not here to kill me—a legitimate shock, to be honest—what the hell is he here for?

"I have been sent with a message, from your queen."

I purse my lips. "The Queen of the Whisperwood? Sent me a message?

"Yeeeesss," the black form hisses.

Well, this conversation has not been what I'd expected.

"For many years there's been a campaign to reinstate your status. The Shadow Court argues that your actions were that of a soldier's in war and you should not be punished so harshly."

I blink and take a step back. That's ludicrous.

"Of course, the High Court would have nothing to do with it, but your name is quite popular, and the movement has gained momentum. So much so that the council has... agreed to a compromise."

I purse my lips. "What does that mean?"

"You see, our world is in peril. A plague we've dubbed the *scourge* is spreading through the land. Magic is failing in the places the scourge touches. Children are dying at an alarming rate. And we are in need of a champion to save the world of wild magic from utter destruction."

"You think I can be your champion? Of what? I'm no healer."

"No, there is only one cure for this disease, and we know where to find it. That is where you would come in."

I hold out my hand, palm up, waiting for the creature to go on.

"It is inside the Schorchedlands."

I swallow. The Schorchedlands are essentially fae hell. With unbearable cold, dead plants and animals that live in a frozen state of decay, where the souls of evil fae are entombed in wraith form—though they're occasionally set free by a bargain. "Only wraiths can go there," I say, "And why would a cure be there?"

"Not *only* wraiths. *Mostly* wraiths."

Of course. If they were going to lift my banishment, this would be what they'd ask of me. Nothing less awful could be considered.

"The illness began with a curse. A curse given by a sorcerer banished into the Schorchedlands. And now we need to get his spell book in order to reverse it."

"Great. Sounds like you have a solid plan. So, why don't you go get it?"

"Because I, my dear, have no physical form." He holds out his shadow hands. He couldn't carry a book. "And besides," he continues in a low hiss, "that would be no fun."

Of course. The wraith is only here for the intrigue. They enjoy the suffering of others.

"So you, a wraith, are here hoping to *save the world*?"

"I care not for the cure."

"Then why are you here?" I say slowly, firmly.

He rushes forward, shadows swirling around me. "I am looking for you," the shadows whisper around me. "The Shadow Court is my home, and I wish to see its power reinstated—or if not, at least make those in the seat of power squirm. I want to see the Luminescent Court's pain and rage as you walk into the competition."

That's what this is all about. Not me. I'd be willing to bet they all know I am nothing close to a hero and my actions had nothing to do with their stupid blood feud—they're just using me as an excuse.

My court was once influential and powerful, but their right to rule was stripped from them several centuries ago. They've been looking for revenge ever since. When I killed the next heir to the High Court, we should have ruled, they used that to fuel their rebellion.

"What competition?" I ask skeptically, measuring his words carefully.

"You will have the chance to escape your banishment entirely, but first, you must prove yourself. They won't choose just any champion, but the high courts have agreed to allow each of the fifteen courts to choose a champion. Any champion. You are ours. Your banishment will be temporarily lifted, and you may enter the fae realm, so long as you are in the trials."

"Trials..."

The smoke over his makeshift head curls into something like a smile. "The Trial of Thorns, to be exact."

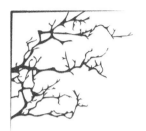

Rev

The moment she walks into the banquet hall, my vision is rimmed with black. Hatred—pure hatred fills my soul, dark and unending.

My father stands and his chair flips to the floor. His expression shows rage matching my own. It's uncommon for us to agree, ever. This evil fae is our one exception. We both hate her more than any single soul in the universe.

My mother gasps, placing a hand over her heart. Several sets of eyes dart to my family's table at the front of the room, then back at the horrendous creature they call *a countess*.

She's petite, with light blonde hair—ironic given her court is one of darkness. Her eyes are dull, dim, and I cross my arms, evaluating.

She killed my brother when she was still an adolescent. My powerful brother who was not only the heir to the Luminescent Court but the chosen heir to the High Court. He was going to be High King for a hundred years.

And yet he was killed by a fae who stands before us openly weak and powerless. How?

I shake my head. It doesn't matter. Though her dim eyes leave me with uncomfortable questions, it also tells me what I need to know.

She can't win.

She'll be easy to beat. Easy to kill.

The blond betrayer marches down the aisle, her eyes straight ahead, face determined. Emotionless. Her body is high fae—skin glistening, nails sharp, eyes gleaming. Her clothing, though, is human. Raggedy skinny jeans, her feet adorned with plain black boots and a black T-shirt with some symbol I don't recognize. Plain. Harsh. Ugly.

I curl my lip, not taking my eyes off of my sworn enemy. She does not even glance towards us. It makes me hate her even more.

A snowy owl soars through the open hall and its squawking covers the silence in the room. "What is she doing here?" my mother whispers.

"She's been invited to the trials," my father says calmly, though he still stands, watching her intently as she finds her place at the Shadow Court table. "I didn't think she'd have the gall to actually show up."

I clench my jaw. "I can't believe they would have the *gall* to invite her," I say. "Or the other High Lords to allow it."

"She is their champion?" my mother asks, her voice a mere whisper.

If I could kill this betrayer from here, I would. In fact, what would be the punishment? Banishment to the human world like she got for murdering a High Court heir? *Worth it.*

Whispers sound through the hall. Some of the most infamous fae in modern history have piled into this room, and yet it's her that holds the attention. Her, because she's the root of a feud. She's no one. Meaningless. Except that my family has sworn to kill her.

And I fully intend to fulfill that vow.

"SILENCE!" WE ALL TURN to face the source of the booming voice at the podium in the front of the room. The queen of all fae stands, facing every important faery in the world. Fae of every kind, from every court, have packed into the Flicker Court estate to witness these historic games.

The queen's auburn hair glimmers as she scans the room. Her face is harsh, sharp cheek bones and sunken eyes. Not a wrinkle in sight, but there are other signs of age. She was over one hundred when she was chosen as High Court Queen. Her hundred years of ruling is nearly passed. She's not anywhere near to death, but her energy runs low. Her retirement will be well met, I assume. Ten more years and still no new heir has been chosen.

"Tomorrow, we will begin the first Trial of Thorns in one thousand years," she announces. The room cheers. This is quite a historic event, indeed.

The Trial of Thorns is legendary. No one alive has witnessed one.

Every one hundred years we choose a new ruler of the High Court—that is about the only thing that remains the same today. How we chose our rulers was quite different a millennia ago.

In the past, all twelve original courts would compete, sending their most elite young people. The winner would become the next high ruler.

This barbaric ritual not only resulted in killing off some of the strongest fae, it often resulted in a very violent king or queen. One who lusted for power and had been willing to rip and steal their way to the top.

Things have changed significantly in the last few thousand years. The courts have changed, and the way we choose our ruler is entirely different—more civilized.

After many wars and splits and betrayals, there are now fifteen courts, instead of twelve, but only eight of those are "ruling" courts. The others are lesser. Weaker. The High Court ruler still changes every hundred years, but they are chosen politically and only from the eight strongest courts.

"Instead of choosing a ruler, we will be choosing a hero. A savior of our entire realm."

I clench my teeth. It doesn't matter what the queen tells us, because she still has not chosen a replacement heir—those of the lesser courts think this is their chance to reclaim their power. They think if a lesser court wins, they'll stand a chance at having a High Court ruler again.

"Our champions have been chosen and will compete to become the savior of our world. Most of you have witnessed the plague known as the scourge. Our forests are decaying, our precious children dying, our cities crumbling."

Much of our infrastructure is based on magic, so not only are fae dying but our very way of life—clean water and crops, transportation and communication—has dissolved where the scourge has hit.

"As the scourge grows, so shrinks our hope to outlive it. But today, I am here to tell you that there is a cure."

The room breaks into applause.

"The High Court, the council, and every ruling court has spent the last several years seeking a way to save our world, our people. We have found the source and learned how to stop it."

The room hushes. Even as heir to one of the ruling courts, this is information I know little of. We've been told of a cure, but not the details of how it was found.

"Deep inside the Schorchedlands, the cure has been hidden. We require a savior to retrieve it. Since the cursed walls of our hell will only allow one living soul to return every year, we will choose only one. The strongest. The most cunning. A champion that will not fail us. Each court has been given the opportunity to choose their champion. The Trial of Thorns will decide only one victor to become our world's savior."

The crowd claps politely, eyes darting to examine the fifteen courts and their supposed champions. Many are well-known and unsurprising.

My brother was the previous High Court heir. Until that no-one betrayer from the Shadow Court murdered him in cold blood.

After his death, most expected I'd be chosen in his stead. But after ten years, the queen has still made no such announcement. Now, the rumors of my weakness grow daily.

I am not weak, and I intend to prove it. The other courts have propelled the rumors that I am lacking to promote their own agendas. *Why else would the Queen refuse me*? They ask. Truthfully, that's a question I'd like answered myself.

"Tomorrow, we will begin, but there is one provision I must make clear here and now. No champion is to be harmed. If any champion dies by another fae's hand—any fae—outside of the trials, the punishment will be steep. The killer will be put to death immediately. Without trial."

I twist away from the queen to watch my sworn enemy. Thin and beautiful. Aloof. Her face fill of disdain. I'm going to kill her at my first opportunity. Though I am not the only one who will try. The queen knows this, which I assume is why she's set this rule so clearly and forcefully.

I can't kill her yet. But I noticed the wording in the queen's warning.

Any champion that is killed *outside of the trials* will incur a steep punishment. But if they happen during the trials?

My lips turn up into a bitter smile and acidic joy fills my heart. I have my plan.

She'll see it coming, of course. But that will only make the hunt that much more fun.

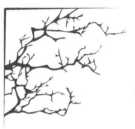

Caelynn

I keep my attention tight on the queen of the fae. Her amber eyes find mine, and I find no solace. She turns away quickly. Of course, she hates me as much as the others—I killed her chosen heir—but her position prompts her to at least *hide* it.

I can feel their heated gazes on me. Fae from all over the realm who hate me.

Reveln's eyes pierce me, so dull they appear more gray than silver.

I hold my gaze steady on the queen as she addresses the crowd, avoiding meeting Reveln's harsh stare. Even so, I can't help but register several things about him in the precious instants my eyes dart his way then back.

He's filled out a lot since the last time I saw him, his body sharper, harder than as an adolescent. That's the thing about coming back here like this—I have a lot of history with the other contestants, even if I haven't interacted with them very much.

Rev— well, Rev more than anyone else.

His hair is dark, his shoulders broad, his eyes a dimmer silver than I remember—though I suspect I can blame myself for that. Seeing me causes him pain. That's a fact I've got to live with.

I may never see the full beauty of his eyes, so very much like his brother's. Eyes I darkened forever.

Finally, he turns his attention away from me and towards his queen, political favor winning out over his hatred. Now that I know he isn't watching my every move; I dare a glance up to the agitated bird perched in the rafter above. Her clucking has calmed into a dull murmur.

Then, I very carefully examine the fae prince I haven't seen in over a decade.

My gaze flicks to his hands first, thick fingers gripped in a tight fist, then up his muscled forearm covered in tattoos. *Those are new.* Black lines twist and curve like a maze of roots and thorns and disappear under the rolled sleeves of his grey tunic.

I continue my search over his body—my competition. My enemy.

I pass over his broad chest and shoulders, covered in a thick leather vest, quickly. Those only tell me what I already know—he is battle ready.

Past his long neck and sharp chin, my eyes linger on his plump lips, soft and delicate unlike every other part of his body. The brutal lines of his cheeks, the anger in his eyes.

Reveln is harsh and brutal and eager to kill.

Me. He's eager to kill *me*.

I didn't need to examine him so closely to come to this conclusion, but I could use the reminder. I'm sure he'll give me plenty of those in the coming days.

"Tomorrow we will begin," the queen says with her smooth, eerie tone, "by introducing each of our chosen champions. A representative of each and every court. Fifteen of our strongest fae will compete in this severe competition. At noon, our first challenge will begin. By the end of this month, our savior will be chosen."

The room begins a frantic whispering. I keep silent, focused straight ahead. Usually the trials would last for a minimum of three months. So this expedited version will prove to be intense.

"We will not cut from the number of trials or their severity. There will simply be less time to recuperate between challenges, which will be a realistic representation of what you will face if you are chosen for this important quest.

"As you all know, we do not have time to waste. We must choose our champion as quickly as is feasible. But even more importantly, we must ensure we choose the *right* one. Politics cannot play a role. Not in this. We must choose the fae that is the most powerful, resourceful, brave, and brutal. Only the strongest fae can survive the Schorchedlands, and so, only the strongest fae will win these trials."

Failure is indeed not an option. I've not yet seen the devastation with my own eyes, but I don't need to in order to understand the fate of faery in all forms is at risk. If they'd told me ten fae children have died from the scourge, I'd justify the trials. The number they've told me—three hundred—is inconceivable. That's nearly a quarter of all faerie children in our world. Because we age so slowly, children are rare. Children are precious.

I had considered leaving this world to their fate—I do not intend to take my place back in the Shadow Court, savior or not. But there are a few reasons I've decided to take the risk.

Firstly—pure pride. I am able to win this, and I will prove it.

Second, because I too believe every court should have the opportunity to rule, not only the most prosperous.

Three, for all the cruelty in this world of wicked fae, their love of children will always remain. And it remains in me.

I might be bad deep down. But I will fight for those that can't fight for themselves. And maybe, just maybe, if I save them, I'll redeem myself from my own condemnation. Maybe I'll be able to live with myself one day.

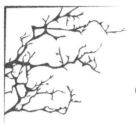

Caelynn

The lights twinkle above my head as I stand over the railing of the Flicker Court balcony, looking out upon the land I lost when I was still an adolescent. The rolling hills flow with magic and talking trees. Lights and power and beauty the human world could never even comprehend.

The trials are being held in the Flicker Court—home of fire fae—because this is the home of the current High Queen. Soon, the power of the High Court will shift to a new home. A new century, a new ruler, a new ruling court. The Luminescent Court should have been next, they still may be if Reveln is chosen as heir. But the Glistening Court, the Whirling Court, and the Crackling Court are all also in the running, from what I've heard. And the trials have the power to turn everything on its head.

A soft wind tickles over my skin like a caress. Magic I'd thought lost fills my lungs in the most glorious way. I'm hundreds of miles from my homelands in the Shadow Court, but I am in the faery realm, and that alone makes me feel whole. For just one quick passage of time, I am home. A blink, and soon it will be gone, like it barely existed at all.

I intend to make the most of it.

Most of the Flicker Court lands are desert, but the western edge of the territory collides with the black sea, which allows for a surprising amount of lush vegetation—all red and orange in hue. To the west is a golden forest and black sea beyond, to the east and for many miles north is barren desert.

I don't recognize the swirl of pathways and the swaying amber trees—bright and glistening. But I do recognize the whisper of wild magic, unwieldy and raw.

A sizzle of heat brushes my neck, and I shiver as his shadow falls over me. I blink quickly, surprised I hadn't heard anyone approach, but I feel his presence now—thick and heavy. His anger ripples off of him in waves.

"You came," is all he says, his voice low and somber.

I close my eyes and suppress a shiver. For a moment, I could pretend there wasn't animosity in his tone. I can pretend that he is glad to be near me. I can pretend my presence doesn't cause him pain.

"It was too tempting an offer," I say smoothly.

"To see your homeland one more time before you suffer a violent death?" His words are as sharp as his obsidian blades.

"Something like that." It will be fitting for him to end my miserable life. "I intend to win," I admit. Because I do. This competition was created to form ruthlessness. It was made to breed violence and sate the most power hungry of all faery.

I am the worst of them all.

And they don't know it yet, but I am also the strongest of them all. The cost of this power was higher than it's worth but since that price is long paid—I may as well use it for something important.

Not that I expect the competition to be easy. No, I am sure I'll face the brink of death a time or two before I end them all.

But I will win.

"Intention and completion are two very different things. The odds are stacked against you, *betrayer.*" He spits the last word, and I wince. A new pet name for me. *Lovely.*

"And I just want you to know," he continues slowly. He takes another step so close now I can feel his warmth. His rage. His power. The Luminescent Court is light and raw power. "When you fail, it will be me laughing over your cold corpse."

"Perhaps."

His warm breath tickles my ear, and I shiver in sick delight.

"I'm going to make your every moment torture. You will lament the day you allowed me to lay eyes on you again."

His stomping feet echo away, and I let out a long breath. "I expect nothing less," I say to the empty place he left behind.

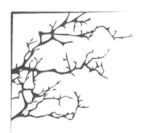

Rev

"I cannot believe she is here. What is Zanter-Leisha thinking?" Brielle tosses her arms up in frustration, her red hair a strangled mess from all the times she's run her fingers through it. "Allowing a fae murderer into her court?"

"Especially *that* fae murderer," Nante adds.

I cross my arms and sink deeper into the cushioned chair by the flickering fire. I don't blame their anger—Brielle hates the betrayer as much as anyone, and the High Queen is her great aunt. To her, this is a betrayal of very different kind.

"They announced pardon for any fae who enters and wins, long before the Shadow Court chose a champion," Rook says in a flat voice. Always logical.

"Absurd!" Brielle says. "They knew. They knew the first moment they could get that girl back through the fae land gates, they'd do it. It fuels their damn rebellion."

I blink at her insight. "True." Although, it's only the beginning of a rebellion, the whisper of discontent. No violent action has been taken. Yet. Part of me wonders if allowing the lesser courts to enter—with the expectation they'll lose quickly—was in an effort to quiet the rebellion, rather than fuel it.

See, we're gracious enough to give you a chance.

My emotions have been so strong for the last several hours that now I am simply exhausted. She is here. She will die. That's all I need to know.

I care about winning. I care about solidifying my place as heir to the High Court.

Today is the final day before the trials begin, and I am already in a good place. I have friends in several of the highest-ranking courts, and we will all work together. Brielle is from the Flicker Court and has been close to our family since before my brother's death. Rook is an old friend from the Twisted Court, which neighbors my own. Both powerful allies. Prickanante is Brielle's tagalong friend from the Frost Court. She's not very strong, but she's a number, and I'll take it.

"How are you so calm?" Brielle huffs, the flames behind her blazing, twisting and then settling back down.

"I'm focused. Winning is what matters now." The sparks flutter through the air before fading into nothing.

"So, you've... accepted it? Your sworn enemy. Your brother's murderer has the chance to become a hero in our world and... you don't care?"

I clench my jaw and sit forward, pressing my forefinger to my temple. "Of course I care," I say with a sharp anger. "I'm simply focusing my rage into something more productive than grumbling."

She rolls her eyes and snarls.

Brielle hates the witch as much as any of us, so I cannot blame her for her passionate reaction. She'd barely known my brother, but they were fated mates. She would have been his bride. His lover. His queen. Together, they'd been destined to have an important child.

That future is gone now, all because of the Shadow Court witch.

"Fine. Whatever. Be all zen about it. But why? Tell me why they'd do this, to you, your family, your court, to me?"

I sigh. "Because this trial is about more than politics."

Her eyes flare, the fire popping along with her. "What does that mean?"

I stand, facing the fire, my hands clasped behind my back. "They want the best fae to win. It doesn't matter what that means for our political world. Feuds and power struggles no longer matter. Our very survival is at risk. That is what matters."

I bite my tongue from continuing, as my father's harsh words come back to me. Words I don't want to recount to my allies. To my competition.

My weakness. My father says that's the reason they've opened the competition to the lesser courts—the High Court's heirs are not strong enough. If I were indisputably strong enough to lead, they'd have just picked me as the savior. They'd have chosen me as the High Court heir.

But the queen isn't impressed with her options, so they devised a competition to prove ourselves.

They let *her* into the competition because I wasn't good enough.

It's bull, of course. My father will just find any reason to put me down.

Brielle doesn't respond, but her eyes watch me closely. I pretend not to notice how they linger on my abdomen. Her mate has been dead for over a decade. I cannot blame her for noticing other males.

"You haven't seen the scourge at its height," I tell her. "I have. I've seen what we're facing. I've seen what will happen to our people if we don't stop it."

"And? You'd let your brother's murderer become a hero in order to save us?"

"No. I'd let you all burn to get my revenge," I admit. At least, to this, she smiles. "I am calm not because I don't care but because I don't believe there is even the slightest chance the shadow witch gets within a mile of the winner's circle. She's weak—did you notice the color of her eyes?"

She purses her lips. "She's from the Shadow Court. I assumed her eye color is black like her soul."

I smirk. "Shadow Court eyes are sometimes dark but always with a flicker or border of light. Flecks of gold or a rim of silver. Dull eyes, even to them, still only means one thing."

Rook stands, a wicked smile crossing his face. "She's weak."

I nod. Even if she did have power strong enough to compete—she's out of practice after living as a human for ten years.

"She's no one. She'll fail quickly and easily. And I'm calm because I have a plan."

"Oh," Nante says, leaning forward to hear the gossip. She's the Frost Court champion, but she's weak. The only reason she'll make it far in the competition is because of her friends—us. "What is it? It's not like you can just kill her."

Rook's eyebrows flick up. "Historically, many fae have died during the trials."

"Indeed they have," I say low, watching the flames dance. "I find it unlikely this girl makes it through these challenges with her life intact."

Caelynn

"You have nothing to prove to us, Caelynn."

I blink and look up to the elderly fae woman. The Shadow Court queen, Queen of the Whisperwood—my home. She is small, feeble, her face sallow, skin thick and scaly. She is nearly five hundred years old and beloved by our people. But her power is limited. We are a weak court.

"You are a hero to us. As only a child you defeated a foe much stronger than yourself. You are what we all aim to be."

I shiver. *They aim to be murderers?*

Yes, I killed the heir to a rival court. I made the highest of fae courts fall into despair. Made them turn their eye to our lesser court. I killed an unkind fae that would have made an awful king.

But I killed a fae when I didn't need to. If I'd known why, what possible purpose his death served, perhaps I wouldn't hate myself so fully. Perhaps if I hadn't known what it would cost me. Perhaps if it had been my own choice.

But none of those things are true. I lost a future. I lost a people. I lost myself. For someone else's gain.

So my people, my queen, they look at me with respect. With appreciation. And I hate every second of it.

I so much more enjoy the hatred streaming from those nameless faces. The sneers. The jabs. Those I deserve. And once the pain comes, I will relish it. I will thrive in the dark despair that has become synonymous with my name.

I am destruction.

"Thank you." I don't mean it, but I know there is no point in correcting her. No point in telling her how much I hate myself for what I've done. The act they so cherish as putting our court on the map is the one thing I hate most about my life.

The fact that I liked it—the moment his life seeped from his body, the rush of power that filled me—makes me hate myself even more.

"I am sorry your family couldn't make it. They had other... engagements."

I hadn't asked about them. I have no siblings, and my parents are less impressed with my actions than the rest of my people. Especially considering, along with my banishment, I was forced to be disinherited, leaving my now barren mother without even the possibility of an heir. Never will my ancestors have another queen.

I've doomed them even as I lifted my court out of obscurity. Ironic.

A large male fae walks into the room, his chin lifted high.

"Brax here will show you to your room in the estate. You'll be on the same floor as the other champions. Which I understand may cause some... interesting situations. All of the champions know the cost if they attack you outside of the challenges—they will be put to death without trial.

None would risk it. But even so, to be safe, I am appointing you a guard who will be stationed outside your room at all times."

A single guard? What exactly will that do? The champions are supposed to be the strongest of all the fae in the land. Of course many were picked for political posturing when others are really stronger, but Rev and his allies? They hate me and would easily overpower any single guard my court could provide. No, the High Queen's warning is my only saving grace here. Because those two wouldn't risk their lives or their positions in order to openly kill me.

For that, they'll wait until the trials to begin.

A bird squawks, and I turn my head, grimacing.

Its beautiful white feathers ripple as it soars over us, circling like a bird of prey.

"Friend of yours?" The queen asks, and I cross my arms.

I take in a long breath. The queen isn't a threat, but what if someone else has made the connection? The owl dips down and lands on the banister beside us. "Shoo!" I tell it, swatting the creature away. It screeches in annoyance and flies away.

Brax chuckles, an eyebrow raised.

"Do you require anything else before I retire?" The queen asks.

I swallow. "No, thank you." I bow, my light hair swaying toward the ground as I do.

"I am looking forward to watching you defeat your enemies tomorrow. You will be great. I'm certain of it!"

I smile. That is the only thing I can agree with her on. I will be great.

Strategy may push me to conceal my true power as long as possible to keep the entrants guessing. No need to make my target any larger.

But by the end of the trials—I will be remembered for my power.

If the queen wants a show, I'll certainly give her one.

I MARCH TO THE WINDOW the moment the door to my chambers shuts behind me. I wave my hand out the window, and the snowy owl lands on my arm, talons scraping against my skin. I wince, but pull her inside.

I twist my neck, cracking it even as I flick my wrist. With a quick sizzle and pop, the bird explodes into the form of a slight female.

I leap onto the bed as her human squawking begins. "What the hell is wrong with you?" Raven squeals. "A bird? A BIRD!?"

My lips curl into a smile. "Hello, Raven. It's so good to see you again."

"I asked you to bring me to the fae realm, but I didn't mean as a flipping BIRD."

"It was the only way." I shrug. "I couldn't just bring a human along for the ride. Do you know how many people want me dead? Anything attached to me is in danger, which is why you need to stay away from me in public. And for God's sake stop squawking everywhere you go!"

I couldn't leave Raven behind, not when she looked at me with those big puppy-dog eyes, begging me to take her along. When her bottom lip trembled, I was reminded of the last time her mother relapsed. She nearly died from the overdose.

Raven found her mother unconscious, called 911, then me. I can't unsee the state she was in. Curled into a ball, shivering. Eyes red.

I vowed I'd do anything to stop her from feeling that way again.

So, when I told her I was going to the fae realm she begged me not to leave her—I couldn't do it.

"You couldn't even make me a *raven*?" she shakes her head. "My name is Raven, and you turn me into an OWL? What the hell is that about?"

"Quiet your voice," I scold her, attempting to hide a grin. "No one can know you're here. Humans aren't allowed to return to the human world—ever—once they see this place. So, if you still want a regular life, you'll remain quiet."

She opens her mouth to respond, but I beat her to it. "Unless you'd rather go back home now. I can't promise you'll be completely safe here, there are dangers everywhere. So just say the word, and I'll take you back."

She heaves a huge, dramatic sigh. "I don't want to go home."

"Even if it means being a bird during the day?"

She purses her lips in a silly pout. "Fine. But seriously, can I be an actual raven instead? Those things are so *cool*."

I smile, warmth growing in my chest. "I chose an owl because it's less likely to be linked to me. Ravens are the bird of my people. If they see you as a raven, they may think you're my spy, and you'd become a target."

Raven stumbles over to the bed and flops down on her back, hair flying.

"Maybe I'll change you into a raven later. Changing your form so no one notices a pattern isn't a bad idea. But you're going to have to wait until at least after the first trial."

"Fine." She sighs.

"Do you forgive me for turning you into an owl?" I roll to face her.

"At least you didn't leave me behind." There she goes, looking at me like that again. Adoration that awakens me and terrifies me at the same time.

"As long as you want to be with me, I won't leave you." I'm desperate for friends as much as she is. "Unless... unless you'll inevitably die if you stay. This place is... harsh. And if I win, you cannot enter the Schorchedlands with me."

"Why?" she whispers, turning her dark brown eyes to me. Our faces are only inches apart. I smile as I meet her soft eyes. I'm quiet for a long while. She's nearly an adult in the human world, but she's still so young. Innocent. Lovely. She deserves so much more from life than she's been given.

"Besides the fact that it's basically fae hell? Full of decay and evil spirits of ancient and powerful fae?" I turn my gaze back to the ceiling.

"Yes, besides that."

"Because only one person can enter and return. That would include a human masquerading as an owl."

"So, if I followed you, I'd never be able to leave that place?"

I pause. "No, you would."

I watch her eyebrows scrunch up in confusion.

"*I* wouldn't," I clarify. "I wouldn't leave you there."

She swallows. The Schorchedlands won't be pleasant, but I know I'll end up there eventually. My fate as a wraith has been inevitable for several years. So, if it was between me and her? This beautiful young woman who hasn't had a chance at life? I would choose her without hesitation every time.

"You'll come back, though, right?"

"Yes, I'll come back."

"So, who's that guy?" Her voice leaps, full of energy and life once again.

"Which one?"

"THE one. Come on. The one who came to you all smoldering on that balcony. The one who watched you the whole meeting today."

"The one who threatened to make my life miserable and implied he'd kill me?"

"Yup, that one."

My lip ticks up into a half smile, but there's no life in it. No light. That's a damned loaded question if I ever heard one.

"I heard the others call him Rev. He's could rev my engine any time."

I snort, uncharacteristic laughter bubbling up in my chest.

She chuckles alongside of me and I thank God for Raven, not for the first time, and not for the last, I'm sure.

Every moment I'm with her, she pulls me out of my own despair. I don't think she even realizes she does it.

She continues giggling, and I can't stop smiling as I watch her, the life inside of her glowing in a way only I can see. Here, in this realm, she's dim and lacking because she holds no magic. But I see the truth that's more than physical. Raven is bright.

"It's true." She shrugs. "But seriously, who is he?"

I take in a long breath. My moment of joy dies too quickly as the acid of reality swirls back through my stomach.

"His name is Reveln," I say flatly. All laughter gone. "He hates me, and those threats weren't idle. He's going to make my time here torture."

"Why?" She sits up, watching my expression.

"Because I deserve it."

"Stop it. No you don't!"

"I killed his brother."

She's quiet for a long while, watching me. Studying me. "How? Like a car accident?"

"No." I sit up, my back facing her. "Like I shoved a dagger into his chest and watched until his life left him."

I don't have the courage to look at her expression. Will she hate me like the rest of them when she realizes what I am? Will she fear me? She knew I'd done something bad to be banished from the fae realm, but I'd never told her what. I didn't want to.

I didn't want it to change the way she sees me once she knew I was a murderer.

"I don't understand," she whispers.

"It's a long story, okay?" I stand, walking to the window looking out over the world I'd lost that day.

"How long ago? How old were you? How old was he?" She's trying to rationalize it. But the truth is, it doesn't really matter how or why. It doesn't matter that he deserved it.

I did it.

My hands ended someone's life.

"Over a decade ago. I was sixteen. He was thirty-nine—which for fae is adult, but still very young."

"Was he bad?"

"Yes. But that's not why I did it."

"Then why?"

"Because I had to."

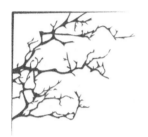

Rev

Despite my calm demeanor yesterday, the moment the sun set the anxiety surfaced.

I wasn't able to relax for even a moment last night. My muscles continued to clench, and my head ached, keeping me awake for hours until I finally gave up on sleep and sat in the common room next to the roaring fire. I stared at the flickering red flame, sunken into my new favorite cushioned chair until dawn. I wonder if Brielle sent her comforting magic to the fire place to keep it going so strongly all night.

"Rev, you awake?" Rook waves a hand in front of my face.

I blink into focus. "What?"

"I've been talking to you for five minutes. You must have been sleeping with your eyes open."

I shake the fog from my mind. "Yeah. Didn't sleep much last night."

"I told you, you should have taken a sleeping draft. You'll be hurting during today's challenge."

"I'll be fine," I rub my face. I'll be forced to run entirely on adrenaline and magic but I have no doubts in my ability.

I can't keep up with that for all five challenges, but today, I'll make it through just fine. "I'll take you up on it for the next challenge."

"Good." He nods sharply. "And with any luck, that witch won't be here to bother us anymore."

I sigh.

"Anyway, as I was saying." Rook plops onto the couch beside me. "How about a run? We have two hours before the banquet, and I wouldn't mind starting off the day with a good workout."

"That sounds perfect."

"She came by not long ago," Rook says lightly. "I gave her a good glare. I thought you were just ignoring her, but now I wonder if you were just too out of it to even notice."

My shoulders deflate. "Where did she go?"

He shrugs. "For a workout like us, I'd guess. Maybe we'll see her out there." He flicks his eyebrows up.

"Save it for the challenge." I roll my shoulders.

"Come on, don't you think getting in her head a bit is a good idea? Make her fear us. We don't need to kill her to make her regret her choice to come here. A little champion intimidation is not frowned upon."

I purse my lips. "All right." I nod. "If we see her, we'll make our message loud and clear."

Rook's lips curl into a cruel smile. I'm one part grateful to have friends this hateful and bloodthirsty, and one part terrified. Remind me never to get on their bad side.

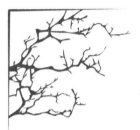

Caelynn

I run through the winding trail around the Flickering estate. The trees here have permanently deep-golden leaves that hang down like weeping willows. The water is clear, the stone below a deep red, making the rippling water of the lake shores look like varying types of flame. It's beautiful, if not intimidating. And of course, fitting for the Flickering Court.

Sweat drips down my temple, my thighs roar in protest, but I don't stop moving until the pain becomes one with my body. I don't stop running until my mind stops whirling.

I welcome the discomfort. I enjoy the sharp bite of wind on my tear streaked cheeks. All emotion must be dealt with before the trials begin. They cannot see my weakness. I won't let them.

They can take everything—my dignity. My future. My comfort. My joy.

But I won't let them see inside.

I'm the villain in this story. There is no other option. And if it's a villain they want, it's the part I'll play.

Footsteps sound down the trail behind me. Shades of black flash behind the twisting golden leaves around the bend and I stop. My heavy breath puffs out in wafts of mist in the chill morning air. Two males are sprinting down the trail behind me. Are they after me or working out their anxiety before the trials as I am? I'm not sure it makes much difference.

I wipe my cheeks of any evidence of my emotions and look around for a place to hide. I could press against one of the tree trunks in hopes their low hanging branches will veil me from sight, but I find it unlikely to work, and I'd rather face whatever threat is coming than for them to find me cowering.

I could go for a swim, but it's rather cold, and I don't know what dangers lurk beneath the surface of this lake. I have very little allies in the fae world. I doubt kelpies would enjoy my presence in their waters.

So, instead, I find a mostly bare tree, and casually lean against the bark. I cross my arms, empty my face of any emotions except annoyance and watch them approach. The two males slow to a walk to moment they see me. Or perhaps "march" is a more appropriate term for their heavy stomps and clear attempt at intimidation.

"Look what we found," the taller of the two says. I don't know him. I don't know his power, or his court, let alone his name or why he holds the disdain on his expression. Except for the fact that he's with Rev. Just being friends with my victim's brother is enough for him to hate me along with the rest of them. "That human-loving, pathetic prince murderer," he spits. "You know, I can't even remember her name?"

My eyes drift to Rev, whose face is full of fiery hatred. His black hair drips into his darkened eyes. I look away from him before I betray more emotion than I intend to.

"But you have heard of me," I say with a wink.

His lip curls into a sneer. He didn't get the reference, I assume. I smile at his reaction. Exactly what I want.

"You're nothing," Rev says, his voice low and husky. "A murderer, whose days are numbered."

I allow darkness to fill me. My eyes hooded and lazy, a bitter smile still on my lips. I put my hands on my hips. "And?" I flick an arrogant eyebrow.

At this, his anger erupts. His carefully controlled manner is gone as he stomps towards me, power rippling from him. I accept his hatred. I let it fill me. Surround me.

His hand is around my throat before I blink a second time, my head slammed against the tree trunk. The pain that shoots down my back chases away the fear. The insecurity. It fuels me. Empowers me.

In only moments, my lungs struggle for breath. "And you're in my world," he whispers, and I shiver at the feeling of his breath on my neck. If he only knew how much I liked it.

I grit my teeth, unwilling to fight back or show weakness. My body begins to squirm involuntarily as air remains absent from my burning lungs. He presses harder, and I grip his forearm. "You are weak. You will lose much more than this competition before your time here is done. I look forward to watching you writhe in pain."

He throws me to the ashen pathway and spits at my fallen body. My ankle twists as I go down. I gasp for breath, fingers clawing into the muddy forest floor. Nameless guy howls with laughter, but Rev says nothing more as they continue their jog as if it never happened at all.

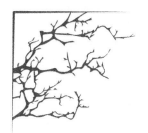

Rev

I sprint the rest of our run. I don't stop until my lungs are raging, my legs burning and my head throbbing. At some point in the last mile, I lost Rook. I stand outside the steps to the back of the manor, hands on my knees as I pant.

"Damn." Brielle skips down the steps towards me. "I'd wondered where you went off to. Looks like you're torturing yourself before we begin." Her laugh is light as bell. Delicate. Annoying.

I don't respond, in part because I can't stop heaving in massive breaths.

"Where did Rook go off to? I assumed he'd be with you." She tilts her head innocently.

As if on cue, Rook rounds the corner, shoulders slumped and face red. He stops next to me, his chest heaving in breaths to match my own. "What the hell, Rev? You'd think you were running for your damn life."

I roll my eyes. "Just because." I suck in a breath, "you couldn't," another breath, "keep up."

Brielle laughs again. "You know you only have a half hour until the banquet begins. You might want to *bathe*." She wrinkles her nose at our sweat-drenched tunics.

"Beat you to it!" Rook says, jogging up the stairs. Damn, how does he still have energy? I follow behind slowly and

Brielle falls into stride beside me. She's already dressed in her glammed-up warrior garb. She's the Flicker Court's chosen champion, but I know she's displeased with the fact that she can't wear a dress for this first banquet. We'll begin our trials immediately after and she can't battle in a skirt. Not that she wouldn't be willing to try.

I was there while her family fought her—literally— into wearing those leather pants, which she only conceded to once she called her seamstress in to add in a removable shear skirt over top, beaded belt, and low-cut satin top. She's still not pleased, but perhaps she'll change her mind when she realizes she's easily the best dressed champion to date.

Annoying. Vain. But lovely.

She's also one of the strongest fae in the competition, and as the High Queen's niece, incredibly influential, so I forgive her vanity. We all have our vices.

Beauty without substance is a weakness. Beauty with power behind it? That's what faeries are all about.

"So, what happened? Something happened, right?"

"We ran into the murderer on the trails."

Her eyebrows flick up. "Is she alive?"

"For now."

Brielle nods, fire burning in her amber eyes. "If you don't do it, I will you, you know?"

I don't respond to that.

"Or Rook. Or Nante. Or Crevin. Any of us. If you ask it, we'll do it. We want her gone. We want her dead. And we want you as king."

"You want me as king, but how many of my friends will lay down this competition to assure it to me?"

She purses her lips. "None."

I nod. "I very well may need this win. The queen is not a fan of mine. My father's outbursts have not helped my case. And with little to no accolades to my name, other than a famous dead brother, I need this."

She sighs. "We won't lay it down, but we will work together. We'll cancel out any threat other than each other. Starting first with that witch. Then we'll work it out from there. You need to prove yourself more than you need to win."

"I need both."

She nods. "Prove yourself first. Trust us in the beginning while we have a common enemy."

"Then we turn on each other." My voice is low, harsh. I won't be looking forward to that part of the trials, but I know they'll come. I know my own friends will rip my head off in order to win. Each one of us want to be the hero.

But only one of us can have it.

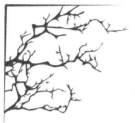

Caelynn

A snowy owl chirps from the rafters of the banquet hall as I walk in and I suppress an eye roll. She's quieter than before but only just.

Heads turn to watch me as I march forward in the same clothes I wore yesterday, all the way to the front of the cavernous room to the champions' table facing the crowd. I have no allies here.

The loudest whispers I've ever heard fill the hall.

I am a shadow fae with a soul to match. And I'll let that be my strength. I'll use my anger, my lack of fear, my emptiness, to my advantage.

I study the champions sitting along the front table. I don't recognize any of them, but based on their expression, they sure as hell know who I am.

Each fae is risking something important to enter the trials. Each one needs this.

I don't.

I have nothing to lose.

And that will be the reason I win.

I reach the table and claim my place between a redheaded female—fire fae for sure—and a stalky, bearded male. His hair is unwieldy enough that, paired with his short statue, I assume he's part dwarf.

The redhead clenches her jaw, eyes pinned straight ahead like she's trying not to attack me. Wonderful. Another member of my fan club. Beside her is a male with long, straight white hair, blue eyes, and sharp cheek bones who openly sneers in my direction.

Yes, this is going to be a lot of fun.

The dwarfish fae on my left has a calm demeanor but keeps his determined gaze straight ahead, neither looking to me nor to my enemies at my right.

He doesn't wish to choose a side. That's fine by me.

Based on the plaque in front of him, he's from the Crumbling Court—one of the non-ruling courts. If I don't win, I'd like another fae from a lesser court to win. A fair consolation prize. Perhaps the dwarf feels the same.

"Did you not bring any other—do you call those clothes?" the redhead asks, keeping her nose high enough to be thoroughly ironic.

I smirk, eyeing her ensemble. Tight, black jumpsuit with a plunging neckline and multi-colored glistening beads adorn her belt. "Do you think your pretty gems and tight clothes are going to help you win the trials?" I ask sweetly. "Or did you only enter as an excuse to attract a husband?"

This was apparently the wrong thing to say. Every muscle in her body clenches, hands in fists, back bent in a crouch. "I'm going to rip you to shreds," she seethes, low enough that only I—and perhaps our immediate neighbors—can hear.

I smile and turn from her just as her white-haired neighbor settles a gentle hand on her forearm. "I'm looking forward to it."

I take a moment to note the clothing of the other champions. They are either in fighting leathers, armor, or black-tie appropriate apparel. I am the only one who sports the just-rolled-out-of-bed look.

I'm in jeans and an Avenge Sevenfold T-shirt, but my boots are thick and sturdy. Admittedly, I should invest in a jacket of some kind for any cold weather trials, but that's a problem for another day. Today will be a short trial. A few hours at most. They'll want to cut down the entrants with one swift blow. Meaning today will be intense and extreme but quick. It will not be an endurance challenge.

The obsidian doors fly open to reveal a large statured male in nearly as casual attire as I am. His pants are leather but that's typical fae apparel, his shirt a white tunic, and a simple black jacket that hangs low enough to cover his ass.

I pull in a long breath and hold it. I steady my expression into one of cold indifference as Rev approaches. The whispers he fuels are quiet, blending together to create a low hum, vibrating with authority.

Considering his family rules one of the most powerful courts in the fae world, odds are on him to win this, despite the questions of why he hasn't yet been named heir. But the effect of his presence is more than his family. There is a sense of power about him. In his stance and his bright eyes. Gone is the dull black of pain and back is his bright silver gaze.

Fae eye color holds a major clue to their power. The color matches their court and their magic elements. The brightness showcases their strength. Clear and bright equals strong. Dim and dark means one of two things—pain or weakness. It's important to distinguish the two or you risk greatly underestimating a foe. A potentially fatal mistake.

I watch his features closely. He holds a confident calm; the only evidence of his tension is in his jaw as it clenches tight.

He's controlling his emotions in order to posture his strength. It is no secret how he feels about me, but letting his emotions take over could make him appear weak to the court.

It's all about politics in the fae world.

As for me? I steady my anger and pain. My empty, scorched soul on full display. Complete opposite strategies.

"Welcome, fair folk!" a puck with streaks of purple in her mane, matching her deep purple horns, says bright and excited. Her legs are thick and long, ending in hooves. "And welcome to our champions. One of the folk sitting at this table will become a hero to our entire world. History and the spirits will honor you greatly!"

I roll my eyes.

Most fae do not believe in benevolence. They seek power. They seek true immortality—to be remembered as a hero for all of time. The people at this table? They're here for what the notoriety could do for them.

"The competition and the quest that follows, will require sacrifice," the puck female continues. "You must battle against dark forces, push through pain. You will battle your own nightmares made real. You will be tormented from the moment you cross the thorn gates until the time you return. Today's trial will test your strength and speed and magic and intelligence and endurance. We will test your willingness to sacrifice *everything* to achieve your goal."

I smirk, knowing they are not seeking flawless heroes.

They stopped the Trial of Thorns a millennia ago because they believed it too barbaric—to test a future leader on their physical strength and ruthlessness alone. It made for great leaders, but not *good* ones. Because great can, and often does, mean terrible.

But for this—where entering the land of evil spirits and betrayers is the reward—it's perfect. To enter hell and return, you must become one with the nightmares. You will only survive if you are wicked enough to face the darkness and *own it*. The Trial of Thorns is brutal. And only the most brutal will win.

They won't be looking for the perfect angelic fae. They are looking for a fae damaged enough to have nothing to lose.

They are looking for me.

All I have to do is prove it to them.

There is a long pause as the puck runs her eyes over the champions. "Will you accept?" she says slowly, asking us honestly. "This painful and harsh game will result in notoriety, but you will be required to endure even harsher pain and torment as your reward. Please stand if you understand and accept the risks. Stand if you are willing to give up everything in order to win."

I am the first to stand and a murmur cascades through the crowd.

I gave up everything that I was a very long time ago.

At the end of the table a very handsome fae prince stands, his nose wrinkled in disgust, a silent growl clear on his expression. He's mad I beat him to it.

For a long moment it is only us, standing together but apart, facing a sea of fearful inhuman faces. Rev and me.

A dark haired male next to Rev is next to stand—the one from the forest today. Followed by the dwarf beside me. In the next moments, several others stand that I couldn't name.

There are fifteen champions in total, one for every court. There was once only twelve courts, but civil war or quarrelling heirs have split three over the last millennia. Several courts were disinherited by the High Court, whether as punishment for rebellion or due to perceived weakness. Now, there are only eight courts with the ability to take their place as a ruling court.

That is one of the reasons people in my court have expressed pride in my murderous actions. They see it as a political move. Rebellious.

The Shadow Court has feuded with the Twisted Court for hundreds of years. Our last Shadow Court High King was over five hundred years ago. His ruling cycle included a drought, mass poverty, and a failed war with the dwarves. The next king was chosen from the Twisted Court, and he disinherited us, claiming our entire court weak. Not fit to rule. And he convinced the entire council of it.

Since then, our power has dwindled due in part to forced marriages—our strongest Shadow Court women married to other courts, taking their power with them. Our court lacks high education and opportunity, making it near impossible to overcome our disadvantages.

The redhead next to me is the last to stand, apparently enjoying the drama. She gets the loudest applause as the last, ensuring her expression shows it wasn't cowardice that made her wait—it was spectacle. I roll my eyes and cross my arms.

"Thank you, champions!" the purple puck shouts over the roar of the crowd. "Next, we will introduce each court's champion. This will be your chance to showcase your court's magic!"

Oh perfect. A chance to show off. *Just what I want.*

Rev's turn to be introduced to the cheering crowd comes first.

"Reveln of the Luminescent Court." Rev stands. His expression shows bored annoyance, but his body lights up in a white glow so bright the crowd gasps and covers their eyes. That's just a party trick, but the crowd seems to enjoy it.

I twist my back in discomfort as I remember his brother's ability to paralyze you. He could pin you down with his light. Unable to move—or scream. Does Rev have the same power?

Murmurs of discontent rumble through the crowd—originating at my court's table—before the next champion's name is even spoken. "Rook of the Twisted Court." The male next to Rev smiles, handsome but cruel, his green eyes shining. A vine twists its way up his arm like slithering snake. It curls over his shoulder, around his neck and up to his head where it curls into a perfectly placed crown and grows thorns. He winks dramatically, and the crowd laughs through their cheer.

"*Clever*," I mumble, and the dwarf-fae beside me snorts.

"Prickanante of the Frost Court."

I can't help but chuckle at the girl's name—so many easy puns.

She glares at me but then beams with a massive smile to the crowd and holds out her hand. Ice crackles and twists, forming into a six-inch-high carving of a blue ballet dancer.

I begin wondering if we were supposed to plan and practice these little party tricks. I don't have anything planned, but then, maybe that's the best plan of all.

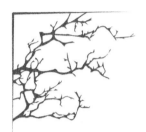

Rev

I cross my arms and wait for the other champions to be announced. They each have their little tricks. Enough to showcase their court's magic, but not enough to give away their power.

"Drake of the Whirling Court," Miss Koran, a puck I've known since childhood calls out. I hold back a grimace. Drake is easily my biggest competition for the crown, and therefore, the one I'm most concerned will win the trials. He's not the strongest physically, but he's smart, and he knows politics better than anyone. Drake smiles big and bright as he tosses his hands into the air, thrusting a small cyclone into the crowd. It whips and pulls at the spectators' clothing and hair, even pulling up a female's skirt.

Pig, I think.

"Kari of the Crystal Court." Drake's closest ally. She looks up to the ceiling as deep purple crystals grow down like stalactites, then all at once they shatter and fall to the ground sending up a puff of harmless glittering smoke. Crystals have many uses, but I know from experience that Kari also has several types of earth powers. She's a formidable opponent.

"Crevin of the Crackling Court." The oldest fae in the competition, a contender for the crown himself, although I've heard rumors of an alliance with Drake. I suppose we'll have to see about that. His white hair flies back as he sends sparks sizzling up and around the room, twisting through the lights and then finally raining down on the spectators. They ooh and ahh and hold up their faces to feel the heat—unafraid of being burned. The sparks fade into nothing before they touch anyone, and the crowd murmurs their approval.

"Brielle of the Flicker Court." Brielle holds out her hand and flames erupt into a moving sculpture of a couple dancing. The male flickers and glows with a white flame that I know represents my bother. Tears well in Brielle's eyes as they dance. Red flame and white.

Then a black flame creeps over the male, and he disintegrates leaving only the red-flame woman standing still.

I blink and swallow, and my eyes drift to the next in line. My brother's murderer stares at the flame, and though the rest of her face is smooth and calm, her pupils are dilated. Does she realize what Brielle's performance means?

"Caelynn of the Shadow Court," Miss Koran's voice betrays her pain at having to say the betrayer's name. Speaking a fae's name is a sign of respect. It's something I will never do for the shade witch.

The crowd boos and roars at her.

The female stands there, looking straight ahead. Even as her court attempts a cheer, they're drowned out by the rest of the room's jeers. Everyone hates her. Everyone but her minuscule and worthless court.

She doesn't move. She doesn't blink. No power comes from her in anyway.

I narrow my eyes, watching. A deviled-egg flies from somewhere in the crowd and hits her shoulder, splattering bits of yolk. She doesn't even blink. She doesn't move to wipe it off.

I watch her closely. What is she doing? What point is she trying to make?

Does she have no power to show? She used none to defend herself today in the woods, and she shows nothing in the showcase. She must have had some magic if she'd been able to kill my brother.

She's been in the human world for over a decade. Perhaps her magic is rusty from disuse? Perhaps she emptied her well so thoroughly to kill him she wasn't able to regrow it—maybe she doesn't have anything left.

That's a comforting thought.

We all wait, wondering if she's doing something we haven't noticed yet—shadows twisting or dancing. Lights dimming. But no. There's nothing.

She has nothing. My lips curls into a sneer of a smile.

Brielle glances to me, her expression just as pleased. She will be an easy opponent.

The showcase finishes with the last few courts—the weakest ones at the end. The dwarf pretending to be a fae from the Crumbling Court spins rocks around his head without moving. The Beastly Court fae grows wings, nearly knocking the dwarf next to him over. Brielle snickers.

And lastly a petite dark-skinned girl from the Webbed Court—weakest of them all. She opens her mouth in a silent scream as a massive spider crawls out from under her tongue and onto her cheek. The crowd gasps, and even I shiver.

Creepy, but worthless.

"We welcome you all, champions!" Miss Koran announces proudly. *Well, most of you.* "We will eat in your honor, and in one hour, our first trial will begin."

THE CHAMPIONS ARE SERVED first. Plates full of several types of meat, vegetables, and a basket of rolls for each of us. I take a few bites of poultry and one roll from the full plates they serve us. I could use the energy for the challenge, but I don't want to overdo it.

The rest of the champions shove their faces with the luxurious food. Except the betrayer—she doesn't touch the food at all.

Now that's an interesting strategy. Perhaps her stomach is too uneasy to eat. I'd certainly prefer to be weak than to throw up in front of everyone.

Acidic warmth fills my chest at her discomfort.

Perhaps I'll enjoy this challenge more than I'd anticipated. I am eager for her downfall.

The champions are led from the banquet hall and into the training center. My friends Brielle, Rook, and even occasionally Nante have worked in here together for weeks, preparing for the trials. I'm quite familiar with the place. I spend my minutes before the first challenge stretching and bouncing on my toes to get the blood moving.

"Can you believe that?" Brielle says. "First she laughs at Nante's name—wench." She rolls her eyes as she pulls off her beaded belt and sheer skirt, leaving a quite flattering leather jumpsuit. "Then she does nothing. Nothing. Like what even was that?"

I shrug. "I'm hoping it means she has no power to speak of."

"None?" Crevin says. "She has to have something."

"I'm certain she's out of practice, living as a human child for years."

He nods. "Maybe she just didn't want to embarrass herself."

I turn to find her among the crowd, still keeping close to the dwarf—one of the only fae in the competition not ready and willing to take her head off at the first opportunity. But she doesn't look at us at all.

"Lord Reveln!" a small voice calls. I look down to a young puck, his horns barely curled at all. "Which sword do you want?" Charlie asks me with a big grin.

He's a squire apprentice and a big fan of mine. "You should know that answer already," I say with a wink. He smiles big and runs off to grab my favored sword and belt. He skitters back, and I strap it onto my back in one smooth motion.

"How do you know which to choose?" Brielle asks. "They haven't told us anything about the challenge yet."

"And I don't suspect they will," I admit. If they haven't yet even hinted at how they'll first test us—it's likely going to remain a surprise. At least to us. "I just chose my most familiar weapon. Light, powerful, and versatile."

Nante purses her lips, unsure.

"I wonder if the eclipse has something to do with the trial?" the puck murmurs. "A hint maybe?"

"The what?"

"Oh! While you were in the banquet there was an eclipse. My mom told me that's super rare. Do you think it was for the trials?"

My eyebrows pull down. "What do you mean, exactly? Can you describe it?" I hadn't seen any eclipse—though we were inside the Flicker Court banquet hall with the curtains drawn—nor have I heard anyone else remark on it. Surely that would have been a major event, if there were even a partial eclipse this year.

Charlie shrugs. "The sun went totally black for like a full minute. All the servants stopped to watch it, waiting for something big to happen, but it never did. The sun came back out a minute or two later and still nothing. Then my brother and sister were ordered to serve breakfast, so we gave up waiting."

I press my eyes closed, trying to puzzle it out. The sun went entirely dark while we were inside—apparently no one had known about the major celestial event.

There are several possibilities. It could be some dark magic that has to do with the scourge —a scary thought, but perhaps the most likely. It could also have been planned magic as a way to celebrate the trials, but badly timed—why would they do it while we were all inside?

Or... my eyes drift over to my brother's murderer, her face severe, her blond hair pulled back into a ponytail and a generic sword in her hand. Her eyes are black, as usual. Her frame is slight, her eyes big, her clothing plain and even raggedy. Everything suggests she's weak and pathetic. Someone to be protected or ignored—certainly not someone to be feared.

Is this all a farce? Is there more beneath the surface?

Based on Charlie's timing the eclipse happened around the time of the court showcase. Around the time Caelynn did *nothing* with her power.

It's not possible she is the one that blacked out the sun. Right?

Caelynn

Rev watches me with an expression of shock and confusion. I'm not sure what he's figured out—there are quite a few possibilities, but I can't afford to be distracted right now. I'm the underdog, I know. Ill prepared but not nearly as weak as they all assume me to be, which is exactly how I prefer it.

Still, I am untrained and out of practice, so I will need every ounce of determination to make it through today.

I return my attention to the weapons rack. We are given our pick of any weapons we'd like, and there are hundreds of options. Blades of so many shapes and sizes, each best for a certain frame or fighting style.

These kinds of weapons aren't exactly my forte these days. I did enjoy my double katana set once upon a time. I handle one of a few small blades, getting a feel for its weight and length. I heave a sigh. I'm not prepared for this part and find myself hoping the first trial doesn't involve hand to hand combat.

I'll add that to my mental notes.

One, get a warm jacket.
Two, practice sword play.

I'm sure there'll be more I need before these trials are through. For now, I add one more item.

Three, survive.

Out in front of us are iron gates studded with rubies, towering at least fifty feet high. The rest of the champions are now converging in front of them. I grab a pair of small swords and quickly strap them to my back. Those will have to do for now. They're the closest thing available to my old set. Most likely, I'll have to use one at a time. Using the two together is a challenge, and I'm not at all prepared for it.

I hope I've retained some muscle memory.

The doors crack open, exposing a tall sliver of light. I watch the blinding light with awe. It's beautiful and pure and terrifying. Light exposes the truth. Shadows conceal them.

I close my eyes, letting the warmth of the newly exposed sun settle on my face, taking in long breaths of air.

I pull out one of my swords just to feel the grip, to adjust my hand and squeeze it tightly. Then, I step forward.

I AM THE LAST TO LEAVE the training area. The last to face the cheering crowds roaring down at us. The last to step into the light.

My pain swirls around my soul, wrapping around it like armor. I will use it. I will use my sadness, my hopelessness, to fuel me today. And tomorrow. Until these trials are over. Until this world is saved and I can slip back into those shadows and disappear.

So, I pull it in. Every bad thing that has happened to me. Every terrible thing I've done—for good reason or not, it doesn't matter. Every person whose life I've irrevocably changed. I soak in their hatred. I wear my own like armor.

"We're going to kill you, you know," the redhead says sweetly, without turning to me, as I join the group standing before a massive arc of winding green and black vines adorned with thorns as large as my torso.

"Today, champions!" the puck hollers, her voice magically magnified and even so it's hard to hear her over the roar of the crowds. "Your trials begin. First, you will compete in a basic form of competition. A race."

Whispers erupt from the crowd and gathered champions alike. I don't for a moment I think it will be anything simple. We'll have a starting line and a finish line, with who the hell knows what in between. My only question is how many people will pass this challenge? Only the first three to cross will win? The top six? Ten?

I look around at my fellow entrants. Who is the fastest?

The dwarf will be the slowest, I decide quickly. Though, he isn't even waiting for the puck to finish announcing our trial. He's already—wisely— pulling his armor off and tossing it to the side, leaving only his bulky hair-covered chest. I give him a nod, but his eyes are full of fearful determination. He gives no sign that he sees me at all.

"The course," the puck continues, "will take you through ten miles of swamp and forest. There will be brutal obstacles and some of our lands most formidable creatures there to stop you at every turn. You must be fast, but you must be strong. You must be vicious. All fifteen of you may pass to-day's test. Or perhaps there will only be three or less who succeed. You will have a time limit of one hour. It doesn't particularly matter who comes in first or in last—as long as you make it before the timer clicks to zero. Make it through these gates in one hour, and you will remain a champion. One hour and one second—you are no longer a champion in the Trial of Thorns."

One hour. Ten miles. That's an average of six minutes per mile—that would be a challenge for even the most athletic humans without any obstacles. Fae can run, on average, twice as fast as a human. Even out of shape fae could manage an obstacle-less course of this size. Which means the obstacles will be formidable.

I staring through the gates to the forest beyond. Any manner of challenges could be waiting for us. I consider if I'd be better off waiting at the back, letting the boldest get hit with the brunt of fiercest attacks.

"We expect not every faery who begins this trial will sur-vive to the end. So, while we frown upon direct inter-cham-pion fighting, we wish to make the trials as realistic as possi-ble. During each trial, you may do anything short of death to stop other champions from crossing the finish line. If a con-testant is unfairly killed during the challenge, the queen will pass down judgement. The moment the challenge is over, our strict rules—immediate death to any who kills an active con-testant—will be back in place."

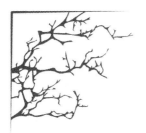

Rev

I stand at the front of the pack, head high and shoulders back, and stare out past the giant thorn arches. But my lips curl into a smile as Miss. Krovan tells us the punishment for killing another contestant during a trial. All I have to do is make it look like an accident and boom, no consequences to my revenge. In fact, I'm fairly certain I'd be considered a hero just for that act alone. Any who ends her life will be greatly rewarded. Unofficially, of course.

The shade witch stands in the back, eyes dull and bored as usual. Why is she even here? She doesn't try, she doesn't care. She isn't strong. She's hated.

The only purpose her presence serves is to anger my family and to fuel the stupid Shadow Court's rebellion. She cannot win.

And if I have anything to do with it, she won't even last through one trial.

The simple rules are finished, the champions set, the betting commenced. My heart begins to pound as the high fae flag is raised and the countdown begins.

In thirty seconds, I will have one hour to run ten miles and fight whatever creatures the courts have prepared. Easy. This trial's only purpose—as was already admitted— is simply to whittle out the weaklings.

I will have plenty of time to ensure my enemies do not make it out of this alive.

In one hour's time, I wouldn't be surprised if there were only eight champions remaining—the ruling courts. We are the strongest. The most prepared.

I take in a deep breath as the last seconds trickle down. The crowd roars, "Three. Two. One."

I am fifteen feet ahead of the next champion in only moments. Running ahead may be a bad strategy, as it will mean facing the brunt of the worst dangers. But I highly suspect the first third of the course will be the easiest, the most dangerous feat will come in at the end, and running ahead will give me the chance to scout out the perfect place to ambush *her*.

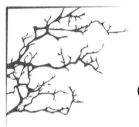

Caelynn

I begin the race at a walk as the others sprint forward. Rev is the front runner immediately, the others in a large pack following his tracks. I am left behind, and I take the moment to wave at all my "fans" in the stands lining the first few hundred feet of our course. An egg lands at my feet, and I step right on it with a smile.

Once I reach the edge of the amber forest, I run.

I hold back my shadow magic that could shoot me ahead a dozen feet at a time and just use my physical strength. Every fae, even the strongest, have limits to their magic. If we use it all on menial tasks, we'll have nothing left to fight with.

The copper trees hang over the path, and I enjoy the view for the entire first mile. Then, the roar of a massive creature causes a shudder to rumble through my body.

It's not him, I remind myself. *He wouldn't be here.*

I've already faced the world's worst ancient beast. I can't say I survived because he stole my soul, but I am still technically alive so, I suppose I have something to say about the experience.

At least I won't be afraid of beasts that most fae would cower before.

With the Night Bringer in my mind's eye as I turn the corner and find three dragons battling with several champi-

ons, I almost laugh. Several of the least imposing champions
are stuck on this first obstacle. The dwarf is cowering behind
a shield in front of the red dragon. The Webb Court female
has the green dragon stuck between a wall of sticky webs.
And two others I couldn't name are dodging the largest
black dragon.

There are many ways we could handle these beasts, but
speed is the game so moving past them is the only option. I
sprint forward, towards the trembling dwarf—dwarves and
dragons are not exactly on friendly terms—and use my shadow magic for the first time. I catch the attention of the red
dragon, my black smoke streaming behind, and I stop to
smile and wave at him.

He blasts a heavy blaze of fire right at me and I twist
away, leaving only black smoke in my stead. I appear in another place and repeat the process.

"Go!" I shout to the dwarf. "Run past them. You don't
need to fight them; you just need to keep running." Him especially, who's largest disadvantage to begin with is speed.

He blinks at me from behind his shield. But then he
looks up at the dragon, and the moment I poof away from
the dragon a fourth time, he sprints for the lake water, where
the trail leads. It's still far off, but if he's lucky, he'll make it
without incident.

The Webbed Court girl follows suit with her dragon opponent stuck well and good in her webs.

I follow behind, reaching the black dragon, who isn't as
impressed or confused by my ability as the red dragon. But
that doesn't matter. I have a new plan.

I shoot forward, leaping up, and land on the black dragon's tail. I call to the red dragon, and then poof away towards the water. The other two champions go wide-eyed, realizing what's about to happen just a moment before it does. They sprint after me, the last one's hood catching fire as he sprints away from the now battling dragons.

Mr. Black Dragon was not very pleased when the red dragon scorched him.

My little mini crew—who by the way hate me as much as the others—make it through the water quickly. I waste no time, unsure of what might be in the dark waves—kelpies or krakens, waiting for an unsuspecting champion to munch. I am the first of this small group to exit the water.

My chest is tight, eyes fierce, but I'm relieved I didn't have to fight something in the water. And even more so that the stretch of path in front of me is open and clear, no obstacles or opponents to be seen.

But my relief is short lived because one step I'm upright and the next—I'm not.

A vine snaps around my ankle, pulling my feet out from under me. My head smacks the ground in a sickening crack.

A sinister laugh rumbles from the forest line as I hang unceremoniously by my ankle. My heart throbs as I realize this wasn't random.

A dark form comes into focus as I twist, swinging in the stupid vine trap.

"Hello, Rev," I say casually, crossing my arms.

Four other forms appear before him: the redhead, the white-haired fae, Prick-a something or another, and Rook, each holding a wriggling creature.

"This is only the beginning if you keep going," Rev says, his eyes dark. Pain. He's in pain. I swallow.

They release the water goblins—the worst! Sharp toothed with long claws that love to sink into warm human flesh. The creatures sprint to me, claws flying. I twist just before one of their sharp claws swipes across my face. The first digs into my back, searing my whole body in agony. I can't hold back a pathetic scream as my focus narrows to only the pain.

Rev and his friends laugh and then march away.

I send a short blast of acidic smoke to my goblin attackers and they drop to the floor, hissing. They won't be deterred for long though, so I pull my body up and pull at the thick vines on my ankle. It won't come free with only my fingers. I could use my swords, but they aren't exactly made for sawing rope-like vines.

A goblin leaps onto my back, his teeth sinking into my shoulder and I fly back down, my head just missing smacking the ground a second time. Dammit!

Three of the fae I helped with the dragons pass by me without so much as a glance my way as I struggle to get free again. *Perfect. Glad I made such good friends.*

Screw this, I think and curl my body as tightly as I can manage in this position, focusing on centering my energy, despite the rips and tears in my muscles. I have the magic to get free of this. It's just magic I may need later.

But what use is saving magic if my muscles are torn to pieces?

My magic explodes and shatters three of the four creatures into little bits. The last misses the full explosion, but one of its legs is torn open and splattering out black blood. It stares at me with wide fearful eyes.

Moments later, it huffs away into the forest dragging its wounded leg behind it.

Blood drips down my temple, warmth soaks my back. I take in a few long breaths before trying to free myself again, but then a set of boots are in front of me and someone is sawing away at my bindings.

I drop to the floor in a heap, only barely managing to catch myself and roll into a semi-graceful fall.

"Ow." I grip my shoulder and back, the two of the worst injuries.

The dwarf-like fae drops a vial beside me. "We're even," he says and then sprints away.

I hadn't expected anything from them for my assistance, but it's nice to know I'd earned it from him, at least. I'll keep that in mind for later in the trials. That is if either of us make it through this one.

I might have to expose more of my magic than I'd planned on in order to survive the first. He, however, is going to have to pick up the damned pace if he wants to continue on.

As he disappears down the quiet trial, I examine the vial he dropped. I pull out the cork and sniff it. I have no idea what is in it. Could he have given me a poison draft and later pretend it was an accidental switch up? He could have helped me just to ensure my death.

I *could* make it through this race without it. Maybe. My wound is bleeding pretty badly. I'd have to empty out my magical well, expose my abilities, and I'd be on death's door by the time I reached the finish line, but I could feasibly do it.

I bite my lip as I consider. I've never been very good at judgement calls but this one—this one I'll just have to take the chance. I have several more items to add to my "to-get" list for the next trial: dagger, potions, allies.

Because clearly that's playing a large part in this stupid thing. Rev has his three ruling court friends. The other ruling court candidates are presumably against him. Are they working together? Would they want to take on Rev's enemy as part of their strategy?

I'll have to look into these possibilities, but until then, I have the beginnings of an alliance right here in my hand. I just have to take the risk.

I gulp down the blue potion with a wince. I keep my eyes closed while chanting, *please don't die. Please don't die.*

The roaring pain in my back subsides. I roll my shoulder, shivering at the strange sensation of the blood clotting quickly and strongly. The muscle is still weak and sore, not healed, but the pain has subsided and the blood loss contained. A temporary fix.

I'll take it.

Another reminder: figure out my new friend's name because I can't keep calling him *dwarf*.

I swallow and stand. I've made it maybe a third of the way through the challenge but wasted at least half the time. Now, I'm going to have to race for it.

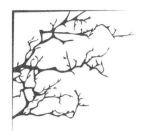

Rev

Rook and Brielle run ahead, laughing as they push at each other. She's in a better mood than I've seen her in days, assuming we've ended the betrayer once and for all.

I am less certain, but I won't dim her joy.

Brielle casts a wall of fire that stops Rook in his tracks. She laughs heartily as she sprints farther toward the finish line. Rook sneers at the flames snaking toward the sky, blocking our path. I blast a jolt of light through the wall that creates a door-sized opening. He winks at me and races through. He has a little catching up to do.

I, on the other hand, am not worried about time. I'll push through, running through the next few miles, but if anyone passes me, I am not concerned.

I'm more worried about whether the betrayer made it out of my trap alive. She shouldn't have, but you never know. The most evil fae tend to be the slipperiest. And the most beautiful. Go figure.

I won't feel the relief until her corpse is removed or at least when her name is crossed from the champions' board.

I climb up a wall of thorns and swing over an acid pit. These obstacles are easy.

No fae pass me from behind for several miles, even though I'm taking my time, which I find comforting. I pass up one of the lesser court's champions and another that's trapped in a sinking sandpit. That leaves only seven ahead of me—all ruling courts. That works for me. If we could get all the weak courts out of the competition, any political grumbling would end quickly and easily, and I'd be able to focus on my real competition.

I pass the six-mile marker, followed quickly by the seven-mile marker only minutes later. Too easy. I'm now three miles from the finish with twenty-five minutes to go. At full speed it would take me ten, max.

I hear scuffling and yelling up ahead.

Perfect, this must be the climax.

I stop as I realize the trial ends over a cliff. In the massive canyon below, smoke rises. The inhuman screech of some dark creature causes a shiver to run down my back. I spy bat-like wings flickering into view and then out. *Great. Shadow-vyrns.* Flying lizard-like creatures, fast and vicious and dumb as rocks.

Across the cavern, there is a metal-wire bridge already half torn to pieces. One side is destroyed entirely, leaving two wires—one a few feet above the other, stretching across the void with bits of metal and scorched wood hanging off of it. This is going to be interesting.

"Come on, Rev!"

I blink, as I notice Brielle standing at the edge, waving at me. I sprint to her, eyes wide. By my estimation, the canyon is half a mile wide and several miles deep, with the vicious creatures swarming the place. We'll have to inch over this wire while fighting these things. There's no other way across unless you're a lucky wind rider. I'm assuming Drake's already long past. Not that he'd help if he was. He's as desperate for the crown as I am. He'd enjoy ripping it from my cold dead fingers.

"Come on. We'll cross together, and I'm going to torch the thing once we're across."

I give her a sharp nod. Good, we'll be the last to cross. No one else will be able to make the finish line in time. Even we're cutting it close now. This half a mile will take at least ten minutes.

A female fae comes into view behind us, and my stomach drops until I notice her dark skin and curly hair. Not the betrayer. Good.

It's the webbed girl.

"We could probably use the help," I tell Brielle, nodding towards the female fae racing towards us.

She sneers but concedes and we pause until she reaches us. "We'll fight them together," I shout to the girl. I don't know her name. I don't care.

She nods, her eyes wide, but she doesn't speak.

We begin inching across the wire bolted to the cliffside. It shutters and sways as I step out from the rock-side cliff, all my weight on the small wire. The first shadow-vyrn bolts towards us, and Brielle sends a roaring wolf of flame at it. The wyvern dodges it and squeals, diving down and rising with a few friends. *Dammit.*

"Move faster!" I shout at Brielle. We need to take the inches we can get before the real fighting starts. We're only fifteen feet out when the three wyverns attack. I explode with light, and they squeal in pain, eyes closed. Shadow creatures hate luminescent light. They're not fans of fire, but so long as it doesn't touch them, they're able to deal.

My light is from the sun. The antithesis to their magic. "Move!" I shout again as we take long steps. I cover all three of us with light, and the wyverns swarm around, looking for a weakness but not getting close enough to strike.

Brielle's hands shake, her feet unsteady. Dammit, I should have gone first.

"Stop," I tell her. My light still shines brightly around us. "I'm going to pass you, just stay still." I carefully step around her, holding her by the waist with one hand, the other only holding tightly to the top wire. She whimpers, but spider girl helps to steady her, and when I'm clear, I move forward. The flying lizards are angrily trying to get past my light shield. It's taking up a lot of my energy but for the moment, it's working.

By the time we get across, I won't have any magic left. But that's a problem for future-me. I move quickly across the wire, Brielle's hands on my shoulders. Around us, my blinding white light is all that's visible. Which is good because it means we can't see *down*. We can hear the high-pitched screeching of the shadow-vyrns. We can feel the unsteady wire. But it does help to focus. One step at a time. Big steps, as quickly as we can manage.

A set of shining black teeth suddenly chomp through the light barrier and graze my right shoulder. I jerk and nearly send us all flying off the wire. Brielle screams and bends forward, hyperventilating. The nameless fae shoots a blob of black magic at bodiless teeth and the creature roars, reeling back.

"Keep it up!" I shout. They will break through my shield at some point, but the more we can delay it, the better. I keep taking long steady steps. Brielle's breathing is shaky, and I wonder if she's trying not to cry. "Keep walking. Just one step at a time," I say in a soothing tone.

Another sticky-black blob of magic flies past my ear, into a snout I hadn't even seen until it was already pulling back. "Good job." I can't tell how far we've gone or how far we have to go because the light blocks the view, even for me.

It doesn't matter. We'll keep moving until we hit solid ground. We will keep going until we don't have to.

I don't know how much time has passed. Again, I don't care. I'll go as fast as I'm able. Another snapping jaw comes at me, and another shot of web magic pushes them back.

This girl is from one of the lesser courts, a branch from Shadow Court if my history is correct—she's not someone I'd usually ally with, but at this point, beggars can't be choosers.

She's doing well, and I don't care where she comes from. I need her help. Brielle is surely not doing much for us at the moment. I'd be screwed without spider-girl.

A claw slams through my shield, and my balance wavers. My light splinters, and I shudder as I watch the darkness crackle over the shield. Webbed girl cries out as she shoots everything she has at the monster pulling at the light, peeling it away. Several blasts hit its claws, and it roars in pain, but it doesn't stop.

My teeth chatter as cold washes over me, my vision blinking black. "I have to let it go," I shout. "Get ready! One. Two. Three."

I drop the shield suddenly, and the shadow-vyrn stumbles forward, claws flying. Brielle shoots fire from her hands, raging over the attacking wyvern and tossing it to the side, but there are more waiting. Claws and teeth bombard us until I can't tell which creature is which. I fall to the wire, hands shaking as a roaring fire covers us. A piercing scream digs into my ears, and I turn to see my new nameless ally topple over, black teeth ripping into the flesh of her bicep. The creature drops her, and she falls into the mouth of another, her screams of agony rippling through the cavern.

"Dammit!" I shout, but it's way too late to save her.

"She's nothing. We're almost there," Brielle says, her voice steadier than I'd have expected. "And she's distracting them."

"She saved us. You know that, right?" She's right though, we have a moment to breathe while they rip her body to shreds. There will be nothing left to bury.

"It's doesn't matter now! I have enough energy for only a few minutes. We'll have to run."

I look up, we are more than three quarters of the way across. "I can do another minute once yours fails, but we'll still have to move fast."

I stand and press on, Brielle's fingers clawing into my back as I march. Her fire shields us as the creatures resume their attack. I pull out my sword this time, knowing they'll bust through the fire easier than my light, and I'm ready when teeth attack. I shove my blade into the first's jaw, black blood splattering.

I step. And step. And slash as claws fly. Step. Step. Step. Slash.

Brielle's fire dims to a flicker and I measure our distance. One hundred feet or so. I take a larger step and blast every ounce of magic I have left in my body. It takes down two creatures and gives me the space I need to take another ten feet. I do it again, another ten feet. My well is drying. Each blast is smaller. Dimmer. We're fifty feet from the edge.

We can do it. We have to do it.

A massive black shadow blocks out the light of the sun, and we pause to look up to find a wyvern twice the size of the rest. "Run!" I shout. We abandon our shields and our balance as we sprint the last fifty feet. Brielle screams, losing her balance and pitching to the right. I reach for her.

Our hands clasp, but it throws me off balance and we're both falling towards the pit below. A vine whips out in front of me and I grab it as I fall. One hand holds Brielle's arm and the other the vine, and we swing into the cliffside, my right shoulder taking the brunt of the blow as we crash into the amber stone.

Brielle's body is limp, and I can't climb up while holding her dead weight. And that's besides the fact that my shoulder is roaring in pain, muscles ripping, possibly out of socket. I use every ounce of magic I have left in me to shield us once more, but it's only delaying the inevitable. Except, I have friends left in this thing, and the vine I still cling to retreats, pulling us toward the summit.

I hold tight to both, forcing my magic until hands grip me under my arms and my vision flickers to black.

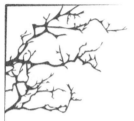

Caelynn

There's only fifteen minutes left in the challenge, and before me is an impossible obstacle.

The wide-open canyon is filled with shadow-vyrns. This... is going to be interesting. Across the opening, a blinding light glows, pulling up higher and higher until it reaches the top and then flickers out. It's hard to even tell what's happening but every shadow-vyrn swarms the light.

The moment it puffs out the creatures dive below into the dark smoke veiling the bottom of the open cavern.

Three fae are shifting slowly across the one metal wire connecting the two sides, balancing precariously. The wyverns turn their sights onto these fae, only a quarter of the way across.

I curse when I notice those on the other end of the cavern aren't leaving. The fire bearer is over there. Her heat would be more than enough to burn this metal wire and send those fae still crawling across falling into the pit of shadow-vyrns.

My chest heaves, and for the first time I wonder if I can make it. One challenge and I've failed. I have fifteen minutes to run three miles, and that includes crossing this now impossible cavern.

Shadow-vyrns use magic similar to my own. In my homeland, they live and breed in the caves between us and the human world. A distant cousin of mine made a name for himself by taming one.

The fae over the middle of the cavern seem to have noticed their predicament as the wire shudders, the red dot on the other end glow growing brighter.

The top wire goes slack with a pop, and the fae in the middle scream and scramble for balance. One of the fae falls into the pit with a horrifying scream.

"She's melting it!" one of them yells. The red glow begins anew—the wire beneath their feet is next.

They can't make it. Even if they sprinted, they wouldn't make it to the other side before the rickety wire beneath them fell to the depths, taking them with it. They're as good as dead. Unless...

There is only one way to make it across now, and if I'm going to do it, I may as well do it while I have the chance to take one or two of the helpless fae with me.

I sprint across the wire in front of me, getting as far as I can before the wire goes slack, the connection of the other end loosened. A chorus of screams echo through the canyon and I dive forward, past the careering fae and my form turns to shadow. I jerk, using the shadow-vyrns magic against them, and I jolt forward until I'm on the back of the closest one.

I don't exactly have time to make friends with the creature, but darkness will calm it, and if it's calm, I might be able to influence its movements with my magic.

It roars in anger, but my shadows cover its eyes, little stars twinkling soothingly. "It's okay," I whisper to it, and the creature's muscles still. I pull my magic around the skin under its wing. I have just enough control to pitch the creature into a dive, towards the fae falling through black smoke.

I reach for a young fae and the dwarf as they free fall. I use my magic to influence my new wyvern pet, pulling his wings back to induce a quick dive, and using it to steer beneath the falling fae. The dwarf sees, eyes wide but stare determined and grips my shoulder the moment I'm in reach.

I groan as his fingers dig into the injured muscle, the pain potion not strong enough for this. I hold strong as he grips me and attempts to hold onto the smaller boy by the forearm, but he slips through his grasp and drops into the smoke below.

The dwarfish fae cries out but immediately pulls himself the rest of the way onto the creature, arms around my waist.

The wyverns around us gawk confused but quickly begin to turn on us, so I cover us both in darkness. This confuses them enough to allow me to push my pet's wings up and down to rise above the cavern. We soar seamlessly through the air, not bothered by anyone. Even my wyvern seems content to be controlled by my soothing black magic.

"We should jump just before the edge," my nameless friend shouts over the wind. "The creature can't fly past the barrier."

He points over my shoulder, and sure enough, there's a slight glistening to the edge of the far cliff going high into the sky. That's why the wyverns turned to new prey the moment the others reached the edge.

"We don't have enough time!" The challenge ends in minutes. Ticking away. I don't think we can run the last two miles and still make it. "Do you think we can go over it?" Maybe I could fly high enough.

"No!" he shouts. "Or they'd all be doing that."

Shit. My heart pounds as we approach the barrier, I slow the creature so we have more time to think. "Go down!" he shouts in my ear. "Ram the cliffside as hard as you can manage and I'll do the rest."

Well, shit. If you say so, dude. I don't have another plan so I follow his instructions. I flow extra soothing magic into my shadow-vyrn and I steer it straight down, taking every ounce of momentum I can obtain. I might die, I realize, as I crash the creature into the cliffside. We'll be splattered onto the stone with nothing left to identify us.

But the stones on the cliff shudder, vibrating violently until a hole forms right where I'm aiming. No, not a hole. A tunnel.

I steer the shadow-vyrn straight into the dwarf made tunnel until blackness surrounds us. "You'll have to tell me where to go from here!" I shout. Because all I can see is black, I have no idea where we're going.

"Just fly straight," he yells, annoyance clear in his tone. I consider being offended by his anger, but I realize he's doing some big magic at the moment so he probably needs to concentrate.

We fly underground, a sheet of pitch-black shadows surrounding us. The wyvern's wings graze stone, and he squawks in fear. "A little further!" the dwarf shouts.

I can hear the count down, dim and echoing. The crowd cheers above us—they have no idea we're just below them.

"Thirty. Twenty-nine. Twenty-eight."

"Go up!" he shouts. I obey, as stones fall around us, slamming into our skin. Dammit, now I could use some armor! The creature roars as a sharp boulder smashes into its shoulders and head, but he continues to move. Sunlight blasts us as we emerge from the ground only feet from the finish line arch.

"Ten. Nine."

The crowd roars so loud at our appearance I can no longer hear the count. We're moments away from losing.

I whip my magic against my creature's wings, and he swerves right, straight through the arches.

"Two. One!"

We made it. Elation fills my being so intensely that my veil falls and the shadow-vyrn thrashes wildly at the champions standing at the finish line.

They scream and run from the panicking monster—not at all where he's supposed to be. Fae soldiers run out to control the beast. I toss the veil back across his eyes, attempting to sooth him, but the roar of the crowds is enough to keep him thrashing in panic.

The dwarf jumps off his back as I steer the creature into the sky. I leap off once he's about a hundred feet off the ground and land in a crouch before the crowd. I wince at the impact through my already pained body.

The crowd roars with excitement and disbelief as the shadow-vyrn soars back towards the cavern.

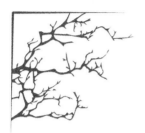

Rev

My mouth falls open as I watch the shadow-vyrn fly off, the dwarf and the betrayer safely on the ground past the archway. They join us in the winners' circle.

Brielle's expression matches my own. Fury. Disbelief. Everyone else is wide eyed and slack-jawed. Impressed.

Dammit!

How in the world did she do that? When Brielle melted the wire across the cavern, I thought there was no way anyone would follow us. We were already celebrating the defeat of the betrayer.

But here she is. In some ridiculous miracle.

She rode a damn shadow-vyrn! If I didn't hate her, I'd be impressed too. Young fae everywhere are going to idolize her for this.

This is bad. This is so much worse than just her continuing in the competition. People are going to start *liking* her. That's the worst thing that could happen.

I press my eyes closed as the announcements are made. Eight of us made it through the challenge. That's just over half. Eight is even the number I anticipated—it's just the wrong eight.

Six of the ruling fae courts. And two from the lesser courts. The dwarf and the betrayer. I ignore the names as I listen. Only two of the missing seven champions are alive. The girl trapped in the thorns and one lesser fae that was freed from the sandpit. Everyone else died there, almost all of them from the canyon.

Some of them don't even have bodies to collect.

Two of them were my allies. Nante didn't make it over the Canyon, and Brielle is teary eyed over that fact. I hardly knew the girl, so I try to hide that it doesn't bother me so much. Crevin was the other ruling court champion to perish there. He was an acquaintance at most and he hadn't declared an alliance so it's not as much of a loss as it could be.

Honestly, I'm more saddened by the girl whose name I still don't know.

I look around, watching the faces of the courts around me. I scrunch my nose at the Shadow Court celebrating. Not that I can blame them. What she did was amazing, even if I hate her for it. I'll turn their joy into acid the first chance I get.

Tears well in several eyes as I scan the crowds. I stop when I see a woman with black, white, and grey webs lining her ears and wrists. I approach the group slowly.

"Where are you going?" Rook asks. "I was planning to go drown my sorrows with a bottle of fire whiskey."

"To see the Webbed Court. I'll join you in a few."

Brielle scoffs. "Why?"

"Because I wouldn't be here if it weren't for her. And she's not here because of me."

Brielle rolls her eyes, mumbling something about a waste of time. I ignore her and continue on. I approach the Webbed Court, and they blink in shock as they stare at me.

I bow slightly. "I'm sorry," I tell the woman with spiders on her ears.

"Are you going to say that to all the courts that lost a champion?" Her eyes are narrowed, anger covering her pain.

"No. Only yours."

Her eyebrows furrow. "Why?"

The crowds waited at the beginning and end of the trial; they didn't see what happened between. She doesn't know how her court's champion died.

"Because we worked together against the shadow-vyrns. I wouldn't have made it past them without her help."

"And yet she died and you didn't."

I cast my eyes low. "I couldn't save her. It happened too fast. But regardless of the outcome, I wanted you to know that I respect her. And in turn, your court for raising such a champion."

Her head tilts as she considers me. Our courts are not at odds with one another, but there is always an underlying bitterness between the ruling courts and the lesser courts. Finally, the woman bows. "I am her mother, and she was my heir."

I swallow, understanding. This is the current ruler of their court, and she was to be the next. Their loss was more than personal. It will weaken their court forever.

"I will honor her however I'm able." She knows I am the next heir of my court, which means I will, someday, have the ability to use my influence for their benefit. Maybe by facilitating a strong marriage for their next ruler. Or simply by aligning with them during a conflict. I owe them a favor.

She nods, accepting my implied offer. And I turn in search of Brielle and Rook, ready to drown my sorrows along with them.

Caelynn

I shift off to the side of the arena, away from the crowds before my court can surround me. I have no desire to hear how amazing they think I am.

I'm relieved I made it through the challenge, but I don't want to celebrate. I wouldn't mind a comforting beverage before a bath and a long nap, but I don't want to face those who treat me like a hero when I am anything but.

I scan the gathering crowds, each court surrounding their champions. Pushing through the crowds, I listen carefully to the announcer, naming all of the successful contestants.

"Tyadin of the Crumbling Court."

Good, now I have a name for him. The cheer for him is like a battle cry, echoing over the arena. I smile as I find him among his countrymen, some stalky and hair covered as he and some clean shaven, fair and slender as the stereotypical fae. They laugh and cheer, and I smile just watching the exchange.

He smiles, but it doesn't reach his eyes.

Many of the entrants today died. I think that's a sobering reminder for the remainder. These trials are not a game.

They very well may be sacrificing their lives in order to make whatever point they're trying to make. But together, my dwarf-fae friend—Tyadin—and I have certainly made one. We are the only lesser courts to make it past the first challenge.

I bite my lip and then turn away, shifting through the scattered outer crowds mostly filled with the mourning courts. Some of the stronger courts are those who've lost their promising challengers. But it's the lesser courts who mourn the most. For some, it was a major loss.

I pass a group of Webbed Courters, who shift to allow me plenty of room. I hold my head high, face blank as I march towards the estate.

A snowy-white owl glides over the stands, squawking. She finds me as I dip into an empty nook behind the stands. She swerves down expertly, and she lands on my shoulder, her wing tangling in my hair awkwardly.

"Well, I was going to compliment you on your new flying skills until that debacle," I say, trying to pull my hair free from her talons and gently set her wing back to her body.

She shivers and clucks softly in my ear.

"I'm glad to see you too," I whisper. She is the only one I want to be around after today.

I'm certain I'll be the first to our rooms, which means I might actually get a chance to bathe without much conflict arising.

I jog up the stairs towards the estate, where several fae are scrambling to do last minute set up for the upcoming party.

Several fae nod in my direction as I pass, and I wince, unsure what the sudden vague respect is for. Rebel sympathizers? I don't know, I don't think I want to know.

RAVEN SOARS HIGH OVERHEAD as I enter, and I make sure to stop in my room to meet her. She's already on the windowsill, waiting for me.

I wave my hand, and she pops back into human form, clunking to the ground awkwardly. "Ow."

I smirk.

"Why do my feet feel so weird now?"

"Getting used to your bird form, huh?" I wink. "Come on," I tell her, already pushing my way back out the door. She scurries after me.

"Where are we going?" she whispers breathlessly. "Can I come out here?"

"Most of the time, no. But right now, the other contestants should be out of the way for at least an hour. I figure it's the best possible time for us to risk a bath."

"A bath?" Her eyes grow large, her lips twisting into a pleased smile.

"Come on!" I rush through the opening, and strip my clothes instantly, hopping into the communal soapy water.

Raven stops, staring at the room. Basically a cave with a massive hot tub covered in pink and purple bubbles. "This is how fae bathe?"

"Not all of us, but it's an old tradition."

"The water is going to be disgusting with you in it." She wrinkles her nose.

"Oh hush," I say, subtly glancing down at my dirt and blood covered arms. "It's magically cleaned and heated. Totally sanitary."

She purses her lips.

I flop back, splashing water and floating there for a moment, the bubbles barely covering my most intimate parts. Raven swallows.

"Come on. This might be your only chance at a fae bath."

She sighs and sheepishly strips down to her underwear and climbs in. She shivers as the warm water covers up to her shoulders.

"What is this stuff?" She holds the bubbles up to her nose, sniffing. "Lavender?"

"Close. It's probably the fae equivalent." I shrug.

"So, tell me about today," she says, drifting closer. "What the hell was that?"

"What?"

"All of it? Those guys tying you up and setting those things on you. Then those dragonish creatures? You RODE one. No one else even tried that."

I shrug. "Well, I didn't have much choice. The wires connecting the two sides were severed."

"So, you just thought: if you can't beat 'em, join 'em?"

I chuckle. "Something like that."

"And the popular kids trying to torture you to death?"

I shrug. "I already told you about that."

"Barely," she mutters. "They're really going to go out of their way to kill you?"

I nod slowly. "I knew I wouldn't have any friends here."

"What about the hairy one? He's your friend now, right?"

"Maybe. We haven't spoken. I hope we can be allies for the next couple challenges because apparently that's something I need. If the others are banding together, I'm going to need some help."

She dips her head back, sudsing up her hair. "Yeah." She bites her lip, watching me as I attempt to scrub the sticky blood and mud off my arms.

"Want some help?" she asks, her eyes pinned to my shoulder. I watch her carefully, but she schools her features, giving away no emotion.

I nod slowly and then shift to the side of the tub and grab a red rag from a basket near the wall.

She dips the towel into the water, and I turn as she gently pulls it across my skin. "Is even that going to be enough?" she says quietly. "Is this whole thing... really worth it?"

I bite my lip. "I don't know."

She doesn't respond to that, just cups some water, trickling it over where she recently scrubbed.

"That first challenge was exceptionally intense, but it was designed that way," I say.

"Meaning?"

"They invited all the courts to enter, even ones they don't want to win. So they can weed out the weaklings as quickly as possible. It'll make the rest of the challenges simpler."

"They don't want some to win?"

I shrug. "The queen seems to be intent on the strongest winning, no matter who they are, but that usually means the ruling courts. They're the most powerful, with strong bloodlines and magic and influence. They'll want to make sure, if nothing else, a lesser court doesn't win."

"Why?"

"Politics. The powerful courts want to keep their power. If a lesser court wins or show themselves as stronger in any way, it destabilizes their claim to that power."

"Ew. I hate politics."

"I'm pretty sure everyone does."

"What about you? Are you from a lesser court?"

I nod. "Yes, my court has been cast out for a few hundred years."

"So they don't want you to win because of that? Or because of... what you told me last night."

I swallow. "Both."

She runs her fingertips over my shoulders absently. I shiver and then dunk my head under the water. I hold my hand out for the towel and use it to scrub my lower back and legs.

"You made it past this one... does that mean the next will be easier?"

I turn to face her, noticing a smudge on her nose. She's markedly cleaner than I am but still—being a bird hasn't done her any favors in the cleanliness department. I reach over and grab her a fresh towel. "I'm not the only dirty one," I wink.

She turns, but I think I notice a blush on her cheeks.

"The next challenge will definitely not be easier. But... I suspect it'll be less likely to result in my death."

She turns back, smiling faintly. "Well, I suppose that's good news. When will be it be?"

"Three days, I think. They've scheduled one day of full rest tomorrow. Then a ball the next day, which will be all posturing and annoying but whatever. It'll probably give me a chance to recruit an ally or two."

"I thought everyone hated you?"

I smirk. "Oh, they do. But some have other motives beyond destroying the lesser courts. I'm hoping I can solidify something with my dwarf friend, but maybe I can get someone else as well. Rev is my biggest enemy—or well, I'm his."

"You don't hate him back?"

I dip lower in the water until my lips just graze the surface. "No," I whisper.

She narrows her eyes at that response, but I don't give any more explanation and she doesn't pry any further.

"But Rev is also the favorite to win this competition and to win the crown. There has to be someone else in the trials who is determined to beat him, and knowing how I affect him— "

"The enemy of my enemy is my friend."

I smirk, my eyes shining.

She tilts her head. "Why do your eyes grow brighter sometimes?"

I blink and adjust my emotions, and Raven watches my eyes closely. "How do you do that?"

"Fae eyes are a window to their souls. The color shows their element and their court, and the brightness is evidence of their strength. The strongest fae have very bright eyes."

"You're pretty strong, then? Cause your eyes were like glowing just now."

I take in a long breath and nod. "I don't want anyone else to see that, though. I don't want them to know, especially if I'm to gain an ally or two. If they think I'm a threat to win the trials, they won't align with me. If they think of me as only a tool to distract Rev—their real competition—and they can easily dispose of me later... it might work in my favor."

"So, how do you hide it?"

"Pain," I whisper. "Eyes dim, appearing dull when a fae is in pain."

"You hurt yourself?" Her face crumples in an adorable pout.

"No. It's not only physical pain that does it. Emotional pain can also dim eyes, and I've learned to channel it."

"Are you stronger than them?"

"Yes," I whisper.

"Then you're going to win this?"

"I intend to."

Her soft brown eyes glisten as she studies me. "That's what I'm afraid of."

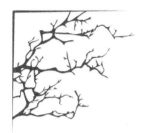

Rev

After a challenging trial and a night of drinking away my sorrows that the shade witch survived, my body is more than spent. I sleep almost the entire next day. I finally wake to bathe near evening and head for dinner with all of the reigning courts. Well, at least those left.

The Cracking Court and the Frost Court, whose champions lost yesterday, have already shipped out. They sent me their support in the upcoming trials, but I suspect they'd sent the same message to the other six champions, just in case they're the winners.

My father frowns in disapproval at my disheveled state, but I ignore him. "Did you need to drink so heavily last night?" he asks under his breath as I sit beside him.

"Yes."

My mother gives a polite laugh, but my father silently snarls. He can't reprimand me here the way he does at home, not that I care if he does regardless. I stopped seeking my father's approval long ago.

I'll never live up to my brother's reputation—in his eyes at least—so why keep trying? I may as well live by my own expectations. By my own goals.

He doesn't even realize that his and mine are aligned. He only sees what he wants to see. A failure of a son. A pathetic heir.

Why does he want to see that? Because he feels the need to continually feel sorry for himself and the loss of his true heir years ago. Poor, poor soul.

I loved my brother, flaws and all. He was arrogant and powerful and charming when he felt the need for it. Those could be extremely worthwhile attributes in an ambitious fae heir. His short temper also made him a force to reckon with if things didn't go just right.

In fact, he was a hell of a lot like my father.

My mother loved me, but my father, most of the time, despised me. He's put on a good face in front of the other courts, if only to avoid weakening our reputation. One day, I will rule. He has no other heirs aside from a set of bastard twins he bore before he married my mother. According to fae law, they can't inherit unless there are no other options.

They are trained and educated like all other heirs, just in case.

Over time, my father has shown his preference for them a bit too heavy handedly, and I am all but certain this attitude has played a role in why I haven't yet been named heir to the High Court.

"It really is in your best interest to keep your body as healthy and fit as possible," my mother says, agreeing with my father in a more reasonable manner. "You know how those hallucinogens affect your body with so little time between trials." My mother speaks low and smooth, quiet and calm enough the other courts don't stop to listen. When my father badgers me they all turn to watch and snigger under their breaths.

I'm over it, and I've learned to ignore it entirely.

"There are emotional and social aspects to these trials far beyond physical. I'm prepared. I am strong. One night of drunken debauchery will not cost me the title. That much, I promise you."

My mother gives a low nod, almost a bow, and her black hair falls forward. "As long as you keep it to one night." She studies me.

"Of course."

And that's the truth. I had intended to eat and head immediately back to sleep for the night. Tomorrow, I'll wake for a workout and a long hot bath and take it easy until the ball.

"No more drinking until at least after the next trial." I hold my fist over my chest in promise.

My mother smiles, and my father sneers. "I'll believe it when I see it."

I roll my eyes. It's in two days. I'm pretty sure I can withhold drinking until then. Even the ball won't be that much of a temptation. As a champion, I'll be expected to show up for an hour or so then allowed to come and go as I please. I fully intend to take advantage of that.

After a polite meal, the room packed with only reigning courts, Brielle comes to sit beside me. "Have you heard about the next challenge?" she whispers.

"Not a word. Have you?"

"Yes. Meet me in the common room in an hour, and we'll talk about it."

I nod, and she laughs giddily like I've just told the funniest joke. She places her hands on my forearm—a fairly intimate gesture in such company. I eye it suspiciously.

My mother notices, her stare settles on the delicate hand resting on my arm. My father glares at me.

Brielle winks, then shuffles off to socialize elsewhere.

My father approaches, leaning low to whisper. "Well played," he says with enough acid that I wince.

Brielle is strong—though she could use more courage out on the field—and influential in her court. If she doesn't marry another heir, she very well may end up queen of her own court. Her mated pair is dead, which means she is open and free for anyone. Whomever she marries will have quite a bit of power.

If she were to marry me, my father would have no choice but to concede some of his ruling power or risk alienating a massively powerful court.

That's not something I've ever considered. Something about a romantic relationship with my dead brother's betrothed seems... unnatural. But politically, it makes a lot of sense. Brielle is smart enough to know what she's doing, so I should be grateful, but I worry that isn't her only motive. I've seen the looks she gives me. Of course, she gives the same to Rook, so maybe it's just her positioning herself, but even so, I can't help but entertain the unnerving idea that she desires me.

I WANDER UP TO THE champion's common room on the fifth floor of the Flicker estate around the time Brielle said to meet. The hall is quiet except for a small human female in strange clothing that freezes when she sees me.

I smile awkwardly, and she scampers off. Weird creatures.

The fire flickers softly as I enter the common room. Both Rook and Brielle are waiting for me, drinks in hand.

"There you are!" Brielle says dramatically, and I raise my eyebrows. "I wasn't sure if something had kept you behind."

"You said an hour. It's been fifty-five minutes."

She rolls her eyes. "Well we've been waiting fifteen minutes."

"If you meant forty-five minutes, then next time, tell me forty-five."

She grimaces, and I wink in her direction—if only to deflect her annoyance. In truth, I waited as long as I could to come up, just in case she was alone when I entered. I still have a lot to wrap my mind around.

If her spectacle at dinner today was more than just trolling my father, I need to figure out how I feel about it.

Logically, it's a win-win. She's beautiful, certainly. And being with her would greatly strengthen my resume in the fae world, but there is still something about it that causes my skin to crawl. Could I love her? Could I be with her? I don't know.

I wonder if that's the real reason she is upset at my on-time-ness. She thinks I'm avoiding her. I was, but I don't want her to be suspicious of my motives.

"I'm sorry if I crossed a line," she says, sitting in the cushioned chair, her shoulders slumped. The crackling fire beneath the stone chimney dims to a dull, low flame.

"Not at all," I say quickly. "No... Well, it took me by surprise, but I recognize how... advantageous it would be."

She smiles, though her eyes remain dim. Light amber, pretty but without its usual luster.

Don't alienate your best ally, Rev. "What would you think about accompanying me to the ball tomorrow?" I spit out.

Her smile turns wicked, and of all the reactions she could have, I like that one the best. The mischievous expression twists my belly in a way her usually sweet demeanor never could.

Maybe I could get over my aversion to her after all.

She nods in acceptance.

"Now, about this challenge," I say, changing the subject. "What have you heard and from whom?"

"My pix friend overheard the queen speaking with her advisors about the lack of physical exertion the second challenge will hold."

She has a pixie playing spy for her, does she?

I nod. "Some of the courts have expressed worry that two physically intense challenges so close together could spell disaster. Of course, I say that would simply test our resolve and endurance thoroughly. It still doesn't surprise me that they would vary the intensity of the trials. But the question remains—what? Will it be mental? Emotional?"

"Fear," Rook says with a low voice as he stares at the fire. I examine his stance, tense muscles, arms crossed, averting his attention from us. Is he bothered by Brielle's new affection towards me? That I asked her to the ball?

"That's what they're going to test?" I ask.

He nods, finally turning towards us. "My father's spies have reliable information on this. They will be testing our fears."

I swallow. "Well, that will prove unpleasant."

Brielle nods. "We can't lose."

"We won't," I say, though I mean myself more than anything. Brielle hasn't always proven to be in full control of her emotions. "If we fail, and she doesn't..." I say it only to motivate Brielle. Her golden red eyes meet mine as her lips curl.

"She will not beat me."

I stand and take a step towards her, towering over her thin frame. "Good. You're better than her. Stronger. One of us—one of us is going to win." I turn my intense stare to Rook, who finally meets my eye.

"We will."

I hate that the betrayer made it past the first challenge in spite of us, but she got through on nerve more than anything else. She's still not proven to have any of the strength I worried she'd have.

"Do you think we'll be able to get to her during this challenge?" I ask.

"It's possible we won't," Rook says. "Unless we each have to face each other's fears? It's unclear how it will be done, but I imagine it will be a less dangerous challenge based on the spy's information, so that makes me think it will be individual. But we'll take whatever opportunity that arises. There will certainly be more challenges with plenty of opportunities. We will get to her, one way or another."

This time, it's my turn to give the wicked smile.

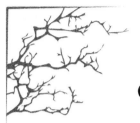

Caelynn

"Take me with you, pleeeease!!"

I roll my eyes at Raven, literally on her knees begging me. "I'll go as a bird, even!"

"A bird at a ball? Come on." I hold my hands on my hips as she crawls closer. I scooch back. "Stop it! You can sit on the terrace as a bird. You'll be able to see inside from there, and all the best drama happens outside anyway. I'm not even going to stay long. I'll come back and hang out with you later."

"Seriously," she says, still crawling forward. "It'll make my LIFE if you make me into a raven and let me sit on your shoulder as you enter. Please, please, please. I promise once you get to the crowd, I'll fly out the window and then sit at the gazebo to watch all the hookups."

I sigh and narrow my eyes at her. I could make her into a raven easily enough. She's done a good job of keeping her distance from the other contestants in public so I doubt anyone has any suspicions yet.

She notices my consideration, and she inches forward, gripping my hands in hers. "Please, please, please, please, please."

I pull my hand back and point in her face. "You stay on my shoulder, completely still—stoic, even—and the moment I'm at the bottom of the stairs, you fly off." She's nodding eagerly already. "You'll be a flashy stunt in their eyes, a magical accessory. NOT a pet. Not a friend. Not anything significant in any way. Anything that brings more attention to you than necessary is dangerous. Do you understand?"

"Yes!" she whispers desperately.

I take in a long breath. "Fine."

She tosses her arms up dramatically, like she just won a championship game, her head hanging back in pure bliss. "Yessssss."

"Okay, Napoleon Dynamite."

"What?"

"Nothing," I murmur.

"I can't believe I get to go to a FAE BALL. OMG." She spins around the room; her arms open wide. This is what I get for bringing a human teenager to the fae realm.

"Now, help me get ready. The dress my queen sent is... intense."

I could magically create a different dress, but it would be impolite to ignore a gift from my court's queen. As much as I dislike my role as a symbol of rebellion, I am still proud of my homeland and the Queen of the Whisperwood.

"I wouldn't put that thing on until you're about to walk out the door. You won't even be able to sit."

I sigh. "I hope I can sit. I have to for the procession."

"Worry about your hair and makeup first. Dress last."

I shake my head. "I'm not trying that hard, Raven."

"What are you talking about? It's a BALL."

I roll my eyes. "And I'm only going because I have to. They made it part of the trials. Stupid fools, just looking for a chance to showcase us like prized cows. How much do you think the crown is making off all that betting?"

"Millions of dollars?"

"We don't use dollars."

"Oh." She stops to ponder. "What do you use?"

"Gemstones. It's a complicated system. Either way, I'm sure the High Court is profiting well from this show they're putting on."

"You were quite dramatic in your last trial. If they want a show, you're doing a good job of it, right?"

I nod. "I'll always be the villain. But then again, everyone loves a villain."

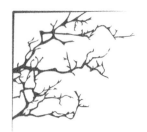

Rev

My whole body is tight as I descend the stairs with Brielle on my arm. The crowd watches with wide eyes and soft murmuring. She and I together make a massive point, but I can't stop the pit in my stomach.

I have never cared for Brielle in this way, so isn't this wrong?

I don't think I'm leading her on. I'm confident she knows my feelings are not true, but she's using the situation to shift herself close to me. Sometimes, it feels as though she's taking advantage of *me*.

But I can't deny how even the hint of an implication of our union would boost my status among the courts. I can't not use it to my advantage, right?

I sigh. Win the trials and none of this will matter. I'm already well on my way to winning. Brielle and Rook are my allies. Rook could be a contender, but we've sparred enough for me to know his weaknesses inside and out. I'm confident I can beat him. My only real competition is Drake, the Whirling Court heir. He also has two high court allies, Caspian and Kari, Glistening and Crystal Court respectively. His allies are possible contenders, but only if the trials work to their advantage. It'll take pure luck.

Still, at the end of the day, it's Drake who I have my eye on. And he clearly has his eye on me. Literally. He's watching as I walk down the stairs, arm in arm with Brielle. Regardless of our relationship status, she is my ally and will remain so, as long as she continues in the competition. Honestly, this fear contest has me concerned for her, especially if it's independent. And if I go into the next trial with only one ally while Drake has two... that might do me in right there.

At the bottom of the stairs, we are greeted by several high ranking fae. We bow and nod and smile politely, but Brielle never takes her arm from mine. Will we be attached like this all month?

I grip her arm tightly, if only so she doesn't notice my anxiety. My smile is big and bright as we mingle with all of the most important fae in our world.

"Odds are on you, boy," Mr. Copper, a Flicker Court official, says with a wink. "So long as that girl doesn't distract you, of course."

I blink, surprised. "Brielle is an ally. She won't be a distraction. That much I can promise."

Brielle beams.

He tsks. "I didn't mean Brielle."

I swallow and follow his attention to the entryway where a dazzling light-haired female in an elegant black dress descends. She's beautiful, the dress hugging all the right curves. Sexy, though the neckline is so high even her collarbones are covered.

My stomach drops. My heart hammers in my chest. *My betrayer*. Why do the most beautiful girls have to be evil?

Brielle also seems rather annoyed at how good she looks. "I cannot wait," Brielle whispers as we watch her gain the attention of everyone in the room, her eyes still dull of life, her expression blank. Bored. Too good to be here. "To snuff her life from this earth."

I snicker in return, but I'm glad that my ally isn't examining my face as I watch my enemy enter the ball. I can't pull my eyes from her, the black jewels on her dress glimmering as her hips sway gently. On her shoulder is a blackbird. It watches the crowd with as much disdain as she does, its wings glistening with hues of purple and blue.

Brielle suddenly pulls me away from the staring, silent crowd, toward the drinks.

"What are we going to do about her?" she whispers.

"You know what we're going to do."

"But how? We need to make a plan. Now. I need a plan."

I sigh. She needs something to focus on before she explodes. That I can sympathize with. She grabs a bubbling purple drink and hands me one. I wave it away. "I can't."

"You're expecting to get through this night entirely sober?"

I chuckle. "I told my father I wouldn't drink until the end of the next challenge. He didn't believe me, so now I must prove him wrong."

She smiles. "He's manipulating you. He only said that to make sure you don't drink."

That very well may be true, actually. I shrug. "I'll keep it in mind for the next time. The challenge is tomorrow, though. So, I can also see the benefits of withholding for another twenty-four hours."

She raises her eyebrows. "I don't know. Knowing the content of this next challenge, I say a bit of drink might be a good thing."

I chuckle at that.

The Shadow Court blackbird flies over our head and into the moonlight out the window above the courtyard doors.

I watch as it settles on a crystal lit tree of the terrace, watching through the windows.

"What are you looking at?" Brielle asks.

I pull my attention back to the room. "That bird, *her* bird, watching us."

Brielle rolls her eyes. "Ravens are always creepy dicks. Don't worry about it."

I turn back toward the ball, knowing she's probably right.

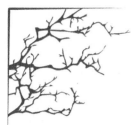

Caelynn

The crowd parts as I pass them. My stomach sinks as I watch Raven fly overhead, just like we talked about, and right out an open window as planned—because Rev's thoughtful eyes linger on her for too long.

I bite my lip and force myself to turn my attention elsewhere.

A set of golden eyes settle on me, bright and thoughtful, through the crowd. Drake, the Whirling Court champion winks at me and I stumble in shock. What the hell is that?

"Hello, mi-lady," a little voice calls from knee level. I find a young pixie, his translucent black wings shuttering in nervousness.

"I'm not a lady," I tell him quickly, despite the pleasant stirring in my stomach at the admiring gaze he's giving me.

"That's not what Mama says. She says you're a hero."

I squat down beside him, "You're from the Shadow Court?" I ask. He nods eagerly. "There are some amazing things from our court. I'm proud of it."

He beams.

"But I am not one of them," I say sternly, and his lips turn to a pout. "I am not a hero, and I never will be. Don't idolize me."

I straighten and sweep away from him in an instant, dipping through the crowd quick enough that I won't need to see the disappointment on his face. When I finally stop, face flushed, and scan the room, I find a set of angry silver eyes.

Rev. Always watching. Always noticing.

What does he make of that? Another reason to hate me, I suppose. *She's so evil she even makes children cry.*

No one in this room is a friend. I have no true allies—expect those from my own court whose worship I despise. But I might be able to create an ally, if I play my cards right.

I search for the Crumbling Courts banners, hoping I can find the dwarfish fae—Tyadin, I remember—among the sea of angry inhuman faces. I cross through the hall, the crowds parting for me. The Queen's speech will start in about twenty minutes, so I have that long to try to align something with him. I don't intend to hang out here long afterwards, so the faster I can get this done, the better.

"Tell me, *dwarf*," I hear a low voice say not far away. I turn towards the sound. "How hairy is your back, really? Enough to make a full cape?" I wrinkle my nose at the rude comment, though I can't see the face of whoever spit it.

There are some actual dwarves in this court, though they're often looked down upon. Faeries and dwarves have never been overly fond of one another. Dwarves are considered second class, among fae. There was actually a dwarfish kingdom across the ocean a hundred years ago, but in more recent years, it's been destroyed by some fell beast.

The Crumbling Court's yellowish-brown banner hangs to the far right of the room, in the general direction I heard the insult from. I push through the crowd quickly, leaving a few aghast fae courtiers glaring at me. I turn back and wink when one female gives me a particularly loud squeal.

A fae from the Twisted Court stands with his arms crossed, towering over a younger fae. They wear the same colors as Rook—Twisted Court green—and the same lifted nose. Near them is a fae with a dwarfish build, but younger than Tyadin.

"Simply barbaric," one fae says to the young stocky male, who looks to the ground uncomfortably. "How do you even fight being so short? You have to swing up, just to spar." They laugh and the young fae drops his elbow onto the dwarfish fae's cheek. "Oops!"

I reach them with one more step and without even speaking a word, I sweep my foot beneath the tallest of the bullying fae, knocking him to the floor. "Oops!" I say loudly. "Maybe if you weren't so busy looking down on someone, you'd have been smart enough to pay attention."

"You're going to pay for that, witch!" the kid says from the floor.

I smirk. "I'll be awaiting your vengeance eagerly. But you'll have to get in line." I shrug. The group scampers off, and I turn to the younger dwarfish fae.

He blinks in shock. Behind him approaches a familiar face, his arms crossed. "You okay, Torin?"

The younger male nods quickly. Now that they're next to each other I see the resemblance isn't just in their race. The slant of their eyes and shape of their nose is identical. They're clearly related.

"I suppose I owe you a thank you," Tyadin says, his face harsh—not at all appreciative.

I wave at him passively. "Not at all. I need no excuses to put a reigning court jerk in his place."

He nods sharply. "Run off to Mama, okay?" he tells the youngster who I now assume to be his brother. The kid nods and pushes through the crowd towards the Crumbling Court banner.

"You came looking for me and found my little brother instead?" He looks over my shoulder as if he doesn't want to look me in the eye.

I nod, not feeling any need to lie. "I heard their sneers from several feet away."

"What do you want, then?" he asks sharply and I wince. I was hoping for a better reaction.

His arms are crossed, expression annoyed. "We're the only lesser courts left. We worked well together during the first challenge. The others are aligning, working against us."

"And you think that means we should work together as well?" He turns his hardened eyes to meet mine.

My stomach sinks.

"Normally, I'd agree. But I am not keen on tarnishing my court's reputation with an alliance so tainted."

I don't speak, don't respond at all. I just watch him.

He doesn't expect to win, then.

I pull in a long breath. "Wouldn't it be better if either one of us won, then one of them?"

"Why? Because we're the underdogs? Not a good enough reason to befriend a murderer."

The breath leaves my lungs, the pain in my stomach like a dagger digging deep. I recover quickly and pull in a long breath. He watches me closely as I school my features, hiding everything.

"All right then. I suppose there's no more that needs to be said." My voice is steady and bored.

His face softens just slightly as I turn my heel in search of the champion's table.

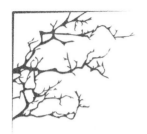

Rev

I find myself unable to turn away from my brother's murderer. She's beautiful, a fact which causes no end to my torment. The back of her dress dips all the way to expose the small of her back. Still, I know despite her outward beauty, what's inside is petrifyingly hideous.

She shouldn't be allowed to breathe any longer, let alone schmooze among the fae realm elite. It gets under my skin, and I find my mood souring the longer I watch her. And the night has only just begun.

"You're distracted," Brielle says, her arm still curled around mine. "What have you learned from your spy-like focus?"

"More questions." I watched the murderer make a child from her own court cry—is she simply that heartless or was there something more to it? The more I think about it the more I realize I have never seen her spend any more time with her court than necessary. She didn't celebrate with them after the first trial, she twists through the crowd as if to avoid them now. They adore her, but does she resent that? It's a strange thought, but I suspect it's true, somehow.

I'd also watched the evil blond beauty defend a dwarfish child, only to be snubbed by her would-be-ally. I'll have to thank the dwarf champion for his loyalty later.

An announcement rings from the rafters, prompting the champions to find our seats so the queen can make her appearance, say some pretty words, and then the dancing will begin.

As I swing Brielle towards the champions' table, I lean in and whisper in her ear, "Also that our enemy has lost her only ally."

Brielle flicks an eyebrow up. "Well, that's good news indeed."

Now, she's alone. With no power. No experience. No allies.

I take my place beside Brielle, causing the other champions to scramble to find a new place after I upset the court order. Brielle grins widely at their distress.

Finally, Drake joins us, seamlessly taking Brielle's old place—beside the betrayer—without so much as a shift in facial expression. He wouldn't dare align himself with the outcast, would he?

As if reading my thoughts, he grins in my direction, his eyes a bright. My stomach sinks. If I am snubbed as heir, he would be the next best contender.

He wants to be king. He wants to beat me in this competition.

How low would he sink to achieve it?

The lights dim, the front of the ballroom glowing with orange light as the queen descends. Her dress is white with a long train that is embellished with literal flames rising all the way up her back like moving scales.

She walks slowly and the whole room quiets. Her reign is coming to an end, and I can't help but feel like she's eager to shed the responsibility. After all, this plague is no game. I can't imagine the kind of stress that would put on a ruler. The doubt. The guilt.

If she can put a stop to it—even by means of finding the champion to save us all—she'll be remembered as a hero. A great queen.

If she doesn't, she'll be blamed for all time.

It's easy to forget here, in this untouched lovely court, the terrors that are spreading through our world.

"Welcome again. Congratulations to all the champions who succeeded in the first trials." A roaring round of applause sounds through the room. "It was a horrid thing, losing such promising young fae, in a competition of all things. It's one of the reasons we did away with the trials generations ago. It was not worth the loss of life. When we resurrected the ancient tradition, we knew there would be loss. We knew that many great fae would die in the process. It was a difficult choice to make, but I believe that it was the right one. These trials are a worthy cause to die for. These trials will choose a savior. If we were not willing to sacrifice ourselves for the betterment of our people, for the survival of our people, our choice of champion would be a farce. So, to those courts who have lost a champion, I want you to know they will be honored. We thank you for your sacrifice."

An image appears on the wall—images of the fallen champions.

"Crevin of the Crackling Court. Prickanante of the Frost Court. Jarsali of the Root Court. Finn of the Winding Court. Willow of the Webbed Court. And still living: Emmett of the Beastly Court and Aaliyah of the Venomous Court. You will *all* be remembered as heroes."

The crowd claps politely.

"Tomorrow we will begin a new trial. The second of four. The first was intense. This will be a quiet challenge, testing your mental fortitude. Until then, let the merriment begin! Good luck, champions."

The queen quickly descends from her throne, now practically speed walking towards the exit and up the stairs, her dress still blazing.

She finally exits and the lights brighten. Music begins gently rising and falling, growing louder and louder. Purple sprites line a circle in the middle of the floor where couples are already racing to be the first to dance.

I hold out my hand to Brielle. "Are you ready?"

"For dancing with you or the challenge tomorrow?"

"Both." Her eyes shine with amusement as she takes my hand and I lead her out onto the dance floor.

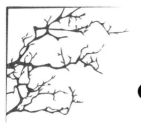

Caelynn

R ev pulls Brielle out onto the dance floor. Faery lights sparkle above, stringed instruments being a soft purr and I slip away from the crowds and onto the quiet terrace. The door shuts with a soft click, and the magical stir of music is muted behind me. I shiver as the cool air hits me.

The ground is paved with mosaic tiles, depicting important moments and people and symbols in Flicker Court history. I could lose myself in all the details displayed in this beautiful abstract artwork. Bright colors and confusing patterns. If you follow it, you'd uncover the whole story of this powerful court.

Trees bank the terrace, covered in glowing crystals of varying colors. Bright purple, red, white, yellow, green, blue—each representing the remaining champions' courts. One single tree isn't lit at all, a dull void set between yellow and red. I draw closer to the dim tree, cast in shadows. At first glance it looks like a flaw in their elaborate decor.

It's mine, I realize.

I run my fingers over the rough bark absently. Instead of taking time to understand my court and finding a way to represent us respectfully, they left it bare. Shadows are its only embellishment. Lack of light its only worthy quality.

A quiet stirring draws my eyes up to find one other decoration to represent my beloved court—a raven sitting on its lowest limb, watching me closely. Her wings glisten with translucent colors mixed with the black, purples, and blues shifting with such beauty it takes my breath away.

If you didn't look closely, you wouldn't even notice it at all.

I smile, my heart soaring for one quick moment. Did Raven understand which tree she chose to rest on? Did she do it for me? I'm not sure I even want to know because intended or not, it means everything to me.

I curl my fingers over the thin trunk, magic shifting through them. I'll add one more embellishment. Raven shivers and hops from the tree to the stone below, as a murmur shutters through the leaves. Indistinguishable whispers dart through the leaves making them rustle in a swirling pattern, just like in the Whisperwood. This is just a silly charm that won't last more than an hour, but it's an echo of the homeland I lost.

The world inside the banquet hall is distracted by whatever spectacle is happening on the dance floor—something I know without a doubt I do not want to witness alongside them. Not an eye is turned toward the glass doors to the terrace. My lips curl into a wicked grin, and I close my eyes imagining the dress in my mind's eye.

Dark blue, almost black, with purple and blue stones scattered across it like starlight. Sweetheart neckline and black ribbon around the middle where it extends into a tool skirt.

A gasp sounds through the terrace, and I open my eyes to see Raven in my purple dress creation, spinning and giggling.

"It's amazing," she whispers. When she stops, she looks into the banquet hall, her eyebrows pulled down. "Is it dangerous?"

"Not if no one sees you." I wink. "There are humans in this world too. Rare in a large fae court, but they're around. Two girls talking outside wouldn't be enough to cause much suspicion."

I take a seat on the short stone barrier at the edge of the terrace.

"Someone seeing you leave my room, though..." I side-eye her, knowing she'd left the room the other day while I was sleeping.

She stares at the ground, biting her lip. "Sorry," she murmurs.

I step closer, and brush a lock of hair behind her ear. "I just want to keep you safe."

"And near you."

I smile, watching her brown eyes, dull and yet incredibly beautiful. Sometimes I wonder if I should be thankful for Raven's brokenness. Otherwise, how could someone like her love me?

As if reading my thoughts, she grabs my hand, curling her fingers in mine.

"Your eyes are glowing again," she says, wonder and awe in her expression.

I blink and shake my head, remembering myself. I'm in public. If someone sees, my secret will be blown.

I'm bad for her, I remind myself. I'm taking risks with her life, and if something happens to her because of my own selfishness... I swallow.

The door to the terrace opens, music growing louder and then muting again. I spin to face Drake, his long golden hair draped over his shoulders.

"Why hello there," he says sweetly, eyes darting between the both of us. My stomach sinks, though I'm secretly grateful he didn't come out only a moment earlier when he would have seen my bright eyes.

"Who is this lovely creature?" he asks, head tilting to the side innocently.

Oh, hell no. My fingers tighten into a fist as Raven ducks her head and shifts behind me.

"We've just met," I say, eyes pinned to his harshly. Territorial. *She's prey*, that's the act I'll put on for him. "She is quite lovely, isn't she?" I puff my chest out.

"What's her name?" he asks.

"Rael," I answer quickly.

His harsh eyes turn back to me and he smiles, exposing sharp canines. My expression turns darker. *You want to fight me for her? I'm willing. Try to take me.* My chest heaves up and down with menace. I hold back a literal snarl.

Drake chuckles and waves dismissively. "Take your prize. Humans aren't my cup of tea."

My shoulders relax as he sits on the stone near the shadow tree, but I will not drop my guard entirely. "You on the other hand..." He purses his lips. "You are quite interesting."

I sneer at him.

"Relax, I'm not a threat." He winks. "Not right now."

Important distinction. I resist the urge to roll my eyes, remembering I may be inclined to align with him at some point. At the very least, being his enemy is a step in the wrong direction.

The music in the hall grows louder again, and I blink as a new form joins us on the terrace.

"Making new enemies, Drake?" a dark skinned fae female in a purple gown says.

"I hope not," he says, clicking his lounge, examining me. "That was not my intention."

I narrow my eyes.

"Good, because we are always in the market for new allies." Kari's purple eyes turn to me, considering. "We only take those that make us stronger, though." She shrugs, like it is all hypothetical.

Is she making fun of me for my weakness? Or inviting me to prove myself?

Raven grips my waist with tight fingers, and I pull in a long breath, breaking my concentration. "As fascinating as this conversation is, you've interrupted something... personal." I smile, savage and cruel.

Kari's eyebrows raise, her attention skirting to the figure behind me. "My apologies. Oh my, I love her dress!"

I'm taken aback by the honesty in her tone at that compliment, but I shake it off and pull Raven through the trees behind the estate.

Behind us, I hear Drake chuckle. "I suppose we shouldn't be surprised she has a taste for humans."

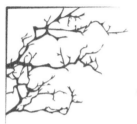

Caelynn

I spit Raven's hair from my mouth as consciousness returns to me, sunlight streaming through the windows. The bed is soft and warm, but I pull myself out of it with a groan.

Last night was an epic fail.

I'd achieve my goal of approaching Tyadin about our alliance, and his message was very clear—*screw you*.

As much as it hurts, I can't blame him. I'd likely feel the same in his shoes. An alliance with me might be his only chance at winning these trials, but the sacrifice would be hefty. Throwing in his lot with the most hated fae of our time.

I had hoped his court would be sympathetic to the rebellion. That may have been enough to make it a worthwhile arrangement. I got the feeling he didn't snub me out of worry for his reputation, however. He refused an alliance out of his own moral code.

He didn't want to befriend a murderer.

"You okay?" Raven rolls over to face me.

I nod, but there's a knot in my stomach. After our conversation with Kari and Drake, I took Raven directly to my room, not at all caring who saw. She'd been noticed as my prey, so it fit the story. It just can't happen again.

I can't let any fae read anymore into our relationship. We can't be seen together again or I'll have to send Raven home. I told her as much last night.

"There's something off about that guy," Raven says, rubbing sleep from her eyes. "He was up to something."

I swallow. "I suspect Drake is always up to something."

"I don't like him."

I nod. "Good. You should never trust a fae. Any fae."

She purses her lips. "What about you?"

I chuckle. "Probably not me either, but it's a bit too late for that."

"I never got a chance to tell you what I heard before you came to meet me last night."

"Oh?"

"The golden-haired jerk was talking with a kid with horns about a meeting tomorrow—well, today now. I don't know what it was about, but he was really mean to the kid. I didn't like it."

"What meeting? Where, when?"

"Somewhere called the pits? And oh-eight hundred, whatever that means."

I run through the conversation with Kari last night. Maybe it was a test. They want to know what value I'd bring to an alliance. They want to know if I could figure it out.

Maybe.

That or I'm about to just show up to their secret meeting unannounced and really piss them off. I pull on my new tunic, one small part of my new wardrobe supplied by my court and a few generous rebel sympathizers. I have a new set of swords, much like my old. I also have a warm jacket and potions.

Still missing those allies, though—for now.

"Where are you going?" Raven asks.

"To find that meeting."

RAVEN FLIES OVERHEAD, back in her owl form, just in case, as I march through the palace grounds.

I'm not well versed in this kingdom, having never visited in my childhood—we weren't good enough to be invited. And now that I'm here as a hated outcast, I wasn't exactly given a tour of the place.

Usually the term "pits" would imply a fighting pit of some kind. The two most likely places for that would be out across the grounds or in the dungeons. I'm not eager to explore the latter and I hadn't seen anything relevant during my workouts around the lake, so I start out at the south side, looking for any large structures that could be an ancient amphitheater.

Raven squawks in the distance, and I increase my speed to a quick run, my sore back roaring in protest. Only five more minutes until the meeting time.

I'm hoping I didn't get the worst injuries during that first challenge because I'm already the underdog here. After my dwarf friend rejected me, I'm all on my own.

Although, as a massive, old stone structure comes into view around the east side of the estate, I find myself hoping for a change in fortunes.

I WALK SLOWLY THROUGH the arches. I keep my breath even but a drip of sweat rolls down my temple.

The browned stone had crumbled in places, but the architecture is quite fascinating. Just knowing how old a building like this is, astounds me. Humans think their ancient structures are old. This one may be twice as old as the colosseum, if not older.

Stone in the form of seats stretch around in a circle like a stadium with a dirt-covered arena in the middle. The whole structure is probably only large enough to hold a few hundred spectators. That would imply this was a piece of Flicker Court culture long before the Flicker Court even existed.

Standing in the middle of the dust-covered arena are three forms. I suppose I successfully found the "pits."

"You came," Drake says. His lips curl into a quick smile, telling me he isn't at all surprised to see me.

He's the perfect fae prince charming, in a golden tunic, matching his gold locks which are tossed into a man-bun. His striking blue eyes examine me closely. He is powerful, and he wants me to know it.

"Let me introduce my team. Caspian of the Glistening Court and Kari of the Crystal Court." Drake waves his hand dismissively. "I am Drake of the Whirling. I assume you know that already."

"Why would you assume that?" I tilt my head innocently. We spoke last night, but had a never a formal introduction.

Kari snickers, and Drake shoots her a glare. I smile wide, making sure to hold on to my veil of anger and pain swirling inside. My sources of joy are limited mostly to wicked enjoyment, which doesn't affect my eye color, but I can't take that chance right now.

If this is what I suspect, the deal would be off the moment they caught even a hint at the extent of my power.

"How did you know about our meeting?" Kari asks.

I shrug. "I have my ways."

She chuckles. "I'm sure you do. The Shadow Court has always been known for their ability to wield secrets. I'd wondered if you held the same ability."

If only they knew my spying abilities came in the form of a human masquerading as a bird.

"It's certainly not my only talent."

"I assume you're here out of desire to align with us," Drake says, examining his cuticles.

"Perhaps."

"We are three of the strongest champions in the competition. As I suspect you'd already gathered, alliances are forming within the trials. You do not have any, do you?" His voice rises in pitch. An attempt at innocence or condescension? My guess is both.

"I do not," I say honestly, resisting the urge to leer at him. He's right. I need alliances, and I don't have any.

"If the dwarf were smart, he'd have aligned with you," Kari says. "But I noticed your interaction last night. It didn't seem very... cozy."

"It wasn't," I admit. I examine the Crystal Court champion. She's smart, poised, her eyes a lovely purple and likely underestimated. She'll be a difficult opponent to defeat. "He said he wasn't willing to befriend a murderer."

Drake grins, but Caspian curls a lip in disgust. Apparently, he feels the same.

"So sad when past mistakes continue to bite us in the butt, isn't it?" Drake says.

"Not really," I say. "That's simply called consequences. Without them, our world goes to shit."

Kari narrows her eyes as she examines me. "Do you not wish to win the trials, then?"

Drake turns a glare to her. "Why wouldn't she?"

Kari doesn't take her eyes off of me. "Are you just trying to make a point? Or do you have another goal?"

I shake my head. "I intend to win."

Caspian rolls his eyes. Drake grins—he doesn't think I have a chance. Kari continues to watch me with quiet consideration.

"Winning the trials is as much a punishment as it is reward." And I believe I'm the right one to enter hell in search of a cure.

"You seek redemption," she says with a nod.

I shrug. "A form of it, I suppose." I clamp my mouth shut after that, knowing if I continue, I won't be doing myself any favors. I want them to think they have something to give me that I'd sincerely desire—other than winning the trials. Let them think they have the upper hand, that they have what I desperately desire in the palm of their hand.

Confident people make mistakes.

"What makes you think we'd want you with us?" Caspian says, clearly annoyed. "You're visibly weak. What value would you bring?"

I raise my eyebrows.

"I don't know," Kari says. "Riding a shadow-vyrn? That was pretty badass."

I smile but ignore her interjection. "Distraction," I say, answering Caspian's concern directly. "So long as I'm in the trials, Rev and his allies are distracted with their bloodlust."

Kari crosses her arms but smiles widely. She likes this answer. Drake too, looks impressed.

I know without a doubt that they'd wanted me to show up to this meeting. They want me as part of their alliance—well, not Caspian, clearly, but the other two. And this is the reason why.

"It's an interesting proposition," Drake says. "We are one of two major alliances left in the trials. The other is Reveln, Rook, and Brielle. Perhaps we could stand to use another on our side."

"They're a pretty tight alliance. Friends for years, and I hear Rev and Brielle are an item now." Kari winks, causing my stomach to sink.

"That's disgusting," Caspian says.

"Why?" I can't help but ask. What would be disgusting about two fae courting?

"Boning your dead brother's fated mate?" He shivers.

My blood runs cold. Brielle was Reahgan's mate? I... hadn't realized.

"They were never together, what does it matter?" Kari asks.

"Anyway," Drake says. "All three of them, I know for certain, have sworn to kill you at the first opportunity. So, I can see how advantageous a strong alliance would be for you."

And why he can trust I won't turn on him. Alone, I'm unlikely to survive. "They've already tried," I admit.

"They attacked you?" Caspian asks.

"They set a trap for me during the first trial." I leave it simple. No need to give them more details than necessary. "It didn't work."

"They'll try harder," Drake says matter-of-factly.

"I don't doubt it."

"They didn't think you had much of a chance at surviving that challenge, so I'm confident their attempt was half-hearted. You surprised us all, if I'm honest."

First honest thing you've said today.

"I, for one, think you've been punished enough," he continues. "You were only a child, after all. Even in the human world they don't judge a child's actions the same as an adult's." His tone is so sweet I almost gag.

I hold my breath, schooling every feature not to show my utter disdain and disgust. I need this alliance. I need them to at least think I'm on their side for another challenge or two. If they'll defend me against my real enemies—who *will* try to kill me—then I have to take it. I clench my hands into fits but otherwise manage to keep my expression calm.

"So, is it a deal?" I ask.

"We'll take it under consideration."

I clench my jaw. They made it clear they have the upper hand. They're interested in the alliance, but they know I need them more than they need me.

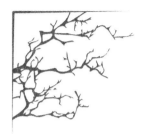

Rev

I stand at the edge of the ruby gates inside the training room, looking up at the intricate design, breathing deep and steady. I am ready.

"You ever think what our life would have been like if she'd never been born?" Brielle's voice is soft beside me. The other champions gather behind us, but my focus is sharp. Facing only what lies before me.

I clench my jaw. "Every day."

"Do you think things happen for a reason?"

"No." I feel her wince at my harsh tone but refuse to look. "I think the world is shit, and we just have to do what we can with it."

"We're going to kill her," she says, the venom in her voice terrifying. She repeats the same mantra every day. *We will kill her.*

"Yes," I hiss. Even if I have to sacrifice my own life to do it. My brother's murderer will meet her end before the end of the month. I'd rather not destroy all my prospects to achieve it—I'd rather not take my own life to steal hers—but I will. If that's what it takes.

The doors swing wide and the remaining eight contestants walk out into the sunlight. I march, my head high as the crowd screams. I lead the pack. The rest of the champions march behind me.

At the end of the massive arena are the thorn gates that marked the beginning and end of our first trial. Below the thorn arch, near the middle of the arena stands an orb of glistening black. Inside are three figures.

A pixie flies overhead, past the champions and over the crowd who cheers for her. She lands on top of the translucent black orb. "Welcome, champions, to your second trial! Today, you will each, one by one, enter the orb of despair. You must face your deepest regrets, and darkest fears in order to succeed."

The crowd oohs and ahhs. "It isn't as simple as it sounds, though. You won't be facing your fear of spiders or heights. You will be facing nightmares made real. Some of you will be forced to reenact your greatest regrets. Some of you must watch the worst moments of your life unfold without lifting a finger. You will not be reversing the darkness in your minds and souls and lives. You must accept them. You must make them part of you. The magic inside this orb can look deep into your soul and learn everything about you in a moment. It will choose your task. Whatever will be the hardest for you to achieve. That is what you must do to move forward in this competition."

The crowd roars. Well, this is going to be interesting. I have a feeling there are going to be a few overlapping events the orb will showcase today. Mine, Brielle's, and the murderer's—will we all be reliving my brother's death?

"The crowd will not be able to see what you face. No one but the champion inside will witness the horrors they face, and none will be forced to share. What we will be able to see is your actions and reaction. Nothing more."

So, they'll be able to guess what you're facing based on what your body does.

I clench my jaw tightly.

"If you cannot achieve the task the orb sets for you, your trials will be ended and you will no longer be a champion in the Trial of Thorns."

Just do as you're told. Simple.

"Come, champions!" the pixie calls. "Approach the orb."

We walk forward slowly. Already, my heart pounds.

As I approach, the three forms slip into focus, their faces clear as day.

In the center is my brother, Reahgan. Tears sting my eyes. I'd nearly forgotten what he looked like. Next to him is *her*. His murderer. And on his other side is me. A younger me.

I swallow.

"What do you see?" I ask Brielle without looking away, my voice shakier than I'd like.

She doesn't respond. I look down at her expression. There are tears on her cheeks, but her expression is one of pure unadulterated rage. I suspect she's seeing the exact same thing as I am.

"It's a clue," I tell her "What we're seeing now is a hint of what we'll face when we go in."

She presses her lips into a thin line. "Why didn't we kill her in the first challenge?" she spits, not taking her eyes off of the orb. "We should have just shoved a blade through her heart and been done with it."

I take in a long breath. "We still have time. We just have to make it through this, and we'll get the chance."

Caelynn

I shiver as I peer into the orb. There are three forms inside. Two are obvious—Rev and his brother. The third is a moving dark monster, shifting like smoke. A hand reaches out from the shifting form, reaching towards Rev's throat.

I tear my eyes from the image. Already, my heart races, my palms sweat, and my stomach twists in panic. Facing Rev and Reahgan is one thing—that beast is another.

For the first time, I doubt my ability to do this.

It's not real, I tell myself.

Not real. Not real. Not real. Not real.

Rev's eyes meet mine from the front of the crowd of champions, hate swirling in his gaze. I swallow down my panic and steel myself with my own shadows. I meet his gaze, steady, unmoved.

Pain ricochets from his face, and I wish I wasn't such a good actress. What would it achieve, though? If he knew how I really felt? If he knew how much I hated myself? How much I wish I could undo what I've done?

Instead, I live with it and I let it become me.

That's what this is testing right? That monster I faced—it took my soul. I took its essence, and used it to survive.

I've lived with this every day of my life. I've never cast it off or pretended to forget it. Never let praises from my own people skew my perception of it.

I know my own darkness and I wear it like a shield.

I'll do the same today and I'll make it out on the other side. My panic still swirls inside of me like a storm but my determination is stronger. I grasp it tightly.

The beast will be gleeful at what he's turned me into. He'll laugh that I ever thought I'd beaten him.

His power to crush my life and my very soul was proven to be beyond reproach. I may have physically escaped, but at the end of the day, he won.

WE GO IN REVERSE ORDER, the weakest courts first, then the ruling courts in their typical order.

This means Tyadin is first. I'll go second.

I barely watch as he steps into the misty orb, magic rippling like water where he entered and then settling back into its smooth translucent gray.

Now, all we can see is Tyadin's silhouette. First, he stands there, his shoulders back, his head high. But then he stumbles back, pressing against the orb's glistening barrier. His chest heaves dramatically.

I can't tell what his challenge is, but suddenly he's holding a sword. He grips it tightly in both hands, his muscles tense. He reels it back, ready to slash through some unseen enemy. But then his muscles freeze in place and he remains like that for a full minute. My heart pounds and it's not even my challenge.

Finally, his hands loosen their grip and the sword clangs to the ground, and he drops to his knees. The crowd oohs and ahhs, unsure. Is he failing? Or is his task inaction?

He holds his hands over his ears and screams in agony.

My teeth chatter as I watch.

He stays like that, screaming until his voice is hoarse, hands over his ears.

Then he stands, his shoulders slumped—defeated. Another moment, he walks to the other edge of the orb, which parts for him.

The crowd is silent for a long moment, then they erupt in a massive roar.

Tyadin is the first to pass the second challenge.

He doesn't seem pleased with his success or the attention as he stumbles to the champions' benches, his hands shaking. Tears stream down his cheeks.

"Next, Caelynn of the Shadow Court."

Nausea sweeps through me as I step forward on shaky feet. I take in three deep breaths and stop before the orb to steel myself. There are some kinds of darkness that terrify even me, but I must embrace even the deepest. So, I allow it to sweep over everything, and my shaking calms.

The black liquid shifts to allow me in, and I enter the orb of terrors.

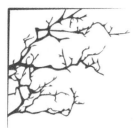

Caelynn

For a long moment, I am surrounded by only darkness.

Hello, old friend, I think to myself and chuckle under my breath.

"Hello," a whisper responds, and my knees nearly buckle as the panic shoots through me. I swallow, eyes remaining closed.

"Look at you, my little pet. You've become just what I'd hoped," the echoing voice of my nightmares rings through the sphere.

Night Bringer.

"Are you ready to face your task?" he asks.

I take in a shaky breath and finally find enough bravery to open my eyes. "Haven't I already started?"

"Oh no." The monstrous voice tsks. "You've not yet begun."

I swallow, watching the shadows shift. Red eyes glow deep within.

Not real. Not real.

He's not really here. He couldn't be. Wouldn't be.

The ancient voice chuckles. "You aren't happy to see me after all these years?"

"What is my task?" I bark with a shaky voice.

"So eager," he chides.

The inky blackness swirls around me and I stand still, growing dizzy. "Oh, I remember a time, so many years ago, when you came to me for a task. Do you remember, Caelynn?"

He laughs, the sound reverberating to my right. "Of course you do. Well, isn't it ironic," he continues his voice curling around me then settling to my left, "that you'd simply need to achieve the same goal a second time."

I wince, scrunching my face up as a chill moves its way up my body, as if an invisible finger runs up my back. I resist the urge to beg for it to stop.

I learned, many years ago begging doesn't help. It just makes you look weak.

"Tell me," I announce with a stronger voice than I thought possible.

"Well, you've certainly grown more of a backbone."

"My TASK," I scream, ready to explode.

"Your task, my dear old friend, is to kill him." Reveln's face appears before me, boyish and innocent.

I shiver.

"No. Not him," the voice instructs. "There will be time for that yet to come."

I turn my attention to the form at the far left of the orb. "Him," the smoke tickles as it whispers in my ear. And my attention focuses on Reahgan.

His silver eyes are as harsh as I remember, his face full of arrogance and hatred. I remember the feeling of his light holding me down so that I couldn't move.

I shake my head. No, that isn't the memory I'm here to face. All I need to know is that Reahgan, the future king of all the fae—is evil. No one else saw it but me.

Kill Reahgan, again. That's my task.

A dagger appears in my hand, a familiar weight, magic rippling through my body as I grip it. This is the act that forever changed my life.

Movement to my right catches my attention. The young Reveln approaches me, his face crumpled in despair. My mouth falls open as I peer into his silver eyes—so different from his brother's harsh ones. So different from the Reveln I know now.

He was young and unscarred.

I am the one who scarred him.

I am the one who shifted his life irrevocably and made him live with this pain and anger until it warped him into the person he is now. I often see his brother in his eyes and that, of all the things that hurt, is what kills me the most.

Young Rev, only a year older than me at the time, drops to his knees and begs me not to kill his brother. "Please, Cae." I shiver at the sound of my name on his lips. "Please don't hurt my brother. Please don't do this to me!"

I step forward, tears already streaking down my face. "I have to."

"Please don't do this to me!" he screams. "Don't you know what we could be?"

The blade loosens in my grip, and I nearly drop it. "Yes," I whisper. Emotion dragging my walls down. I would give anything—*anything*.

I shake my head from the haze. No, there is no going back. This is who I am now.

"Yes," I whisper to the sweet Rev, tears covering his soft eyes. I touch his face gently. "I know what I gave up. But that was lost so long ago."

I shove the blade through Reahgan's heart.

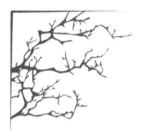

Rev

Brielle grips my forearm tightly as we watch my brother's murderer repeat the crime right in front of us. We can't see his face or his body, but we know he's there—in her mind.

The whole crowd gasps as she shoves a dagger through an invisible victim.

We all know what she just did.

My vision goes black for those moments afterwards. Then she passes through the orb untouched and silence settles in the stands around us.

This is their reminder. This is the evil fae who murdered their future king.

After the dwarf's challenge, there was stunned silence and then an eruption of cheers. After hers? Stunned silence, followed by an eruption of boos and jeers.

Fruits and cups and even a weapon or two flies into the arena, aimed at the most hated fae in our world.

Her face is calm, still, as she passes through the arena to sit beside the dwarf. More items fly at them both, a few getting close to hitting their target. A stone wall raises from the ground, protecting their backs. I sneer but can't blame the dwarf for not wanting their hatred for her to hurt him. Especially knowing that he'd rejected her alliance.

"Brielle of the Flicker Court!"

Brielle tenses next to me, as if it were possible to be tenser. I worry she'll crack her own nails, gripping her sword handle so hard.

I grab her upper arm and pull her to face me. She gasps, her eyes huge. "Listen to me," I say sternly. "They're going to make you face it. You're—" I pause, my voice suddenly lost in my panic. "They're going to make you watch him die," I whisper, my voice breaking, even though it's barely there to begin with.

She winces, a tear already forming in the corner of her eye.

"I need you to remember something: nothing you do will change it. Nothing will bring him back. The only thing we can do is complete the task so we have the chance to avenge him. Complete the task because that's the only way to get to *her*." I openly point to the murderer. She doesn't notice or care. Her eyes are cast to the dirt between her feet like she's just bored and waiting for the chance to leave. The crowd murmurs, and a few jeers in response to my pointing.

Brielle looks me in the eye, only slightly less terrified.

"We're going to kill her," I tell her definitively. "But I need your help to do it. I need you beside me in the next challenge."

I take in a long breath, and then she nods and stomps toward the orb.

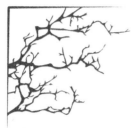

Caelynn

"You see now why I can't be your ally?" Tyadin says as Brielle enters the orb of terrors.

I nod. "I already knew. I get it."

He purses his lips.

"I wouldn't align with me either," I admit.

He narrows his eyes at me but then turns his attention to the orb. We watch Brielle stand still as stone inside.

"Is she facing the same thing as you?" he asks.

"Probably," I whisper.

"It took you a long time, even before the dagger came," he says, a question implied.

"I had to face the monster first. That might have been the harder task." Killing Reahgan, in some ways, felt good. I hated seeing Rev's love for his brother and how I'd destroyed him. But killing his brother after what he'd done to me had always felt good. Sometimes, that's what makes me hate myself the most.

I enjoyed killing him.

"Monster?" Tyadin asks.

I don't respond. That is my secret to know. I realize now that my task had two parts. The voice took on the sound of the one from my nightmares, but it wasn't really him. No, if it had been him, he wouldn't have let me go so easily.

He is real and alive. And waiting for another chance to destroy lives. He is my real nightmare.

Brielle is shaking and crying. "I'm going to kill her," she says clear as day. "We're going to kill her for you," she tells the vision, visible to only her. She falls to the ground, her feet folding beneath her. She rocks back and forth, sobbing. "We'll kill her. We'll kill her. I swear it."

I swallow. How many others can hear what she's saying?

She continues chanting between sobs, but then it suddenly stops. She looks up at some invisible vision and gasps. "No," she says. "No!"

She's standing in an instant, a dagger in her hand—a dagger identical to mine. The one I used to kill Reahgan a decade ago.

She stomps forward but then stops, her muscles freezing, her face crumpling. "HOW DARE YOU!" she screams at no one. She drops the dagger to the ground and moments later she marches from the orb with a look that could kill.

This time there is no pause. The cheers erupt immediately for Brielle.

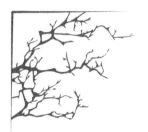

Rev

The whole time Brielle is in the orb, I pace, my hand over my gaping mouth. I curse under my breath at her every mumble. I don't care who hears our plans to kill the murderer. Most of the fae in our world would consider us heroes for such an act. But I'm terrified Brielle will lose. I'm afraid her resolve will flip like a switch and she'll attack.

She stands, like something suddenly changed, and I hold my breath as she screams and almost charges.

When she finally exits the orb, I let out a relieved breath. She doesn't so much as glance in my direction. She stops to catch her breath before taking her place next to the murderer, but she does so looking down at her feet, her face blank and fallen.

I don't watch the next several fae. Instead, I sit and focus on myself. I calm my heart, and I prepare to face my brother's death.

The male immediately after Brielle fails—Caspian of the Glistening Court. He charges some unknown foe and is tossed from the orb like trash from a bin. I am tempted to celebrate his loss—it weakens my strongest opponent considerably, but I refrain because I need to focus. I haven't won this one yet.

Drake passes and exits the orb with a stupid ass smile on his face. Kari passes. Then, it's Rook's turn. I hadn't thought to give him a pep talk—convinced he'd make it through just fine. I let out a relieved breath as he exits the orb on his own.

"Reveln of the Luminescent Court!" the Pix announces, and I stand, my heart in my throat.

I enter the orb and the cheers disappear. I am surrounded by silent darkness.

A form appears in front of me, and my heart pounds. Her face is out of focus but also clear. I squint trying to figure it out. Who is she?

She has beautiful dark eyes with flickers of golden light cascading from them—I'm not sure I've ever seen eyes that bright. Her hair in on the lighter side, but the color is hard to tell with the shadows of the orb cascading over her. She smiles and something about the way she looks at me causes my stomach to flutter.

I'm supposed to feel something about this strange girl. Have I ever met her? I don't know. My mind feels hazy. There is a message here the orb wants me to know, and yet it's veiling it at the same time.

"Hello, Rev," the girl whispers, her voice light and sweet. I take a step toward her, drawn to her like a magnet.

"Who are you?" I ask, so confused. What is my task?

"She's just in the way." I jump at the sudden voice echoing around me. "Dispose of her, little brother." His tone is dismissive. Not an order.

"Reahgan?" I ask.

My brother's voice chuckles around me, filling the orb with strange joy and power that scares me.

"Why?" I ask. I know I have to obey but the task is unclear. *Dispose of her.* Am I meant to kill her? Some innocent strange girl? I'm confused...

"She's no one and she's in the way. She's dispensable." I shiver as the darkness in my brother's voice. The... wickedness.

Another form appears behind the beautiful girl. My brother approaches from behind her, a cruel smile on his face. He grips her hair and whips her head backwards. She yelps in pain, her eyes twisting in fear as my brother throws her to ground.

I freeze. What is this? My brother didn't... he wasn't....

"Don't stop it," a new voice commands me. And I watch helplessly as a bright light shines from my brother's palm, paralyzing the beautiful girl.

I cover my hand with my mouth, appalled. Shaking.

No. My brother didn't do this. He didn't.

I blink as a dagger protrudes through his back. My brother stumbles and turns toward me, the dagger sticking right through his chest. Through his heart.

His dim eyes meet mine. "Avenge me," he whispers.

My body is on fire. Rage and fear and panic fill me. What the...

The girl stands, and her face changes. At first, tears glisten over her cheeks, pain and fear in her eyes, but her eyes grow dimmer, darker. Her face stripped of all emotion. Her features turn sharp, her eyes sallow. She's still beautiful, but now... I choke on a sob.

"Call me by my name," she begs, her voice low and broken, "before you kill me."

I stumble a step back as her features sharpen until I recognize her. She's older, more tired. Angry. Lonely. In pain.

But it's the same girl. The same girl I'd promised to kill so many times before.

A dagger appears in my hand, and the voice issues a new command. "Choose."

Choose? I thought it was supposed to tell me what to do and I obey? I could obey. I could drop the dagger. I could stab her through the heart.

But... choose?

I look her in the eye. My breath shakes, so confused by everything I've seen. That beautiful young girl was her? My brother... did he really do that? Is that why she killed him?

My heart aches terribly as I stare at the dagger.

"Caelynn." My voice breaks as I say her name for the first time.

"Choose," the echoing voice says again, more firmly. I'm running out of time.

I choose.

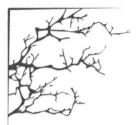

Caelynn

Brielle gasps beside me as we watch Rev shove a dagger into some invisible form. "Was he supposed to do that?" she whispers.

The strange part about this challenge is not knowing what they're commanded to do. Rev walks out of the orb on his own, and I let out a breath. Why did I care? I should want him out of the competition, right?

His hands are shaking as he approaches the benches, his brow pinched with stress. Who had he killed?

The crowds cheer heartily as the challenge ends, but not one of the champions smiles. I don't suspect I'll be the only one heading back to the estate immediately. No private bath time today.

We quietly march through the crowd full of people asking questions. Drake is the only one to stop and talk with his court. Everyone else shoves off the attention and moves along.

I don't know what all of them faced, but clearly it was intense for us all.

RAVEN IS THERE TO GREET me on my windowsill as I enter my room and fall into the bed. I wave my hand, and she pops back into her human form, black hair disheveled, and eyes wide.

She's quiet for a moment, watching me lie there. "What did you see? What was that?"

I shake my head. Maybe one day I'll tell her about it, but not today. Today, I just can't. "A nightmare."

I crawl under the silk covers and curl into fetal position. She joins me, curling up so her chest is against my back, her arm over mine, her chin on my shoulder, breath tickling my ear. Her warmth fills me, and tears well in my eyes.

"You're the only good thing I have," I tell her.

"You deserve more, you know that?"

I pause. Silences stretches between us for a long while. I don't believe that, but I love that she does, so I don't tell her otherwise.

"So do you," I whisper. She deserves so much more than I could give her. More than this world has given her. I don't know how to make her life better. I don't know how to force the world to shift under her feet the way it should. Keep her hidden from the foster system for the final year of high school? At the end of the day, even if I could set her up for life, with a career and money, it's relationships that make life worth living.

That, she'll have to do on her own.

"Are you going to align with the golden-haired douchebag?"

"Probably. It's the only way I can make it through the next challenge."

She sighs. "Why are you doing this?" Her breath tickles my ear.

"Doing what?"

"These trials. They're awful. Those people hate you. That trial today was... cruel. Why put yourself through that?"

I swallow. "That's a complicated answer."

"You want these people to love you? You want them to forgive you?"

"No, I don't deserve that."

"Then what? What are you looking for?"

"Punishment. Pain. Facing what I've done so that I'll never forget it."

Her arms tighten around me. "Stop it," she says, her voice breaking. "Stop punishing yourself."

"Maybe I do want some kind of redemption. Maybe... it's appealing to do something good for a world that I destroyed pieces of, by doing something that causes me pain."

"Punishment veiled as reward."

I smile. "I can't go back to what I once was. I can't be a leader or a hero. I'm a villain, and I'll embrace that forever, but maybe my villainy can have a form of power to it. Maybe I can alter my legacy just a little bit. So, instead of a banished murderer, I can be notorious for several things. Good and bad."

Her soft lips press gently against my shoulder.

She stays like that, lying with me, not speaking for the entire hour it takes for my mind to finally succumb to the darkness and fall asleep.

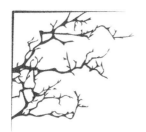

Rev

The next week is fairly uneventful. Brielle has scarcely talked to me in days, but that wasn't overly uncharacteristic for everyone after that challenge. I swear, the emotional challenge was more draining than the physical one. So, I didn't push her, but it's been days, and she still hasn't looked me in the eye. Our next challenge is only two days away, and it's important we are on the same page.

I spent most of my family time asking questions about Reahgan. About his character and what he was like. He was nearly twenty years older than me, and I idolized him. I thought he was good through and through, but I'm still not sure what to make of that vision. Was it real? Was it a trick?

Nothing my parents tell me adds up with the vision.

"Why are you asking this all of the sudden?" my mother asks one night at dinner.

"I just want to remember him," I say. The lie drops in my stomach like iron. But I can't tell her the truth. I won't. Especially because I don't know if it's real or not.

I SLOUCH ON THE CUSHIONED chair by the dim fire in the champions' common room. "Brielle still won't talk to me," I tell Rook.

"Yeah, she's been weird since that last trial."

"The next one is in two days. We're in a good position, three against two, now that Caspian is gone, but if Brielle won't even talk to me..."

Rook leans forward, looking me right in the eye. "She's fine. She's with us, I promise. It's just... weird for her. You know?"

"No," I say. "I mean yes but no. Did she tell you what she had to face in that challenge?"

"She had to go back and face your brother. Her mate. I don't know exactly what she saw, but can't you imagine how awkward that would be? To see him. To be reminded. And then come back to you?"

I purse my lips. "Okay, yes." I mean, it's not like we have some sweeping romance but still. It had been ten years since she'd seen him, and she didn't even know him. So just those few minutes may have been the reminder she didn't need.

"You've talked to her, though? She's onboard for the trial? I hear talk that it's a long one."

"Yeah, we got a message this afternoon to pack for a several-day challenge."

I sigh.

"But yes, I've talked with her, and I'll talk to her again before the trial. It'll be fine. One of us is going to win this. It's a sure thing."

"I hope you're right."

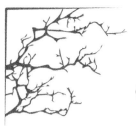

Caelynn

Two days before the third challenge I find a note in my room. I look around, uncomfortable with the idea that someone has been in here to sneak it to me—particularly with Raven hanging around.

I don't know what would happen if someone found her. I do know what would happen if Rev or one of his allies found her—they'd use her against me. And it would work.

I open the note quickly.

Right turret. 22:00

Dammit, stupid military time. That's ten p.m.?

Drake wants to meet to plan out the next challenge? He lost an ally during the last trial, which means he really may need me in this one. It only solidifies my position with him. Even though he disgusts me enough that part of me wants to betray him before we even start.

Too bad I don't have any other options.

I REACH THE STEPS OF the northwest turret of the Flicker estate at nine fifty-five, still hoping I understand military time. An owl screeches in the distance, causing me to shiver. It's not a pleasant sound.

Shadows cascade over the stone stairway, and I pause, my heart pounding. I shouldn't be this nervous meeting my "allies." The rapid fluttering of wings grab my attention, and I quickly shift to the side, into the shadowed alley beside the turret stairs.

The snowy owl crashes into my chest, and I gently cocoon her. "What the hell are you doing?" I whisper, even though I know she can't respond in this form. "Are you okay?"

Her little bird head bobs up and down, but she clucks nervously. Is she trying to warn me of something?

Footsteps stomp down the spiral stairs I'd just nearly ran up and I pause, holding Raven in her owl form tightly.

"Are you sure about this?" a male whispers.

I swallow, listening and pulling shadows over Raven and I both.

"We have to do it," a female voice says.

I blink back my surprise. Brielle. That was Brielle's voice.

Was the note not from Drake? Is this an ambush?

Rook and Brielle march right past us without so much as a glance in our direction and disappear around the corner, back to the Flicker palace.

Raven is the first to move—she leaps from my arms and flutters into the dark sky. I don't know what would have happened if they saw me, but I don't suspect it would have been good.

Now, the question is do I still go up? Raven is careening through the sky without a care in the world now. No screeching or squawking, so I'm going to take that as my clue that the danger has passed.

I ascend the spiral stairs slowly and quietly, just in case. The moment I reach the top, moonlight shining down on me, Drake steps forward, followed by Kari, who had been casually reclining on the ledge.

"Hello there, ally." Drake opens his arms dramatically.

I cross my arms but blink in shock. What were Rook and Brielle doing here? Are they Drake's allies now too? When did that happen? How?

"The game is about to flip on its head," he tells me with clear joy. "I have some information on our challenge tomorrow and wanted to settle a game plan."

I purse my lips, afraid to ask too many questions. This alliance is good for me for several reasons, but if Brielle and Rook are now with Drake...that would change things.

I decide I'll take his information but give none in return. Let him think I'm pliable or stupid. Then decide how to proceed when I need to make that decision.

"Tomorrow's challenge is going to be a maze," he tells me.

"The queen announced it would take several days. It's that big of a maze?" I ask.

"It's a massive maze stretching hundreds of miles. So, yes, it will take several days, and there will be an element of survival. We'll also be given free rein to injure or openly kill any champion we desire."

My mouth falls open.

"Interesting twist, isn't it? They're going straight up *Hunger Games* with us this time."

I roll my eyes, although I'm secretly impressed he made a human pop culture reference. This certainly changes things and... makes Brielle and Rook's presence all the more concerning.

"I have a list of supplies you should bring, if you don't have them, try to get them. As a last resort, ask me and I'll smuggle you some—but this alliance is to remain a secret until the *opportune* moment." He hands me a piece of paper.

"The maze will begin as a scavenger hunt in the desert. Our quest will be to find an ancient well. There will be another clue inside the well, which will take us into the mountains twenty miles beyond."

How does he know all of this?

"We will ambush our enemy at the well. I'd like for you to bait the other alliance into slowing down so that Kari and I can make it there first and set a trap. Go running off to the east, they'll chase you for a mile or two, and that should be plenty of time."

Enemy. Singular.

"It should be easy. We will then work together to extinguish the dwarf before we reach the mountains." He puts his hands on his hips.

I raise my hand like a kid in school.

"Yes, Caelynn?"

He actually called me by my name. Is it another part of his act? Or does he actually respect me? "Why were Brielle and Rook here?" I ask as dimly as I can manage. "Are they... new additions to our alliance?"

"In a way."

My brow pinches together. I tap my hand on my thigh, considering how to proceed here. Their bloodthirst for me was one of the most compelling reasons I agreed to be his ally to begin with. Surely, he realizes this would be disconcerting for me?

"So, this new challenge, the queen will allow complete amnesty for any champion death?" I repeat. Surely this provision was for the benefit of *my* enemies. The crown knows they all want me dead, and she's obliging. "Brielle and Rook were here to discuss killing me."

"No," Drake says dismissively. "They have another target in mind."

What?

"It's true." Kari steps forward, her face calm, considering. "I don't doubt they'll still want you dead, but we've negotiated a truce on your behalf for a short time."

"Truce. You mean to tell me there is someone Brielle wants dead more than me?" I find that hard to believe. There are very few options here, but honestly, none of them make sense.

"More than you? Perhaps not. Or perhaps yes—scorned women and all." Drake chuckles, and I hide my cringe. "But this someone, well, it's in everyone's best interest to eliminate this target sooner rather than later. Brielle and Rook have agreed to put a hold on targeting you in order to receive help removing the greater threat first."

The greater threat.

My mind spins. Rev's own alliance is turning on him.

Drake folds his hands behind his back and begins to pace as he speaks. "Yesterday, we received a message from a high-ranking courtier requesting the death of a specific champion. The reward is large, for you in particular, Caelynn." He smiles like he's doing me some big favor. "And it goes above all of our heads, though I admit it's rather convenient for us."

They want Rev dead. My stomach clenches, lungs struggle to pull in breaths. Who? Who wants him dead? Who ordered it? I clench my jaw and pull my own darkness tighter around my soul. Keep calm.

Rev wants me dead, I remind myself. He will kill me if I give him the chance.

I don't have any other choices. If everyone else decides Rev must die, there is nothing I can do to change it. I need this alliance.

"So, during the trial, our first order of business will be to eliminate our opposition."

"You want to kill Rev," I say, annoyance clear in my tone. Mostly, I'm fed up with his games, but I have to make him believe I don't care.

"Yes."

"What is the reward?"

"Money. Influence. For me, it lands the crown right on my head."

Obviously. Though, I notice Kari's jaw clench. She's placating him too, I realize. She wants the crown.

"And for me?" I ask.

"A promised pardon."

Chills wash over me. *A pardon*—meaning all of my crimes would be forgiven. I could go back home and live a normal life, *without* winning the trials. All I have to do is go along with this plan and survive and I'd have the freedom to return to my homeland.

"The queen promises this?" I ask, prying perhaps harder than I should. There are very few people who could grant such a pardon. Right now, the options are the High Queen or the ruler of the court the crime was committed against—Rev's father. A third option would be Drake, if he is presumptuous enough to assume I'd wait for him to win the trials, survive the Schorchedlands, and inherit the crown.

"Yes."

"How?" I whisper, my whole world shifts under me as I consider this. "Why?"

"She too recognizes the threat this enemy holds over us all, and it's a worthy sacrifice."

Rev. A threat to the whole realm. I shake my head, not understanding.

I am Caelynn of the Shadow Court. Murderer of the High Heir. The symbol of rebellion in our realm.

And somehow I am the lesser threat? To other champions, I understand. He's likely to win. But to the queen?

I'm not sure I believe him. Perhaps he can obtain a pardon, but is it really the queen's promise? Is this really the reason? I consider the possibility that Drake just doesn't want to tell me that it's really Rev's father orchestrating the hit on his own son. Because that's what I'm thinking is more likely.

I know one of his secrets. Does Drake now know it too?

"She'll marry you off to another court," Kari admits. "You'll have to agree to this in order to earn the pardon."

"Ahh," I say quietly. That's unfortunate, but it does quiet some of my questions. A marriage to a court official with little power would absolve the rebellion threat. But I would be free.

And trapped in a new way.

The fae take royal pardons seriously. They would assume if I was pardoned, it's for good reason so the hatred would—eventually—dissolve. Only the Luminescent Court would continue their hatred.

"This is the redemption you seek," Kari says.

"By killing the other Luminescent Court heir?" That's how I redeem myself? Kill the male I missed the last time? I pinch the bridge of my nose. This is so screwed up I can't even think straight.

"Some enemies hide their danger until it's too late," she says. I swallow. That's how I justified Reahgan's death all those years ago.

"Rev needs to die for the betterment of us all."

"We need to know if you're in," Drake says, stepping forward. There is no doubt in his eyes. Why would I decline? Rev is my enemy. Rev wants to kill me.

I swallow, heart aching but somehow I keep my head high as I answer. "Of course."

AN OWL CRASHES INTO my chest the moment I reach the bottom of the spiral stairs. I fumble to catch her without breaking one of her wings. My mind is still reeling over everything I learned during my meeting with Drake. She wiggles in my arms.

I blink and grip Raven's owl wings tightly. "What?"

She squeals quietly. Disconcerting but only for me. She's getting better at keeping her presence unnoticed. "I'm not in the mood for this, Ray." My voice is weak.

She stretches her neck up, nipping my ear with her sharp beak. "Ow!"

She leaps from my arms and flies down the path in front of me, away from the estate and into the forest on the edge of the grounds. I groan but follow her.

Dark trees with yellow and orange leaves surround me as I reach the little snowy owl sitting in the middle of the path. I look around quickly and then wave, removing the magic on her form.

She grows into the lovely human I know in one quick click. She's on her feet, poised, but with an angry expression on her face. "What the hell was that?"

I close my eyes, shoulders slumping, standing awkwardly five feet away. She doesn't move closer. "What?" I ask tiredly.

"You're going to kill Rev now?"

I swallow, watching her expression closely. "What do you care?"

The wind whispers through the leaves around us, rustling gently. It reminds me of the Whisperwood, where the shadows whisper, bouncing through the trees. I could go back there, if I do this. I could go home. I would be free of this curse.

"I care about you!" she says. "You know you can't do this—it will *kill* you."

I bite my lip and pause. I don't know what I know.

"You told me you hate yourself for what you did all those years ago. And you're going to do it again. You told me you want to change how people see you, and you're going to double down on your old reputation."

I pull in a long shaky breath. I've never seen Raven so passionate. I've never heard her speak so deliberately.

"I've seen this before, Caelynn. I've seen people I love give up. I've seen them fall back into the void again and again."

My stomach drops. She's comparing me with her mother.

"I never said I was going to go through with it!" I shout quickly, panic rising my chest. It's not like I could tell Drake I was going to betray him. I still haven't decided. I haven't... I don't know what to think.

"Not with your voice. But your eyes give you away." Her bottom lip trembles. "You're giving up, just like my mom gave up," she whispers. "But I won't let you." Her hands clench into fists.

"It's not that simple, Ray. I... I don't have a choice."

"Of course you do! You always have a choice."

"I can't," I say, my voice so small now. So brittle. "I can't stop it. I'm not strong enough."

"That's what my mother said," she whispers. My heart shatters but my darkness strengthens me. I accepted this part of myself a long time ago. I suppose it was only a matter of time before it cost me the last person who loves me.

Raven won't forgive me if I do this. And yet, there isn't another option.

"You're doing the same thing. You're going right back to the thing that broke you. Replaying it over and over again."

I swallow, remembering the state Raven was in when she found her mother barely clinging to life. But doesn't she get this is different?

"Cae, please," she whispers, so achingly sad. She steps forward, reaching for me, but I step back. She chokes on a sob. "Don't do it. *Please*," she begs.

Kill him, the echoing voice of my worst memory shivers through me. My teeth chatter.

I'm not strong enough for this.

"You told me you were stronger than all of them."

"I am, but not more than four of them together. If I were to stand against them, I would be committing suicide. And Rev wants to kill me. He *will* kill me if I give him the chance. I can't align with him. He wouldn't believe me if I were to tell him..."

Her face crumples, tears running down her cheeks. Does she finally understand the hopelessness of the situation?

This is the only way I can win this game. I knew it would take ruthlessness. I knew it could rip my soul to shreds again and again. If I could do it differently, I would. I don't want Rev to die. I *really* don't want Rev to die.

But I can't stop it no matter what I do.

"Then let's run. Now. We'll leave the fae realm and go back home. We'll make a life together."

"Rev will still die," I say, voice devoid of life. "It won't change anything, except I really would be giving up."

I allow my anger, my pain, my darkness, to fortify me once again, curling around my broken and scarred soul like armor. I pause to consider before I flick my hand, and force my last friend into her raven form.

She screeches in anger and pain but flies off into the dark night, leaving me alone. Always alone.

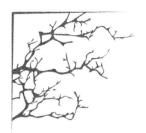

Rev

The morning of the third challenge arrives and tension coils in my gut.

I still haven't talked with Brielle. The only assurance of her continued friendship is Rook's word. I generally trust him... but something still doesn't feel right.

In preparation for this trial—which I suspect will be the most physically demanding of them all—I refrained from alcohol, took a sleeping draft, slept a full nine hours, and declined a run this morning.

I'm the first in the training hall, and I spend a half hour doing minor exercises, mostly because I'm wound so tight.

Brielle and Rook enter the training center next, marching dramatically.

"Hey," I say cautiously as they approach.

"Hey." Brielle doesn't meet my eyes, and my stomach sinks.

Rook slaps me on the shoulder with a big smile. "You ready? This one is going to be fun; I can feel it."

I pull in a long breath. All I feel is barely hidden panic. "As ready as I'll ever be."

He only smiles bigger.

Rook and I spar for a few minutes as the other champions enter the hall. We all stop to watch as Caelynn enters.

I watch her features closer than before. Her eyes are dim, as usual, hooded and uninterested. Her motions smooth and posture confident.

Today, she is outwardly more prepared than before. Gone are her jeans and T-shirt. Now she wears leather pants, solid boots, and a tunic and carries a pack over her back presumably full of supplies for the long trial.

I have no idea what to make of her after that vision. The innocent, lovely female my brother tormented... Was it all a joke to screw with me, or was it real? I close my eyes, and that girl's face stares back at me. Young. Bright. Innocent. Happy.

The fae warrior before me is nothing like the girl from my vision. The only thing the two have in common is their beauty.

When I open my eyes, I find Brielle watching me. Her eyes are wide, but otherwise, her expression is unreadable.

She blinks, her eyes softening. "Now is our chance. She won't survive this challenge, right?"

My stomach twists, but she's right. That vision shouldn't affect my emotions. The second trial's entire purpose was to test us in the most brutal ways. My task had been to choose. It was just trying to mess with my resolve.

I shake my head. No matter what kind of deceptions I face, no matter how believable—I'd have to choose. Kill her, or let her live.

I've already made my choice.

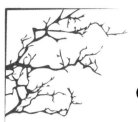

Caelynn

I enter the training center with only ten minutes to spare. I ran this morning and probably pushed myself harder than I should have, but my thoughts were twisting around in my brain so tight I couldn't tell which way was up. The next thing I knew, I was sprinting at full speed.

Today is the start of an extreme endurance challenge—both physically and emotionally—and I've used up more of that energy than was at all wise. Now, I'll just have to live with the consequences.

The queen has yet to announce it officially, but apparently all the fae who hate me will now have an open license to kill me. The last time they tried to kill me indirectly. Traps, wicked creatures, and backhanded attacks. Now? They could all turn on me, shove a blade through my heart and move on—no questions asked.

Like they're planning to do to Rev...

Despite what Drake said, I know I am target number one. The only reason they've added a name above mine is because if they want to kill Rev, they know they're going to need the most power on their side. They think it will be easy to remove me later.

The strategy of hiding my power has been immensely beneficial. I'd be doomed if they knew how strong my magic was.

Over the last two weeks, I've managed to build some muscle and trained with my blades using the training center, even taking advantage of the blade masters when they're willing.

This time, I am ready.

I force every ounce of doubt out of my mind. My pain is my fuel. My darkness my strength.

The champions begin gathering at the gates, and I approach slowly, watching each of my opponents closely. Despite a new alliance, I don't trust a single one of them.

I am Caelynn of the Shadow Court. I have no friends. Not anymore.

I take the spot next to Tyadin, but he doesn't even glance my way. Today, he's in his armor again, and I get the feeling he's more comfortable this way. It'll slow him down, but maybe, today, that'll work in his favor.

Since the first day of this trial has become a planned blood bath, most of the action is likely to be long over if he's delayed. The contestants would like to get him out of the way, but only if it's convenient. They won't go out of their way. Same with me.

They keep assuming they'll have a chance to get rid of me whenever the mood strikes, so they're focused on their stronger enemies. I like this thought process. It works in our favor.

I lean closer to Tyadin only to notice Drake watching me. I stand up straight and adjust my bag. I'd like to warn him, but the champions are too close together. It'll have to wait.

The massive ruby gates crack, light peeking through. Once again, I stand in the center and close my eyes as the bright light streams through and warms my face. This moment, this in-between, one beam pressing through the darkness—it's the only time I can pretend to feel what I've lost.

The sun will forever haunt me, reminding me of who I am. And who I will never be.

I shiver, but soon the light is so bright it hurts my eyes. I wince and turn away from the brightness only to see someone watching me.

Rev.

His eyes meet mine with an expression that's—well, it's not hatred. Curiosity, perhaps? I swallow, unable to hide my emotion for the first time. Just a crack. The smallest sliver of a window, exposing what's inside of me.

Rev blinks, and his face falls into surprise. He turns quickly, once again leading the pack out into the massive arena.

The crowd roars. They're eager for a bloodbath. The last challenge only resulted in one champion loss. They're ready to move on with the competition. They're eager to lose a few more of us.

The sunlight blasts us as we leave the solace of the quiet and dark training center, and my heart begins beating harder. A blackbird soars through the sky in the distance.

I haven't seen Raven since last night in the forest. She won't ever forgive me.

When I turned her into a raven it had been because she'd brought attention to her owl form twice in the hour before. I thought a raven safer. But I hadn't anticipated her avoiding me for this long.

"Kill her!" someone shouts, then another. Until the whole crowd is shouting the chant.

Kill her. Kill her. Kill her. Kill her.

My stomach twists. They've learned about the new rule provision, and it's my head they want on a pike. *Perfect.*

"Welcome, champions!" A minotaur stands on a booth in the middle of the arena, his pitch-black horns massive. "Today is your third and longest challenge of the Trials of Thorns!"

The crowd screams.

"Each day, you will be given a new task. Five in total. Some will be simple. Others excruciating. This challenge will require endurance and intelligence and strategy and basic survival skills. You must follow clues, travel many miles, sometimes in complete circles, and fight both mental and physical battles for days on end."

This is the biggest challenge of them all.

"Your arena will consist of hundreds of miles of wilderness. You must find and reach every corner, following the clues. Do not think this a straightforward challenge—there will be dead ends and misleading clues. Stay diligent. Remain humble, or you will not make it out alive."

Drake described this challenge as a maze, I keep that in mind as I examine the minotaur's announcement for clues I may need later.

"As a reminder of what you're fighting for and against, there are sections of the arena that are marred with the scourge. You will see our world's true enemy.

"And to make it more realistic, to add a layer of betrayal and brutality, we have removed a previous rule. During this trial, there will be no punishment for any death of a champion—no matter the cause."

The crowd roars, and another chant of "Kill her" begins. *Lovely.*

Brielle smirks over her shoulder at me.

Apparently their hatred of me was renewed with the last challenge.

I cross my arms and soak in the bitter hatred. This is who I am. This is who I will forever be.

Tyadin examines me. "You enjoy this?"

"People wanting me dead? No," I say honestly, still smiling bitterly. "But I may as well accept it. I may as well let it be my strength, instead of my weakness."

He purses his lips.

"By the way. I've been meaning to warn you, with this new change on killing—"

"They're going to come for me. I know."

I step closer, but my whisper is easily veiled under the barrage of hatred. "There is a plan for an ambush outside the first clue." I cast my eyes down at his armor. "I suggest using your weakness as your strength, at least for today."

He narrows his eyes, trying to dissect my clue. "It was a mistake, wasn't it? Refusing you as an ally." His words are soft, but his expression is schooled into a scowl. From the outside, our conversation probably looks like classic goading. The others are doing the same.

I wink at him. "Tomorrow, things may be very different."

He takes in a long breath. "I won't turn on you, unless you attack first or the trial openly demands it."

I fully anticipate direct hand-to-hand combat at some point during the trials. Typically, that was done as the last trial, the final decider. But there's no telling what we'll be made to do out there.

"That much I promise," he says.

Well, that's more than I can say for my actual allies.

"Same."

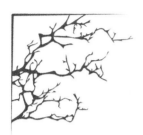

Rev

Rook stands between Brielle and I. He doesn't look me in the eye, which causes more discomfort to stir in my gut, but the cheering, the taunting of the crowd for us to kill the betrayer, has brought Brielle alive again. She's practically glowing.

"Your first task," the minotaur roars over the chanting crowd, "is to find the Ruby Well in the desert and drink from it. Then follow the clue and await further instruction. Each day a new task will be given and must be completed before the sun sets, or you will be removed from the trials."

"How much water did you bring?" Brielle asks.

"Twenty ounces. I worried any more would slow us down."

"It will be enough for the day."

"We'll have to hope we don't need to spend several in the desert."

I am thankful Caspian exited the trials already. His water abilities would have been a huge asset for Drake and Kari.

"Remember, complete the task by the end of the sunset, or you will be rejected from the trials. Let the countdown begin."

WE SPRINT OFF THROUGH the thorn gates, but the
paths beyond are entirely different than the racing trial. We
pass through a short stretch of quiet forest and then into the
open desert. The way is clear, in the beginning. And with
open murder now legal, and the champions this close together, I find myself slowing.

I allow Brielle and Drake to race ahead. At least I won't
have to cover my back so much.

The dwarf falls back, barely running at all. He's weighed
down by his heavy armor, but I find myself wondering if it's
a strategy. You don't have to be the first to the clues, you just
need to make it by sundown. But will the others be willing
to linger in the desert to attack him? Unlikely. Shelter will be
higher in our priorities.

If he's the last to reach the well, he very well may be able
to complete his task without any conflict. *Clever dwarf.*

Too bad I don't have that luxury.

"This way!" Brielle yells, and she drifts off to the east. My
legs are already burning from running on the soft sand, but I
do my best to keep up with her.

"What?" I call, my face already hot. "This is the wrong
direction." Perhaps that's another reason to keep it
slow—less risk of dehydration. We have until sunset to reach
our task, so why exert ourselves this quickly?

"I saw the betrayer go this way. She's trying to avoid us."

I slow to a stop, panting. I literally just saw Caelynn run ahead of us, beelining for the northeast like everyone else. "What are you talking about?" I pinch my brows together.

Brielle turns around, fire in her red eyes. "Do you want to kill her or not?" she says, then spits at my feet.

I narrow my eyes. "What's wrong with you, Brielle? You've ignored me for days. Ever since the orb challenge."

Her lip curls into something like a snarl. Something is definitely not right.

"I saw Ca—the betrayer, run that way," I say. "The way we're supposed to be running. So why are we going off track? Unless you have another motive." My heart rate picks up.

Her face falls. Fear, confusion—panic? I'm not sure.

"Oh, I swore I saw her go this way." Her voice is calmer now. "Sorry, I've been on edge for a while." Her shoulders slump. I'm still not sure what to make of her. What to make of this detour she tried so hard to push us into. Rook hasn't said a word, his face blank.

"You do want to kill her, right?" Brielle whispers.

I sigh, ignoring the tightness in my chest. "Yes."

She nods sharply and turns back the correct direction. "Let's go."

"That challenge really screwed us up, huh?"

"You too?"

I nod. "I wish you'd have talked to me. Now's probably a bad time to work through it."

"Or maybe it's the perfect time." She smirks.

"Do you think what they showed us was real? Or just what was meant to screw with us?"

Her eyebrows pull together. "What did you see?"

I open my mouth to speak but shut it. "Something really screwed up that I'm not sure was real. Then it made me kill her," I say, which is a slight fib. I didn't have to kill her, I don't think.

"That's who you stabbed?"

I nod.

"How did it feel?"

"Not as good as I would have thought."

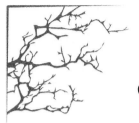

Caelynn

I sprint ahead, fast enough to pass by Rev and his friends but not Drake and Kari.

I find the perfect place to jilt left as Drake suggested, but I continue on. Drake thinks he's controlling this whole thing. He's setting it up for himself, using everyone's own desires against themselves and manipulating every piece of this game.

But I'm not going to let him do it.

He very well may be setting me up for a swift fall. So, no, I'm not going to follow his plan. Let him think I was too stupid to follow his instructions. *Oops.*

Brielle follows the path I noticed but didn't take. Rev and Rook follow.

Uh huh, they're definitely in on this plan, and it's coming into fruition with or without me. My mind is still spinning through so many things.

Do I follow Drake's scheme and let the fae prince—who openly wants to kill me—die? *The Night Bringer would sure be pleased with me.*

But what will happen even if I do? Five of us turn against Rev at the well. Then what? Kari said they'd negotiated a truce on my behalf. Until when? When Rev is dead?

Maybe that was Drake's plan all along. First, he achieves his goal of getting Rev out of the picture. Second, he earns a handsome award and appreciation from some High Court official.

And lastly, with Brielle one hundred and fifty percent against me, there is no way I can swing to another side, I'd be forced to continue my alliance with Kari and Drake or lose.

That would make it three against two.

Once Rev is out of the way, Drake has the power to take down the rest of the reigning alliance. Then, it'll be easy picking the two weakest champions off.

Drake may be a condescending dick, but he's smart.

If I let his plan play out, not only would I have to kill Rev and double down on the tear in my soul, but I'd put myself in a position of fighting Drake and Kari on my own. Maybe Tyadin would finally consent to aligning with me but that's a big "maybe," and even then, we'd be even at best.

But what are my other options? Turn against this alliance of five and save Rev?

I'd like to be that person. I like the idea of redemption in that form but... he hates me. I'm not sure which he'd choose: working with me or death. Which would be a bit of a problem for this strategy of mine to work out.

So, my choices are stick with Drake's manipulative plan and hope for the best. I probably won't win the trials, but I'll likely live to tell the tale.

Or risk my life to save someone who will slit my throat the first moment my guard is down.

A third plan comes to mind—run away. That's something I'm rather good at, actually. I could complete the task while they're distracted, let the big-bad fae alliances work out their own damn issues and weaken themselves in the process.

I sprint faster. That's as good a plan as I can come up with.

A prickle on the back of my neck reminds me that inaction is as bad as performing the evil.

AFTER AN HOUR OF RUNNING, my mouth is dry and my legs burn terribly. I usually relish the pain and simply seek more of it. But right now, I'm not sure what's coming around the corner.

I take a sip of water and catch my breath, the sun beating down on me like a new and salacious enemy. It's like Reahgan attacking me with his paralyzing light again.

He's like a child torturing ants with a magnifying glass. I might have snuffed out his life—a fact I am sickeningly proud of, which is another reason aligning with Rev would be an awful idea—but his grip has been crushing my windpipe since I was an adolescent. His spirit haunts me more than the wraith ever could.

I swallow, my throat still dry, but I want to conserve the water, so I center my thoughts away from the panic and instead harness the rage.

That's why I need to win the Trial of Thorns. To prove Reahgan was wrong about me—I'm not *no one*. I'm not unimportant. I'm not just a doll to be played with, used, and then tossed in the trash.

I am powerful.

And I'm ready to show them all.

Rev

After our quick and pointless detour, our trek through the desert is smooth. We come across a few poisonous snakes, but Brielle singes them while at full stride. Although, she does slow her pace as we go on. I swear she'd usually be willing to go much faster.

Not for the first time, I wonder where her loyalties really lie. I wish I had the chance to ask her what she saw in that orb. I'm not even convinced it showed the truth. And what if she saw something entirely false that turned her against me?

I can't shake the pit in my stomach that tells me something is wrong.

We come to a set of sand dunes, and my thighs burn as we march up the steep slope. At the top we look out at the sea of red sand before us.

"I need some water," Brielle tells me. So we take the moment to rehydrate before beginning our journey anew.

"I can see it." Rook points out to a flash of red, just on the horizon.

"The Ruby Well," Brielle whispers. "I never thought I'd see it"

"You've heard of it?"

She nods. "It's legend. It's said to give those who drink from it one desire. Not always the one you ask for, but something in your heart that you secretly want."

"That sounds dangerous."

"Oh, it is. The stories surrounding the well are... tragic at best. But still, it's something only a select few have seen with their own eyes."

I swallow. Some of the desires in my heart are dark and terrible. I'm not sure I want that well to choose what to give me. I'd rather take none of them.

Brielle shoves her water canister back into her bag and is the first to take off, charging down the steep slope. Rook smirks at me, a challenge, before he and I both race after her.

Brielle seems to have gained a new vigor, and I happily follow suit, glad to be able to pick up our pace. I'm surprised there have been no outright brawls yet with murder entirely allowable in this trial. Other than Brielle following a ghost of Caelynn, there's been nothing.

As we approach the Ruby Well, its red light glowing in the distance, my unease grows to an extreme. A cold sweat drips down my back, hair on my arms standing.

What in the world are my instincts trying to tell me?

Dammit, what am I supposed to do? Accuse Rook and Brielle of conspiring against me? Stop them and demand answers? I don't know. Because I don't even know what the unease is about.

I slow down, and for a moment, Rook and Brielle continue on as if they don't even notice I've fallen behind.

"What are you doing?" Brielle hollers, annoyance lacing her tone.

I look around. Deep in the distance to the west is a set of brown mountains covered partly by white fluffy clouds. To the east is wide open desert, flat for as far as the eye can see. For the several miles around us in every direction is flat desert. There are a few dunes, wind-swept sand piles that shift and swirl but not enough to conceal any enemies.

But then again one of my enemies has earth powers. Can she move sand at will?

The wind can move sand. Drake can control the wind...

"Something doesn't feel right." I slow to a walk, and Brielle rolls her eyes dramatically.

"You've been huffing and puffing about my slow pace all day, and now that we're here, you're stopping?"

"Where are the others?" I ask suddenly. Nearly all of them ran ahead. The only champion behind us is the dwarf. Have they really all completed their tasks and moved on so far they're entirely out of sight? Were we really that slow?

"You're being paranoid," Rook says, putting his hands on his hips, but he sends a glance at Brielle that shakes me to my core. My blood runs cold, suddenly certain of my suspicions.

"Come on," Brielle says. "Let's get this done with so we can get to the mountains before dark."

"Mountains?" I ask her. No one has said anything about heading to the mountains.

Her eyes flare for a moment. More evidence of her deceit. She's been getting information from someone else. Was it her pixie spy? If so why didn't she tell me?

"It'll be safer to sleep there while we wait for the next task." A good cover, but I know a liar when I see one. She shifts nervously.

"You guys go ahead."

"You've got to be kidding me."

I still see nothing out of the ordinary, but my gut is screaming at me to run. How could I run, though? My task is right there, only five hundred feet ahead. I still have a few hours to complete the trial, but even if I ran off, I'd have to come back at some point.

A form appears far to my right, a dark rippling like she stepped out of shadow, and my stomach sinks.

Caelynn stands with her arms crossed, her face a perfect mask of indifference. Her white tunic ruffles in the gentle wind. Always confident, never unnerved. Although, now that I look closer, her expression is one of vague annoyance. She's annoyed I didn't fall for whatever trap she'd set?

Just feet behind her, the sand shifts oddly, catching my attention. There's a ripple. A slight movement beneath the ground like... wind.

I pull out my sword and curse again, but Caelynn holds her hands up in a show of temporary peace.

"I'm going to kill you," I seethe.

She steps forward, hands still up. Brielle is sneering at her, but she's not surprised. Not remotely surprised.

Dammit, I really want to know what's going on.

I look between Brielle and Caelynn. "You're working with her," I say, my voice void of light. How? Why? I don't even have the breath to express those questions.

Caelynn steps forward again, her blond hair waving in the increasingly irritated wind. "Come and get me," she says, with a wink. But her expression tells me she knows I have no intention of doing any such thing. Not right now.

She slides her foot forward, shifting the sand ever so slightly. My gaze darts down to her boot that she very specifically doesn't put pressure on.

Wood. There's a plank hidden beneath the sand.

I let out a breath. Did my betrayer just expose the trap purposefully? Because it sure as hell looks like it.

My heart is pounding.

"I'm going to kill her," Brielle tells me. Well, that's the truth. I can see it in her eyes.

"No one cares," the murderer says offhandedly. "This is between me and Rev."

I wrinkle my nose. "Don't call me that. Only my friends call me that."

Her eyebrows flick up in surprise. "I wasn't aware. These two call you that name all the time. And, well..."

She doesn't complete the sentence, and I hear a huff behind the now obvious shifting sand a few feet back. I have no doubt who's behind it. All five of them against me?

Or is it four?

Time to run and figure out the rest, but just as I tense to sprint away from my pursuers, a vine sprouts from beneath the sand and grips my ankle. I grit my teeth and use my light to shoot the vine away, but Rook and Brielle have already shifted behind me, blocking my retreat.

The sand behind Drake spins and swirls into a small cyclone and laughter erupts. Kari and Drake march to stand beside Caelynn.

The thought crosses my mind for one instant: *I'm going to die.*

Then, I act. I spin, my blade flying into my closest enemies—Brielle and Rook. A roar of fire greets me, searing my
forearm, but I ignore the pain. A groan of rage tears from my
lungs as my blade flies at Rook. He parries with his own, and
I spin toward Brielle, her eyes red with anger and determination. I slice toward her face, but Rook reaches me first. The
sound of flesh ripping wide registers first.

Then the silver glint of a blade through my stomach.

My face whitens as I feel the warmth of blood growing
over my middle. I blast white hot light from my body, holding nothing back—I have nothing left to lose. Panic wells in
my body. My own death pressing down on me.

Not like this. I never expected it to happen like this.

Brielle and Rook dive out of the way of my attack, leaving one small path out.

I don't wait, my brain hardly working. I flee, knowing
that I'm too injured to get far.

Knowing, without a doubt, that I'm going to die.

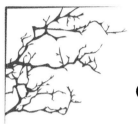

Caelynn

Drake, Kari, and I follow the wounded Rev. A wall of stone erupts from the sand to block his escape and his eyes grow wild with anger and fear. For a moment, I think it came from Tyadin, but I realize that Kari has similar powers. Their courts split into two around the time of the dwarfish civil war. Now, the pure fae bloodlines of the Crystal Court rule over the secondary stone court—the Crumbling Court.

Rev backs into the stone barrier, hands frantically searching for an escape, all the while keeping his eyes on the enemies in front of him. He's trapped and injured.

Maybe if he'd fled the moment he realized something was wrong. Maybe if he'd fled when I exposed the trap. But he waited. He second-guessed. He let the pain of the betrayal get to him.

Now, there's no escape.

Rev is going to die.

The thought sends a pang of regret through me.

I'd never spent much time thinking about what I desired for him all these years after I killed his brother, but the image of his scared face as an adolescent—of the pained expression the orb showed me at his brother's death—rages through me, and I swallow back the pain.

It's too late to change my mind now. He's an injured animal, cornered. He's done for, and he knows it.

"Why?" he forces from his lips as he turns to face us, his whole body feral.

"Animal," Drake spits, and I roll my eyes. *Please.* Put Drake in the same position, and I guarantee the spoiled brat would be sobbing and begging for mercy. The insult seems to hit home with Rev, though, and he stands up straighter. His head high but his eyes still wild with pain.

I clench my fists tighter.

A raven screeches overhead, crying out. I can practically hear her begging me to change my mind.

There's nothing I can do, I repeat to myself. He's injured, blood dripping down his abdomen all the way to his legs. His face is pale. He's weakening quickly.

If I were to try to stop this, I'd be fighting four future fae lords and ladies. Their strength is nothing to be scoffed at. Each of them.

I could fight one or two easily. Four? I shake my head but I notice how close we all stand together and my mind starts spinning...

"Why!" he shouts again.

Drake smirks, crossing his arms, enjoying the game. Savoring his win.

"Your father put out a hit on you." My stomach sinks, even though it's what I'd guessed. "You'd be shocked how much he was willing to pay to get you out of his way."

Rev's lips part, but otherwise he shows no reaction. Is he not surprised either?

"You were never good enough, Rev. Your father doesn't want to hand such a powerful court to a pathetic heir like you. He'd rather give it to his bastards. Sad, isn't it?" Drake laughs. "But of course, he doesn't want the world to know of your true weakness. He wanted you out of the way neatly. And I agreed to hand it to him."

I wrinkle my nose. The fae world is screwed if this jerk is to be their new high ruler.

"And what about you?" I ask, for the first time turning to Rev's friends. "What's your excuse?"

Tears well in Rev's eyes. *Dammit.*

I hate this. I hate it.

They'll blame me for it, I realize.

When this trial is done, they're going to tell all of the courts that I'm the one that killed Rev. I know it. I can feel it in the way they look at me. That's another part of Drake's plan.

I'm the fall guy, whether I live or not.

I pin my gaze to Brielle. "You wanted to kill me for being a betrayer. A murderer. Those are your words. Yet, you stand here, looking your friend in the eye as you watch him bleed out from a wound you supplied," I say. Rook lifts his chin, unwilling to look me in the eye.

Brielle sneers. "I want to kill *you*. But that's not a secret."

"But first... you're going to kill your friend and become what you hate me for?"

"He's not my friend," Rook says, still keeping his attention elsewhere.

"He betrayed us first," Brielle says.

I narrow my eyes, but Brielle turns away, apparently over entertaining me.

"How?" Rev coughs a desperate plea. I don't know why I'm dragging this out. I don't know why I keep asking questions because every second gets me closer to giving in.

The raven overhead soars lower. Closer.

I damn well know anything other than compliance is suicide. And yet, panic has my eager darkness coiling inside of me. Preparing. Ready to fight if necessary.

She's marching toward me before I even notice Brielle turn. Her fists are clenched, eyes ravenous. Rook grabs her by the shoulder to stop her.

Right, this mysterious truce Drake and Kari negotiated for me. "You," she spits at me. Drake chuckles. "First he," she points at Rev, tears now rolling down his cheeks, "tells us all about how he's going to kill you to avenge his brother. He tells me every day he wants it just as badly as I do. Then, in that last challenge, the orb showed me a vision of you two—*together.*"

My stomach drops. I don't ask her what she means by "together." I don't dare turn my attention to Rev. I cannot bear to see the look on his face at this revelation.

Her bottom lip trembles, and she finally turns away, into Rook's chest.

I stare at them—shocked stupid—for entirely too long. Finally, I get my wits about me.

"I've never even been alone in a room with Rev. All he's ever done is hate me..."

"Like I believe you!" she says, the sound muffled by Rook's chest. Rev is still silent, but from the corner of my eyes I notice him fall to his knees with a soft plop.

"So, you're going to murder your friend and apparent *lover*," I say with more acid than I should have, still focused intently on Brielle's back, "over something a scarcely-understood magical being showed you in a vision? The entire point of that trial was to screw us up. Show us what would hurt the most. That doesn't mean it was true."

Maybe I want Brielle to change her mind. If they turn on Drake and Kari now in favor of Rev, maybe I could save myself from this fate. From what I'm to witness.

From the light that's about to leave this world forever.

Drake steps forward, all pompous and proud. "Enough talking."

"Believe me," Kari says more softly. "It is in *all* of our best interest we complete this plan."

Rev's eyes bore into me, and finally, I turn to face him. I can't read his expression. Shock and pain and anger and confusion. Desperation.

My heart still pounds, still aches at Brielle's insinuation. I suspect I know what she saw, and it wasn't the past *or* the future. Meaning Rev did nothing wrong, but he's going to die over it.

"Caelynn, would you like to do the honors?" Drake says.

My blood runs cold. Panic seizing every inch of my body as I stare at the dagger he holds out to me.

"Why?" I stumble over more words. I can't even think.

"Finish what you started," he says.

Even Brielle is staring in shock. I can't breathe as I stare at the same dagger I used to kill Reahgan. Tears well in my own eyes now. How? How could he know?

"Drake," Kari warns. "I don't think that's a good idea."

I look up to the sky for one moment, but Raven isn't anywhere to be seen. My heart aches, it cries. But for the first time, I can see what she saw. I made a choice a long time ago. I wasn't strong enough then.

Now, I'm right back to where I was. And I have to make a choice.

I turn to the four high fae beside me, one at a time. They're in perfect position. All in a line, like a firing squad.

My soul quiets. "I'll do it."

My whole body is burning with rage as I grip the obsidian dagger in my tight fist. I turn to face Rev and step forward slowly, already curling my power within, focusing. Building.

Rev's emotions are clear as daylight now. Hate. Pure hatred fills him. "You would."

I smile.

"What Drake doesn't know," I whisper softly and everyone goes utterly still. "Is that he just put the nail in his own damn coffin."

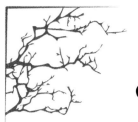

Caelynn

I turn my back to the injured Rev and face the four immensely powerful fae in front of me. This is the most idiotic thing I've ever done, and it's very likely going to mean my death.

Raven flies overhead, squawking again. Does she know what I'm doing?

My regret is so heavy it's hard to breathe. What will happen to Raven if I die today? Because I am very likely going to die in the coming moments. I'd greet death like an old friend. He's been waiting for me, I know. But I'd be abandoning her.

I grit my teeth.

No. I have a plan. I can make it out of this. I hope.

Drake and his allies have set themselves up perfectly, crowded around their prey in a tight circle. All easily within reach.

It's still a massive risk... but I can do this.

Because now is the time to switch up the game. While they think I'm weak. While they think I'm pliant.

"You think I want your damned pardon?" I ask Drake, looking him in the eye, pulling my power tighter. Condensing all of it into one ball of power, ready to detonate. "The opportunity to be some no-one's housewife?"

That's how they've been keeping my court weak for the last several hundred years. They force our strongest fae to marry outside of our court, taking their power with them. Leaving us with less and less.

That isn't freedom. I don't want a single thing he can give me.

"So, you'd rather choose death?" he asks simply, his shoulders relaxed, but his eyes betray his fury. He doesn't care about my betrayal, but it does mess with his plans. Now, after they kill both me and Rev, he'll have to face his remaining enemies on even ground. He wanted me to tip the scales in his favor.

Poor baby.

"Rev," I say. This is going to be the tricky part. He's too close. Too injured. I may kill him, but only injure the others... but then the wall behind me begins to crumble. I blink, shocked as a hole the size of a door emerges right behind Rev.

I smile. "Run," I tell him.

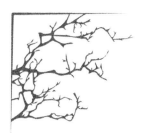

Rev

"Run," my enemy tells me.

My brother's murderer standing between me and two of my allies, two of my rivals. They want to kill me and she... wants to save me? My mind is blown to smithereens.

She's weak. Her dim eyes all but prove it.

But there she is, facing down four powerful fae with confidence that scares the shit out of me. Even I wouldn't face those four on my own.

Is she more powerful than me? Or does she intend to commit suicide to help me flee? Why? What does that prove?

"Go!" she yells, and I sprint through the gap in the stone. Only a moment later a boom shakes the ground beneath my feet, blasting me forward.

I fly through the air, and the last thing I feel before my visions goes black is coarse sand slamming into my face.

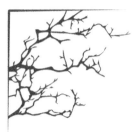

Caelynn

I groan as I pull my body onto my knees. "Ow," I say angrily, even though I only have myself to blame. All four of my enemy fae are out cold, blown back at least fifty feet behind me.

Fighting four powerful fae would have been nearly impossible. But using every ounce of my magic all at once—a surprise attack they didn't see coming—was like a damn bomb. I'd made sure to pull as much hypnosis into the surge as possible so they should be unconscious or at least too dizzy to function for hours.

I'm just hoping that's enough time.

Because my magical well is now entirely empty. I used it all. Every ounce.

I will be weak for several hours and won't be at full power again until morning.

I scramble through the barely-standing stone wall, rubble crumbling down on my head as I pass through the doorway.

On the other side, I find Tyadin struggling to drag Rev through the sand. He stops when he sees me approaching. "What the hell did you do?"

I ignore his outburst. "Finally choose an ally, did you?"

He shrugs, his expression clear he's not particularly happy about it.

"Thank you."

"Why are we saving him? Is he an ally now too?"

"It's us or death." I shrug. "I guess we'll find out which one he chooses when he wakes."

"What happened? They turned on him?" He nods to the bodies lying helplessly in the sand.

"Apparently someone outside the competition wants him dead. Not out of the competition—like, no longer breathing."

"Well, you almost achieved that. He's out cold."

"He'll be fine in an hour or two. Our bigger problem will be getting through the task while he's like this."

Tyadin purses his lips. "Why not just leave him, then?"

"He'll die if we leave him, and then my rebellion would be for nothing."

"Hide him somewhere? So he doesn't make it through the first day of the challenge but lives to tell the tale?"

I consider this. It's not a terrible option, even though I doubt it would work quite like that. He won't be giving up. So, when he wakes, he'll have a little more time to adjust before he faces his new enemies, but he'll still face them out of pure stubbornness and refusal to give up on the competition.

Four to one.

He's still likely to die.

Besides, there's one more aspect to consider.

"Without him, we're two against four, and that's if we stick tightly together. With him... our chances rise significantly."

Tyadin looks around like he's examining the entire competition in the few miles around us. His expression falls as he turns back to me.

"Regretting all your life choices, aren't you?"

He signs. "Pretty much."

"Well?"

"Help me carry him to the well. We'll see if we can get him to complete the task. I'm running for it, though, the moment the others wake."

I nod. Fair enough. "One step at a time it is."

Tyadin grabs Rev under his arms, I grab his ankles and together, we awkwardly carry him the final mile to the first trial task. We grunt and groan, muscles tense with effort as we stumble, sweat dripping from every inch of our bodies under the overbearing desert sun.

"This alliance thing seems overrated," Tyadin says as we finally drop Rev's limp body beside the red glowing well.

My face is as red as the sand on my feet when we finally fall down. A half hour of our cushion time is already gone. We need to complete the task and move away from the area as quickly as possible. Luckily, Rev got less of a hit than the others so he should rouse sooner. And the others will still need to complete the task, which should slow them down even more.

Now, all we need to do is figure out a way to get an unconscious male to complete the task...

Tyadin is on his feet first, he grips the brown paper hanging from the bucket above and reads it aloud. "First Task: Drink from the well and make a wish using a single word."

I purse my lips. That's deceivingly simple. "A one-word wish?"

"This well is renowned for fulfilling wishes in... unpleasant manners."

I bite my lip, considering. That's unsurprising, but it means that legitimate consideration should be taken when making the wish.

The first thing to come to mind is redemption—exactly what everyone thinks I want, and even though it's true in a way, I don't trust it. There are too many ways to define that word. I don't want to be forgiven because I don't forgive myself.

I could wish for something simple like self-preservation. But then I imagine being trapped at the bottom of the well alive but tormented for all time. Nope, definitely not that one. Victory, but one word isn't enough to clarify. Victory in what? Victory in a race off the edge of a cliff?

Tyadin pulls the bucket up and gulps down water eagerly. "Friendship," he says.

I nod. Friendship is simple enough. Difficult for that to go wrong.

Taking the bucket from Tyadin's stalky fingers I fling it back into the shadows below and heave it up one slow pull at a time. It shouldn't be a challenging task, but at the moment my arms rage in protest. Using all of my magic in one blow isn't something I've ever done before. It's not something any fae would ever suggest because it takes hours to recharge, and that leaves us extremely vulnerable.

In this case, it was worth the risk to knock all of my enemies unconscious. But if Tyadin decided to take me out? It would be easy for him. If the task had been to defeat a magical creature? I'd be done for.

Finally, I pull the bucket of glimmering water to the edge of the ruby-studded well. I peer at my reflection in the water. My eyes are dim, just a hint of gold flecks swimming in their depths.

I pull the wood to my lips and take a long sip of cool, sweet water without making a conscious choice—which might be a bad idea.

As the water soothes my dry throat, a gentle feeling fills all my limbs and a word forms in my mind like an illustration, glittering with the swell of magic. "Respect," I say in a near whisper.

I don't immediately know how this word could backfire, so I'm hopeful as I set the bucket back down. Somehow, it felt like the well had told me what I needed.

Tyadin nods sharply. Apparently he approves of my answer.

We both turn to Rev, considering his limp form lying in the hot sand at our feet. How do we get an unconscious ally to make a wish?

"He'll wake before them, right?" Tyadin says. "He's right here. He can complete the task and be on his way before his enemies get to him."

I bite my lip. That could be a better option than trying to force him to make a wish without coherent thought. But then again, if the well had guided me to an answer, maybe it could guide him as well.

I drop to my knees beside him and place my hand on his chest. "Rev?" I jostle him gingerly. "Reveln," I say louder.

He stirs and groans, twisting his neck until his face presses to the sand.

"Pull him up some water," I tell Tyadin, who raises his eyebrows in annoyance. "Please."

He rolls his eyes but nods. Rev turns to his back, his eyes fluttering and unfocused. I brush some of the sand from his right eye, and he groans again.

"What are you doing here?" he asks, voice hoarse.

"Helping you. Here, I've got some water for you," I tell him.

"No." He groans, twisting again. "Nothing," he spits. "From you."

"Good choice of allies," Tyadin comments.

"Hush," I snarl.

Tyadin balances the bucket on the edge of the well and scoops out a swallow's worth of water in his cupped hands. I help Rev sit up, and Tyadin holds it to his lips. "Here, try some," he says quietly.

Rev's eyes flutter again, and the moment the liquid touches his chapped lips, he opens his mouth to allow the fluid to flow over his tongue to his throat.

"What do you want?" I ask the moment he swallows.

His eyebrows pinch together. "Truth."

Tyadin's chin lifts, his expression telling me he's impressed. "All right, let's get the hell out of here."

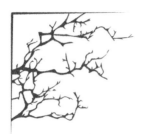

Rev

My head throbs, every muscle aching when I open my eyes. Flashes of memory bombard me—two fae helping me to run through the sand and into shadows below the Winding Mountain range. At first, I assumed it was Brielle and Rook—my allies. But the next flashes don't make any sense.

Brielle and Rook standing beside Drake and Kari and Caelynn.

Caelynn facing me, that stupid obsidian dagger in her hands, poised to kill.

Caelynn turning to face Drake and instructing me to run.

A massive blast of shadow power knocking me out cold.

I groan, more from confusion than pain—though the pain is certainly immense. I touch my abdomen softly, and my hand comes away slick. That's not good.

There's a bandage wrapped sloppily around my middle, but I've already bled through it. I close my eyes and focus my magic to my core. Clearly, I've been unconscious for some time not to have begun the healing process already.

The world around me is dark. It's night. Above me is solid black stone. No stars in sight.

My stomach sinks. I didn't complete the task yet... so if it's night...

Someone stirs beside me. A form sits up, rubbing sleep from their eyes. "Rev?" a soft female voice asks. Not Brielle.

I clench my jaw.

"Where am I?" I ask, my voice barely audible.

"A cave just inside the Winding Mountains."

I close my eyes, every ounce of my body burning with pain and rage and terror. Her eyes give off a soft golden glow. "You saved me. Why the hell would you save me?"

Caelynn sighs. "I just... I couldn't do it. And Drake pissed me off so much... I reacted. I made an instant decision." She lifts her hands in an exaggerated shrug. "Now, here we are."

My mind spins, and I force down my panicked thoughts to stop my body from reacting and retching all over our close quarters. "It's night time," I say, staring out through what I can now register as the cave mouth. Only darkness greets me, but outside there is a blue tinge that hints at sky, a soft glow of starlight.

"Yes."

"Then, why wasn't I pulled from the trials already?"

"Because you completed the task," another voice says. His large silhouette sits up, blocking what little starlight streams through the opening.

I swallow. "How? What was it?"

"Drink from the Ruby Well and make a wish using a single word."

My stomach drops. Those wishes aren't a game. Whatever I wished for might affect me long after the trials are over. "What did I wish for?"

"Truth." Her voice sends a shiver down my spine.

Well, I suppose that could be worse. "Did you tell me to wish for that?" I ask her.

Her face is still shadowed enough I can't see her expression, but those eyes... those eyes are very different than I've seen them before. How had she hiden the glow of power so thoroughly?

"No," she says softly. "You chose."

I close my eyes and suppress a shudder. Dammit, why does her voice affect me like that? She's my enemy. I hate her. I've vowed to kill her. And even though she's apparently my current ally, that's still true.

I'm going to kill her.

"How are you feeling?" the male voice asks. I assume it's the dwarf—the only other fae left in the trials, besides those who betrayed me.

I touch my stomach again, firmer this time. "Miserable. It'll take another day to heal properly."

"That's it?" he asks. "We only gave you a blood loss potion."

Caelynn shakes her head. "He has healing abilities."

I nod. Only those from my court or the Glistening Court have these abilities. I am a fairly capable healer, though I don't use the talent very often. I'm rusty, at best which means not only will it take me longer than it should, it will require more of my magic. Lack of practice means a lack of efficiency.

My father values battle powers more than healing, which he considers a *maternal* power. As in, *too feminine.*

"I could heal it completely if I weren't so drained and didn't mind using all my magic in one go."

"Impressive."

I shrug. It's not really.

"Why did they turn on me?" I ask, running my fingers through my thick hair. Sand scatters onto my pants.

Caelynn pauses, eyes darting toward the dwarf—Tyadin. "Apparently, someone wants you dead."

"Drake?" That's the logical choice, but that wouldn't be enough to turn Brielle.

She pauses, looking down at her hands. "No. Someone more influential. Some political leader who would pay handsomely. They offered me a pardon if I helped."

My eyes narrow. "There are only two people able to do that," I say. "The queen and my father."

Because the crime was committed against my court, it was up to my court to decide if and when the criminal would be pardoned. My father is the leader of my court, so he'd have that choice. The queen is the only person with the power to supersede him.

"Drake said it was the queen, but I don't know that I believe him," Caelynn says.

I nod. "I have no idea why the queen would want me dead. She has the ability to squash me in every way except physically. What could possibly threaten her so thoroughly that she'd want me dead?"

"Your father also seems unlikely," Tyadin says. "Why have his own child killed?"

I pull in a breath through my nose. "I wouldn't be surprised," I whisper.

"Oh?" Caelynn asks.

"He's always hated me. I don't know why. I suppose now I'm going to have to find out."

She doesn't respond further, and I lie back on the hard stone. How had I slept so deeply in such discomfort? I stare up into the dark stone above, my mind still spinning through this new reality. It's entirely changed.

Friend is now enemy. Enemy is now friend—or ally at least.

Why? Why would she save me? It doesn't make sense.

I close my eyes, and an image floats through my mind—of a young version of the woman with me now. She had one request in that vision.

Call me by my name before you kill me.

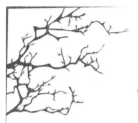

Caelynn

We rise with the sun, pack up, and head out without one word spoken between us.

Most awkward alliance ever. We climb the highest point we could conceivably complete in a day because the clue at the well told us to reach a high point and look for a blue clue in the south for further instruction. Apparently, climbing and finding the next instruction is our second task. Simple and fairly easy. So long as we find it by the time the sun sets, we are good for the day.

The only thing we have to worry about today is basic survival—including avoiding our enemy foursome who are certainly hunting us as we speak.

We climb for hours without a word spoken, each using our own supplies. Our chosen mountain is a plateau with a steep but well-worn path up to the summit. We could take shortcuts up the sharp face of the mountain, but considering the amount of time we have in the day and Rev's injury, we've decided to take it easy. Or, at least no one has voiced otherwise.

Rev never looks me in the eye.

He never says a word to me.

We silently work together to complete our simple task; for the moment, content with our protection by sheer numbers. We edge across a narrow ledge and sweat pools over Rev's brows.

"Are you alright?" I ask him calmly.

He scrunches up his nose like he's disgusted I'd even speak to him. "Fine," he says through gritted teeth.

I raise my hands in surrender, and he rolls his eyes. Yeah, should've seen this kind of reaction coming. What did I expect? He'd all of a sudden swoon over me since I saved his ass?

Nope, I'm still his brother's murderer. I need to remember who I am—to him, the others, all of the fae world, even to Tyadin.

I will die one day and rise as a wraith, destined to haunt the Schorchedlands for eternity—all for one mistake. One decision that I can't take back.

I've come to terms with my past and my future that can't change. Even if Rev were to treat me as an equal. Even if he could forgive me—not happening—it wouldn't change anything else.

I need to win to change my legacy, but my future will still remain.

A raven flies over head, squawking as it goes. "What is with that blackbird?" Rev says, annoyance clear in his voice.

"It's a bird. Nothing to be concerned with."

"Right," Rev says, his tone implying he's not convinced.

I swallow.

Rev's foot slips, sending a scattering of rubble down the side of the mountain. Without thinking, I reach forward and grip his forearm to steady him. He rips his arm away with a growl. "Don't touch me,"

I wince. Tyadin meets my eye but looks away quickly.

"Then get moving," I say, not bothering to hide the acid in my tone.

"I am." He takes another slow step. Annoyance stirs in my gut.

"The others may have seen the disturbance," I say, voice still edged with stress. Presumably, the fae I knocked out yesterday will have revived and are out for blood more than ever before. "We don't want them to find us."

"I'm not an idiot," he seethes, and I swallow.

"No, you're just holding us back with your stubbornness."

"I hold no one back." His feet shuffle more quickly over the edge.

We finally reach the end of the narrow ledge and continue farther up the mountain side. Rev still grumbles beneath his breath.

I march past him and begin an all-out climb up the uneven mountain face. The path is long and winding, and I'm out of patience. Rev and Tyadin can meet me at the top.

Tyadin stops to watch me take the challenging climb, his hands on his hips. "I doubt that's actually a good idea, Cae."

"Why not? Rev thinks he can do anything I can, injured or not."

I hear him grunt far below. I don't know how much he's healed himself already. His injury was potentially fatal without medical attention. The potion we gave him was a mere temporary fix. Some healers are able to heal even fatal injuries in moments but only the most talented and extensively trained. And I can tell is he doesn't trust me. He's saving as much magic as he can to fight me if necessary.

Based on the stiff way he's moving, he's only about halfway to healing his wound at this point.

More than a hundred feet up, I find a reunion with the walking path and I plop myself over the mini cliffside to watch them below me.

From this spot, I'm nearly three quarters up the mountain. We'd reach the summit quickly, if they can follow me.

Rev and Tyadin argue for a minute or two as I dangle my feet over the edge, watching Rev begin to climb after me like it's my evening entertainment. Just missing the popcorn.

He's steady for the first two dozen feet. He pulls his weight up seamlessly, no noticeable issues. But his pace slows once he's halfway up the section. Still over fifty feet to go.

Tyadin patiently climbs behind him, watching closely. "He's bleeding through his bandage," he calls to me.

I shrug. What's that to me?

"This is your fault, you know?" he says, eyes half annoyed, half amused.

Rev doesn't respond, just continues to climb, getting more and more vocal with each pull of his arms. He groans with every move now. He's close enough for me to see his clenched jaw, vein bulging over his temple, and sweat streaming down his face and neck. *Stubborn fool.*

Yet, I know I'd do the same thing.

"You can do it," I say, watching his efforts with renewed eagerness. "Only another ten feet to reach me." His pain is obvious, but he keeps moving. Keeps pushing. The muscles in his back tense and bulge through his tunic. I bite my lip.

Yes, he's a stubborn fool for even trying something this far beyond his current physical abilities. I am probably a fool for baiting him.

But watching him push beyond what should be outside his capabilities has me suddenly on my feet, hoping he makes it. Endurance and tenacity at its finest.

"Keep pushing," I coach louder.

He grunts and growls, his fingers shaking. He has feet left. One more stretch and pull would have him at the top.

"Come on," I whisper, stomach squirming with unexpected anticipation. I'm impressed. He's stronger than I thought.

"Shut up," he spits through ragged breaths.

I chuckle.

His foot finds a rock as a foothold, but as he places his weight onto it, the rock slips, crumbling all the way down the mountain face. I gasp as he roars in pain, holding all of his weight with his right arm, his back pulling through his injury. The back of his shirt now exposing a deep red stain.

I lay down on my belly, reaching an arm out to him. I'm close enough to reach him now. I could pull him up.

"I said, don't touch me," he hollers through gritted teeth. He swings his body, reaching for another stone with his left hand. He smacks my still hanging hand away as he pulls himself up through a roar of pain, finding one last foothold. He lifts himself over the final ledge, falling to his stomach on the flat pathway beside me.

I sit up, watching in awe as he stands without a glance in my direction, wipes his pants, and walks away with a significant limp but confidence in his gait.

Tyadin follows, pulling himself up, eyes examining my expression as I still watch Rev walk away, stomach squirming.

He places two fingers under my chin and pushes my mouth closed. I hadn't even noticed it was hanging open.

He leans in and whispers, "You could at least pretend not to be totally turned on."

I snarl at him, but he laughs and follows after Rev, now out of sight around the corner. "I'll catch up in a few," I call to Tyadin. Knowing I'd pushed Rev much, much farther than I should have—farther than he should have been able to go. So, I decide I should do something to make up for it. Rev is going to need a bit more help now that his injuries have regressed.

I'd seen the red flowers from below—it was one of the reasons I suggested this mountain to start with. Yes, it was a decent medium between easy and high and too obvious, but it also held some significantly powerful healing herbs near the summit.

So, let these stupid red flowers be my olive branch.

He'll still hate me—I still hate me. But at least he'll be in a little less pain while he does it.

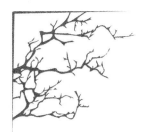

Rev

Pain roars through my body with each step. My vision blinks in and out with inky blotches of black. I'm closer to blacking out than I'd like to admit. But my pain tolerance is high, my annoyance tolerance is low.

I won't let her win this one. I'll make it the rest of the way to the top without her seeing any more weakness from me.

My chest is on fire, my muscles trembling, but I force my mind to steady and push myself through every step.

Almost there. Almost there.

I can make it without her help.

I don't need her. I won't need her.

My focus is so tight on each step, I don't even notice I'm at the top of the mountain until Tyadin places a hand on my shoulder to stop me. We're on a flat ridge at the top of one of the highest summits in the area.

I blink, looking out at the amazing view—miles and miles of expansive forests beyond us. My knees wobble beneath me, and I crumble onto my butt beside a blue maple.

I lay my head back against the bark and pant. He hands me a bottle of water, and I sip it gingerly, wincing with each swallow.

Caelynn doesn't appear to be anywhere nearby, so I venture a question that might make me sound weak. "Can we camp here tonight?"

Tyadin doesn't immediately respond. "Maybe. It would be better if we move a bit farther down the mountain—less likely to be spotted and less travel time tomorrow. But if we have to, I'll back you."

I nod and swallow, head spinning.

"Where is she?" I ask.

"She said she'd meet us up here. Maybe she's giving you a little space."

"Good." I press my eyes closed, entire body throbbing.

"You probably hurt her pride. She didn't expect you to do that."

"Good," I repeat.

"She was clearly impressed. You should have seen her face. Mouth hanging open, cheeks flushed. It was quite entertaining."

I swallow but don't respond. I don't need her to be impressed. I only need her to not think me weak. Footsteps sound gently nearby, and Tyadin stands, but I can't seem to open my heavy lids. I continue to breathe heavily, consciousness slipping from me.

My head spins as I try to rouse myself, but finally, I concede and let the void take me.

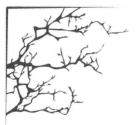

Caelynn

"**C**an you get him to eat some of this?" I ask Tyadin as I finish crushing some of the healing seeds into a fine dust. "And wrap his bandages with this?" I hold up the red leaf.

"Me?"

"He won't take anything from me." I shrug.

"He's passed out now." He nods toward Rev slumped against a maple. "He won't notice."

"Fine, I'll do the wrapping if you do the feeding."

He accepts the arrangement, and we chat about the next day's challenge as we work. He helps to hold Rev's limp body upright as I wrap it.

Looking south, the clue is obvious—three words written out in blue stones over the landscape beyond. The higher you get, the easier they'd be to read. At a lower spot, you could see the letters but the wrong angle could skew the message. We likely didn't need this height to make it out.

SW Black Gate

"The Black Gate is five hundred miles from here," Tyadin muses.

I purse my lips and consider. The Black Gate is on the north end of Shadow Court land, my home. And he's right, it's entirely too far to travel in one day. I take a slow walk around the plateau, examining the landscape around us. Everything seems normal. Except...

We traveled west to reach the mountain range, and we're only a few miles in. I should have a good view of the Fire Sands in the distance... but I don't. It's nowhere to be seen.

Is it just me or is the forest below us much bigger than the one we traveled through?

"I think we traveled farther than we thought," I say. "We're not in the Winding Mountains."

He looks around. "I thought the mountains seemed strange for the Winding Court. The rock is too brittle."

Of course the dwarf would notice the rock.

"Seems more like the Blue Mountains. Between the Glistening and the Whirling Courts."

"So what? The whole arena is fake? They're mimicking real world places? The Black Gate could be only a few miles away."

I shrug. "Possibly. But... if the arena were that small we'd definitely be able to see the desert from here."

He purses his lips, scanning the land around us.

"Is it possible we passed through a portal without noticing?" The fae have used magic to create a sort of portal between lands for thousands of years. There are a few public, well-known doors. Some fae have the ability to create and destroy them. I've never heard of a portal being used in this manner—to pass one without noticing would be impressive.

He purses his lips. "Interesting. I think you might be right."

"So, we travel southwest and look for the Black Gate. Will you know it when you see it?" he asks. "It's from your court."

"I'll know it. I'll be able to find it easily once we reach that territory. No idea how long that'll take if hidden portals are being used. We should keep an eye out for them. If it's true, they could come into play later in the challenge."

He nods.

Raven lands on a branch above us, chippering quietly. Tyadin eyes the bird and then looks to me. "A friend of yours?"

I sigh. "You could say that."

He shrugs. "Better than someone else's spy."

Connecting Raven to me is dangerous for her, no matter who knows.

Anyone who wants to get to me, which is pretty much everyone, would be eager to shoot down an ally of mine—pet or human. Doesn't matter.

I don't want anyone to know about her in any way. If it's only Tyadin, for now, I'll let it slide. Any more than that, and I'll have to send her away or turn her into a damn frog so she can't follow me. If Rev finds out...

Raven chippers more and then flies off around the slope to the side of the mountain. "I'll be back." I sigh and then follow the path.

A hundred feet below the plateau, Raven lands on the grassy ground, hopping on her little black talons excitedly. I roll my eyes and flick my hand. She pops back into human form breathing hard.

"Wow!" she says the moment she's able. "That was... intense!"

Her smile makes me smile.

"You said you weren't strong enough."

I sigh, leaning against the mountainside, arms crossed. "I got lucky."

"You're *amazing*." Her eyes glisten, and my stomach twists. "That was way more than luck."

I shrug. I don't bother to tell her that if one of several things had happened differently, I wouldn't have been able to win that fight.

"I'm glad I didn't lose you," I admit. I'd been ready to sacrifice everything for this. Maybe she was right and I should have run away with her. But then Rev would be dead...

Part of me feels like fate was on my side yesterday. That I was supposed to be here, and I was supposed to defend him.

That's a stupid thought but comforting nonetheless.

"Me too," she whispers and wraps her hand around mine, our fingers intertwining. She giggles. "You should have seen their faces when they woke up."

I whip my head around. "What?"

"Those assholes who tried to get you to kill your hotty friend."

I roll my eyes but ignore her comment about Rev. "You watched them wake? What the hell is wrong with you? Don't you know how much danger you put yourself in by getting that close?"

"I'm just a bird. Come on, no one cares."

I step forward and grip her upper arm. "They do, Raven. Rev made a comment about you just an hour ago. He thinks you're someone's spy."

She shrugs. "I am. I'm your spy." She smiles proudly.

"Yes, but that's the problem. If he suspects, they will too. And they won't hesitate to shoot you from the damn sky to stop you once they even begin to suspect you're with me."

Her face falls slightly. "I'll be more careful."

I scrunch my nose. "Fine, but one more close call, and I'm sending you back home." I flop down on a stone. "So what did their faces look like?" I ask begrudgingly. *Okay, I'm curious.*

Her eyes light up. "They were soooo mad. It was hilarious. Drake started throwing shit. And that snobby girl?"

"Kari?"

"No, the one with Rev before. Red hair?"

"Brielle."

"Yes! Brielle, her whole head caught on fire when she came to and realized what happened. I mean, her hair was perfect when it was over, which was annoying, but it was still funny at the time."

I can't help a small smile.

"They had this whole conversation about how you could have done that. That you must be stronger than they thought. Drake didn't want to believe it—pompous fool. But Kari was the smart one and convinced him you must have been hiding your power all along."

I purse my lips. Guess my secret is out.

"Where are they now?"

"They barely made it to the mountain ranges by sunset, so they picked a mountain near the desert. They're almost a mile east of you now."

I nod. "Thank you for the information, but I mean it." I point my finger at her. "Don't get that close again. And stop chirping and squawking while you fly. Stay low in the trees. Stay silent. Stay far away. Got it?"

She swallows.

"I mean it," I say. "I'll turn you into a damn tree frog and come back for you when the trials are done if I need to."

"Ew!"

"Then follow my rules. Stay safe. Or I'll do what I have to."

She nods somberly. I grip her behind her neck gently and kiss her cheek before marching back toward the summit. I flick my hand and turn her into a black owl with blue eyes this time. That will help a little at least.

Maybe in a few days, if she does a good job of following my rules, I'll reward her with being a raven again.

Because if she dies out here...

I'll lose the last good thing I have left.

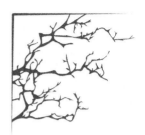

Rev

The sun has set by the time I wake, darkness hanging over the trees. I groan as I stir, although the pain is nowhere near as fierce as it had been.

A small fire burns, Ty and Caelynn sitting beside it, warming their hands.

"It's colder than it should be, isn't it?" I ask.

Ty jumps at my voice. "Welcome back," he says with a smile. "And yes. We've got a theory about that, though."

"Oh?" I ask, not daring to let my eyes move toward the female fae with him. I could like Tyadin. I'd like to pretend she's not here, though. That would make my life a lot easier.

"This isn't the Winding Mountain range," she says simply.

"You can't see it now," Ty says, "but the desert can't even be seen from here."

My eyebrows pinch together. "How?"

"We're thinking some dimensional magic. They want us to traverse the entire fae lands so some points must skip hundreds of miles, while we only walk a few."

I bite my lip. That sounds complicated.

"There was a clue on the horizon. I remember seeing southwest. What else?"

"The Black Gates."

"The real Black Gates?" I ask.

Ty nods. "We think so."

"I guess that's good for her." I nod toward the blond without looking at her.

"I'll know my way around it," she agrees.

"Although, the scourge passed through that area. We might have to face that tomorrow."

"Really?" she whispers.

Did she not know?

"Where did it hit?"

"Just one corner of the Whisperwood and some small mining town before moving on."

She bites a lip and looks down at her lap. Does she care about her homelands? She hasn't set foot there in a decade so far as I know. It's hard for me to imagine her feeling anything at all.

She doesn't look up, so I take the non-threatening moment to examine my enemy closer than ever before. Her eyes darken as she stares at the fire. Her eyebrows gently pinch together. Otherwise, she shows no evidence of pain.

Is that what it is that covers her eyes? Pain? I suppose if someone is full of rage and pain, it would be her. She's so messed up inside, her blackened soul covers the true color of her eyes. Her essence.

I blink away the image of the golden eyes of the girl in the vision.

I can't feel sorry for her. Even as her voice echoes through my head, begging my brother to stop as he held her down.

I stand suddenly. "I'm going to take a walk."

They don't stop me. They don't say a word, and I don't ask what they did to take away the pain in my side. My muscles are still stiff and sore, but my abdomen doesn't pain me at all.

I take a long walk around the mountain top and stare out over the star-streaked sky for several long minutes. The skyline is vaguely visible in the moonlight. I wish I'd had the opportunity to study the valley while the sun was still up. But no, I had to be a stubborn fool and push my body to its breaking point to prove my worth to an enemy.

So foolish.

Their theory is interesting—that we've walked through portals, transporting us hundreds of miles without us knowing it—but potentially ludicrous. Luckily, the clue is transparent enough. Whether our arena is as basic as it seems or something more complex—they did say it would be a maze—southwest should take us where we need to go.

I suppose the real question will be if we pay enough attention to our surroundings to make our way back by the week's end. If there are portals, they might be showing us the way through the maze without us knowing, and we'll need to retrace it to finish the trial.

I consider this as thoroughly as I can, alone with the wind and the stars' calming hue. I close my eyes and think through everything I've learned. Though each task will be a challenge in a different way, testing us physically, mentally, and emotionally, the trial itself is surprisingly simple. The more I think about it, I suspect their theory is correct or close to it. We are meant to notice our surroundings and figure out the difference between real and fake. Notice when what we've left behind has changed. Realize when our paths have switched on us.

A maze that doesn't appear as a maze.

If we are literally traveling to the other side of our country, they've taken out hundreds of miles between making it a y possible journey in the five days. I will certainly be keeping my eyes open for how these planes may have been folded. Are they directing us through small portals? I recall a bridge over a river that may have held some clues. Or are the portals miles wide so we couldn't miss them? Is that even possible? There will either be one route we must memorize or a pattern we must uncover.

They'd told us at the beginning of this trial that we'd need to travel to each corner of the arena, so it's easily assumed we'll travel to the exact southwest corner. We traveled at least ten miles to reach the Ruby Well, which was apparently the northeast corner. We are now moving toward what must be the southwest corner. If we are to hit all four corners in five days, and we've already missed one day, there is no other option.

My eyes begin to grow heavy again, my mind satisfied with enough information for now. I'll be very interested to see how our journey goes tomorrow. Not only the destination but every twist and turn between.

This challenge, much like the trials in general, will easily become more and more complicated as time passes.

Caelynn

I wake to find Rev staring out over the skyline.

"Couldn't sleep?" I ask, as I sit up.

"Slept fine. Just doing some homework."

I nod. "Find anything useful?"

"The desert should be there," he points behind him. "It's not."

I nod. We'd said as much last night.

"There's very little to tell from here. Other than the fact that where we came from appears to be gone, there is nothing else out of place. No signs of shadow creatures in the southwest. No changes in foliage to be noticed. It looks... normal."

"You've kept an eye out for evidence of portals?"

"Yes," he says. "Nothing that I could make out from here."

"They won't want to make it easy on us, I suppose. We'll have to see what we find as we head south. I'll wake Tyadin, and we'll get moving right away. The mountain alone will take two hours to descend, and who knows what kind of distance we'll need to travel."

I nod. "Two hours on the mountain. Then a few hours of running should get us twenty to thirty miles of distance easi-

231

ly—assuming a direct and obstacle-free route. Can the dwarf run for hours straight?"

"We managed the first trial fine."

"Riding a wyvern half the way." His voice remains low and sharp. Anger rises in my chest, even though it's not me he's criticizing. I thought he was getting along with Tyadin.

"It was a tenth of the way. And that tenth, if you recall was entirely underground. In a tunnel that did not exist before Tyadin plowed his way through. And that's assuming riding a Shadow-vyrn is easy."

"I have the two weakest allies left in the trials," he says.

Several defenses and comebacks fly through my mind, foremost that I was strong enough to save his ass, but I bite them back and instead stare at him with disgust.

"With an attitude like that, you will never win the trials," I say with no acid at all. It's the simple truth.

If he can't see beyond his preconceived perceptions of his own allies to understand what's right in front of his face, he'll lose every time.

He curls his lips, his eyes dark and full of rage. "Neither will you," he seethes, hatred clear in his expression. He's imaging all the ways he'd like to kill me. I can almost see them. His fingers gripping my neck, me gasping for breath. The words he'd like to hear from me—begging for my life.

I swallow back the pain those images cause.

"Watch me."

Rev

After another revitalizing potion and some food in my stomach, I feel significantly stronger and we make it to the valley below in less time than we'd planned.

We begin a run through the forest, traveling directly southwest as instructed. We'd discussed the possibility of traveling full west first, then south, for the extra distance we'd put between us and the others, but we decided against it out of concern we could miss a portal.

Finally, we pass the river we'd crossed on the way to the mountain yesterday, and I stop in the middle of the path. Caelynn and Ty stop up ahead, turning to watch me.

The bridge stands there just like it did before, nothing out of place. The water of the river rushes gently. It would have been impossible for us to get this far inland without crossing the river. There are likely a handful of bridges much like this one.

"What?" Ty asks, watching me stare at the bridge like a madman.

Caelynn eyes the bridge along with me. "We crossed it on the way here."

"Yes, and?" Ty says.

"Let's try it," she tells me.

I nod, jog toward the bridge, and cross it in only a moment. On the far bank, I stop and look around. The birds still chirp, the trees are the same species, the sky looks no different. But as I turn back, Tyadin and Caelynn are nowhere to be seen. I tilt my head, watching the other side of the river where I knew them to be. Quiet. Still.

I walk back over the rushing water slowly. Watching each step.

Nothing noticeable. Then, all at once, Tyadin and Caelynn appear into the path before me.

"Whoa," Tyadin says, his eyes wide where I assume I'd just appeared in the same manner.

"They worked hard on that one," I say.

"What?"

"It's seamless. I couldn't tell you where one portion starts or ends, the forest looks exactly the same. How did they find two bridges with the same angle and build, where the trees are so similar?"

"Could you see us on the other side?" Caelynn asks.

"No, that was the only clue. One moment you weren't there, then you were. Is it an illusion, do you think? Every tree is exactly the same as what I see now, but it's obviously not the same place."

"An illusion makes sense." She nods.

"Well, the only question now is will they continue to corral us through the portals like this one, or will we be expected to find them?"

She bites her lip as she considers, her intelligent eyes darting around like her surroundings will have the answers she seeks.

Truth. I'd asked for truth from the wishing well.

I hope it's her truth they give to me. My stomach squirms, knowing there is no truth in her that will fix my hatred. It'll only make my life harder—and that's likely the exact reason the well will give it to me.

I steel my heart for what she'll expose eventually. Truths I know I don't want. And yet, can't possibly walk away from.

"Let's keep moving," Ty says. "We'll have to puzzle it out as we go."

Our steps are swift but light as we careen down the pathways, compasses out. It bothers me how seamless the portal was—sights, sounds, and smells didn't change in the slightest. Which means we might not notice the change even now that we know what we're looking for.

I almost want to go examine the bridge portal again—there had to be a clue we missed. But it's best to keep moving, putting distance between us and where we assume the others to be.

I've somehow swapped from the strongest alliance in the trials to the weakest. Four of the strongest fae are hunting me. Though, I'm almost at full strength, my climb yesterday set me back, and my two allies are lesser court fae. Weak.

I shake my head at my ridiculous predicament.

At least I'm alive, I suppose. But death very well may be just around the corner.

"Could we destroy it?" I ask suddenly. Ty and Caelynn turn to me. "The bridge, the portal. If you're right that they're behind us, they were likely on the other side of that portal and if we destroy it, they may never find the right course."

Caelynn presses her teeth to her bottom lip. I stare mercilessly, then shake my head. *Stupid.*

Yes, she's attractive. Yes, she's smart. Yes, she's strong. And probably more things I've never expected from her—but she's still my enemy.

She destroyed my life for her own gain. She's a damn terrorist.

"We don't know that will work," Ty says.

"That's not a reason not to try."

"What if we have to go back through it later?" Caelynn says, flecks of gold flickering in her eyes like fire.

I purse my lips.

"This is supposed to be some kind of maze," she says. "So far, it doesn't seem very complicated. I'd be willing to bet these portals will become more and more important as we complete the challenge."

"We'll have to follow the same route we used to reach our tasks, you think?"

"Possibly."

I nod sharply, content with the reason not to destroy our known portal.

"Should we leave clues for us to find later?" Ty asks as we continue our swift pace.

"Maybe," I say, "but then we run the risk of the others following our hints. I'd rather trust my own memory and instincts. Brielle has a particularly sharp eye. She'll notice something out of place."

We cross another small body of water, but after a few moments of testing, we decide there is no portal here. We keep moving. Our miles take much longer than we'd have liked, but figuring out the keys to the portal maze is easily worth it.

Our pace is more of a swift walk than a run, but we still travel several miles before deciding a meal break is in order.

"Does your bandage need changed?" Tyadin asks.

I pull up my shirt to examine the gauze over my stomach. "Looks fine to me. Did you change it last night?"

He nods. My shoulders relax slightly, knowing it was him that aided me while I slept and not Caelynn. For all I know, she'd poison me while she did it.

I don't want her to touch me, at all. Ever.

"Did you do something different? It seems to be healing better than before." That or I didn't hurt it as badly as I thought while climbing the cliff.

He nods but keeps his eyes low.

"Carnelian," Caelynn says.

My eyes dart to her, blood running cold. Stupid reaction, but I can't help it. The thought of her touching me... "You did it?"

Her gaze doesn't meet mine, her expression unreadable. "No, Ty did it all. I just told him about the flower."

My lips thin, eyes hooded. "Lies," I say. Rage once again flows through my veins. "You expect me to believe the *dwarf* climbed the mountainside to get those herbs? I saw where they were." And if she lied about that...

Tyadin stands. "You should thank her," he says smoothly, but his tense shoulders tell me something bothered him. Was it me calling him a dwarf? Is he ashamed of his heritage? Did he think he passed as a fae?

"I'm sorry if I offended you," I say, looking at the ground. "But I won't thank her. Not for anything. I don't want her touching me, even if it's to save my goddamn life."

Tyadin curls his lip in disgust. "What do you think offended me?"

I narrow my eyes. Trick question? "I'm unsure," I say honestly. "I assume calling you a dwarf."

His hands curl into fists. "I am proud to be a dwarf," he says, his voice a low rumble.

I take in a long breath. "As you should be."

He rolls his eyes like it was a joke, but it wasn't. Dwarves are different from fae, and those differences will always make him stand out among us. But that doesn't make what he is any less than us. If his heritage means something to him, he has every right to be proud. I'm sure I would be if I were dwarfish and knew even a thing about them. As it is, all I know are the stereotypes.

"I do not know why you were offended," I offer. "I only noticed your reaction. Were you defensive for...her?"

"No. You're a fool for how you treat her, but I don't blame you for those emotions. I'd hate her in your shoes too. I hated her for a long time, and it wasn't my brother. It wasn't even my court."

"Yet, you aligned with her."

He nods slowly, arms crossed, still standing. "In part out of necessity. Did you know she was invited to an alliance by the others and I wasn't? Climbing and speed are not even close to the only disadvantages to being a *dwarf*."

I turn my gaze to Caelynn, but she's studying Tyadin closely. What does she see?

"I am offended," Tyadin says slowly, enunciating each word, "because you intended to offend me."

I open my mouth to respond but close it again. *What?*

"If you're going to call me a dwarf, that's fine. It's true. I am half-dwarfish. But do not use the word as an insult."

My eyebrows rise as I consider his words, knowing I've done that very thing many times in the past.

"Don't think the difference goes beyond my notice. Rarely are my people's name used in a positive way."

I swallow. "I'm sorry." I can't say it was an accident, but... "I'll make an honest effort not to do it again."

He nods. "That's all I could ask."

"I did mean it," I tell him. "That you should be proud of who you are and where you come from."

"Even if it's dwarfish?" he asks, amusement on his tongue. I smile.

"We poke fun and belittle what we know little of," Caelynn adds, her voice soft. "Maybe it would help if you told us more about your people?"

Ty smiles sincerely, his eyes lightening.

We pack up and begin a quick walk while Tyadin tells us the story of the final battle that drove the dwarves from their homeland over a hundred years ago. They'd had a massive country within the mountains, caves winding deep with uncountable fortunes. Dwarves are renowned for their stone wielding ability. Nearly all the precious jewels in fae possession were mined by dwarves.

Many believed the dwarfish city inside the mountains would be crude, as the dwarfish culture is generally considered unrefined. But every soul that entered those gates was astounded by the intricacies in the stonework built into the mountains.

The precious city of legend was destroyed over a hundred years ago by a shadow monster that attacked from below, cutting into the supports and destroying their throne room, and with it, their king. There were two princes taken by two rivaling dwarf courts, and they vied for leverage, each claiming their prince was the true heir and that their mountain should be the new capital. Civil war began.

That was when the goblins invaded and took what was left of their crumbling society.

Their divided people were never able to kill the shadow monster, so it still lives in those mountain ranges, driving out any dwarves who remain underground overnight. The fae, instead of helping the dwarves, scavenged through the remains of their city and took the most precious items for themselves while denying the dwarves any right to their own handiwork. Some were given jobs, helping to build the fae's own architecture—which they then took credit for.

The rest were scattered. Some lived as nomads near the mountains of their now-abandoned homelands. Many assimilated into the fae courts—the most welcoming being the Crumbling Court.

Time is lost as I listen to Ty's story. I'd heard pieces of this story but never from a dwarf's point of view. The sadness in his voice as he speaks of his lost heritage, of the missing people, of how they were treated in the aftermath of their tragedy, sends a pang of pain through my gut.

I am so caught up in his emotion that I almost don't notice the rumbling sound of pounding footsteps approaching us from behind. I only have a moment to realize what's happening when a solid wall of rock blocks our path, and I spin to find three very angry fae rushing us.

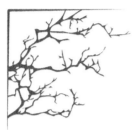

Caelynn

I turn to face our enemies bearing down on us.

Both of my swords are unsheathed in an instant as a calm settles over my body, magic bubbling beneath the surface. Hungry.

A blast of fire roars toward us, and I dive out of the way, rolling to my feet off the path as leaves fly.

"Run," I tell Rev and Tyadin. Rev is injured, he can fight if he must, but I can hold them back for a short time.

My magic is mostly restored, and a squirming in my stomach tells me my darkness is eager to escape. Eager to destroy.

Kari flies past me and through a hole in her stone wall, following Rev and Tyadin as they flee.

The other three have their sights set on me. They aren't taking any chances this time. I'm the wildcard. They don't know what I'm capable of, and they're planning to take me out quickly.

My lips curl into a smile.

They forget that I am of the Shadow Court—secrets are my biggest advantage.

Shadows curl around my fists, the swirls extending to the blades of my twin swords.

Above us, the sky grows dark, the sun covered by a dim film. Drake is the only one to notice it. The only one whose expression shifts, fear settling over his features.

The only one who knows what it means.

My swords fly, blocking Rook's first slice in my direction. Rook and Drake engage first, I twist and turn, avoiding their swords. Brielle sends a wall of flame up behind, blocking any retreat.

I am not the strongest of swordsmen, but I am fast and I see what most others don't—or perhaps *feel* is a better term for it. The darkness that spreads around me is more than for show, more than a distraction. It whispers in my ear, shifts as their muscles shift, and tips me off to their movements before they make them. My own little spies.

A vine wraps around my ankle, and I nearly fall from the sudden blockage. I grunt as Rook's blade anticipates my hesitation—he sent the vine after all—and flings his sword at my head. I twist, and it hits my upper arm instead, slicing a nice gash into my flesh.

I cast a gathering of shadows at the ground, and the vines retreat. I waste no more time blasting Drake and Rook with walls of black acid flame.

They roar in pain, clawing at their eyes, and I leap toward Brielle.

Brielle snarls at me as she swings her sword at my face—a blade too big for her. She couldn't win this fight. She's good at long range attacks and defense, not close range. Good, I'll destroy her in moments.

She leaps at me and I twist away, slashing through her thigh as I go. She howls in pain and rage, her eyes a bloodthirsty red. Her sword ignites in flame, and I swallow. Drake and Rook are already back in the fray. It's everything I can do just to stop from being gouged with all three swinging their blades at me. Move, spin, duck. Each swing getting closer and closer to their mark. A blade nicks my shoulder, and I curl my lip.

I can't keep doing this without backup. I'll lose, and quickly.

Time for one final trick to get away from my pursuers.

With the quick flick of my hand, the dark film high in the sky is loosened. The darkness falls, enveloping everything around us. I time my last strike, leaping to the side, as we're plunged into darkness. I shove my blade into my chosen target—the only one of the three to leave his stance open.

My blade scrapes against and—with a pop—through male flesh. The cry of agony is the only sound audible in the utter silence of my blanket of shadows.

My eyes glow golden. I know he sees them because Rook stares back at me like I am death itself. His eyes grow wide before they dim, death taking hold so quickly it surprises even me. The other two fall to their knees in defense. I can see them, but they can't see me.

Too bad it won't last, and I need to get away before that happens. If I'm honest, I'm impressed I lasted this long against three of them.

My victim drops to the ground limp, and I sprint toward the blaze, surrounding myself with a quick shield as I blast through the still standing wall of flame and into the forest beyond. My arms and legs burn through the singe of heat.

My shield protected me from the worst of it, but I couldn't stop a minor sear.

It'll be uncomfortable to sleep tonight, but that's the extent of the damage.

I turn around a corner, searching for Rev and Tyadin—where did they go? Atop a hill to the east, I spy a stone arch through the trees. I pause, staring at the obvious, and random, entryway. Was it just me or was there a glistening of magic within?

A portal perhaps? It would be significantly more obvious than the last, but maybe we were supposed to puzzle it out and notice it. If we pass by the arch, will we wander forever southwest and never find our task in time?

I let the possibility fall by the wayside because first things first, I have to find my allies. Then we'll worry about the tasks.

We need to get moving fast. We'll be hard pressed to survive another fight, even with the others down one. Rev is still recovering, and Tyadin isn't nearly strong enough to take them all.

Right now, our choices are to flee or die.

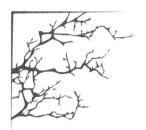

Rev

Tyadin and I sprint through the pathway, not even pausing as Caelynn stops to engage. I don't know what her plan is, and I don't care.

If she wants to put herself at risk again to help us—have at it. I hope she dies in the process. It would make my life so much easier. I'd live with the disappointment of missing the chance to shove the blade through her heart myself. I know what it feels like, thanks to the orb of terrors, and it's not something I feel the need to live with forever if I don't have to.

Call me by my name before you kill me.

Tyadin pulls me behind a boulder, the stone rising to surround us as we hide, listening to the battle waging behind us.

"What the hell is she doing?" he whispers. "She can't beat them on her own, can she?"

I swallow. "She did it once."

He shakes his head. "She had the element of surprise that time, and she had time to build her magic into one atomic shadow bomb. I doubt she'll get a blast like that one again."

"Is it bad that I don't care one way or another?"

"Suppose I don't blame you. It's better for our survival if she's still around, though. She's the strongest of the three of us at the moment."

"That's not a comforting fact." I swallow. "How does she do it? Hide her magic like that?"

"Isn't it obvious?" Tyadin says, brushing hair from his eyes.

I raise my eyebrows, waiting.

"Pain."

I narrow my eyes. "Is she ill?" Chronic pain of some kind? Except that would suck her strength, wouldn't it?

"Pain isn't only physical," he says ominously, and the truth I hadn't dared even consider sends a jolt of discomfort through my chest. The image of a young Caelynn being held down flashes through my mind.

"But she's so..." Several words cross my mind. Listless, apathetic, hard-hearted. "Cold," I finally decide on.

He nods. "The more time I spend with her, the more I suspect she's simply a very good actress. She's hated, and she doesn't fight it. She owns it. Perhaps because she hates herself just as much."

I wince. Dammit. I cannot possibly feel compassion or empathy for my brother's murderer. She killed him, and she doesn't care. I wrap that truth around my heart and seal it there. That's my truth. That's what's going to keep me going. Keep me sane.

Once her heart has stopped beating, maybe then I'll consider looking deeper. A cry of agony echoes through the forest around us, and I freeze. The voice was distinctly male.

"Who was that?" Tyadin whispers.

"Rook," I say, knowing it's the truth as soon as I say it. My brother's murderer has become my friend's murderer, and I am culpable. It's not like he didn't try to kill me first, but the pain still hits hard and sharp as if it were my heart she carved out.

"Well that's... good news, I suppose," Tyadin says, a hint of sympathy in his tone. He turns away from me, peeking through the gap in the stone wall he created. "She's coming—shit!" he spits and then quickly slips from an opening on the side of his created cave.

"What?" I don't dare say it loud enough for him to hear now that he's already on the path sprinting toward some unknown conflict.

"Look out!" Tyadin cries to a figure in the distance.

I watch over a hundred yards from the scene as Caelynn skids to a stop, her eyes darting toward Ty and then to the bolder beside her just before Kari's blade flies at her. Caelynn barley blocks the attack with a fling of her sword and cry of surprise.

Tyadin just saved Caelynn's life. I can't help but feel a pang of disappointment, even though the logical part of my brain tells me it's a good thing. She's still an ally. She's still defending me.

With movements fast as lightning, Caelynn swings her shadow-singed blade at Kari's neck, and she only barely avoids it. Caelynn's second blade clips Kari as she twists away, slicing deeply through her inner thigh.

I wince and sprint to them, knowing the battle is over.

Kari falls with a cry of pain, gripping her thigh as blood pours over her fingers. I brace myself for Caelynn's final blow—ending the life of another enemy—but I blink back my surprise as she slides her blade back into its sheath.

"Just do it," Kari spits, her face white.

"They're coming," Caelynn says through her teeth, annoyance clear at our anticipation. She *doesn't* want to kill her? "We have to go."

"Where to?" I ask.

Caelynn takes in a long breath. "This way." She leaps from the path, into the forest where leaves crunch beneath our feet.

"Where are we going? This is east." As in, *wrong way*!

"I think there's a portal over here," she says, her strides long and even. Is she even tired after battling four powerful fae, defeating two of them? Who the hell is this girl? I'm beginning to understand how she managed to kill my brother. He probably never expected the young pretty thing to have this much power. Did she hide her bright eyes even then?

Note to self—never underestimate her. Never underestimate anyone from the Shadow Court, who uses secrets and deceit as their greatest advantage.

We follow Caelynn through the forest until I see her destination—a stone archway at the top of a hill. It's off the path but otherwise is obvious—if you know to look for portals.

Maybe she's right. Maybe this is right the way, but I'm not entirely certain until we climb the hill and pass through the archway into distinctly different terrain. The shadows are vast, thick with danger.

"Wow," Tyadin breathes in front of me.

I swallow as the twisted trees with leaves black as night tower over me the moment I'm through. It's another world entirely.

Caelynn stares at the canopy above, the sky beyond a dark blue, even though it's still midday. She sucks in a long deep breath, eyes closed, expression serene.

I step forward and can't help but glance back at her, watching her reaction carefully. Her expression as soft as I've ever seen it.

The look of someone who has finally come home.

I turn away, acid filling my veins. *I hate her*, I remind myself. And I hate myself for needing the reminder.

I breathe in deeply, the thick and humid smell of the shadow realm. This forest has a distinct scent—damp wood and fresh foliage. Of wild power and danger.

It's the smell of her.

A smell I am simultaneously disgusted by and in awe of.

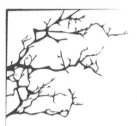

Caelynn

I am home.

Darkness surrounds me. Fills me.

Shadows shift and wind howls past my ears, tossing my hair around in a whirl of power, welcoming me to the world of night and enigmas, where nothing is as it seems. Where power lurks, hiding in the most unexpected places and can be found within every nook, if one is only brave enough to dare.

I open my eyes, studying the forest ahead, trying to get my bearings. I walk forward slowly. It feels as though we've lost our pursuers—we are now a world away—but I know better. Drake and Brielle could come flying through the portal behind us at any moment, and we wouldn't even hear them coming.

Tyadin must have the same thought. "Let's keep moving."

We jog half a mile, and the feeling of familiarity continues to grow, the curve of the path feels right somehow. The trees curl over us in a comforting manner. At least to me.

Murmurs and whispers cascade through the blowing leaves growing louder, filling our ears, allowing us to hear little else.

"What is that?" Tyadin asks, his voice mixing with the mysterious whispers filling the air around us.

"Why do you think they call it the Whisperwood?" Rev asks with an amused tone. "The trees whisper to each other."

"No," I say quietly. "It's the shadows."

As if on cue, a dark mist clings to my legs and shoulders, rippling off of me.

Rev and Tyadin both gasp, looking to their own appendages, only to see them bare of the dark magic.

"Are you doing that?" Tyadin whispers.

"No." They aren't my own—my magic is too depleted to cast that kind of power unnecessarily right now. No, this magic is part of the Whisperwood, a type of sprite, technically. "Don't worry, they're friendly."

He swallows. "Maybe to you."

Whispers circle past my ears, and I stop to listen. *They're coming.*

I pull in a breath and listen again. They know much more than I do, and every ally is valuable at this point. *This way,* they tell me.

I smile and continue my march, shadows and mist sweeping over me and curling into a path ahead.

"Is that..." Rev begins but stops.

"Just follow them," I tell him.

Welcome home, the dark sprites whisper for only me. A comforting warmth fills my chest. A feeling I'm so unaccustomed to now.

I hadn't realized how much I missed this place. This magic.

I sigh, following the shadow path to a nook beside the pathway. It's a dead end.

Hide, the whispers tell me.

I look around the forest, still not quite familiar with our location, but I trust the sprites.

I slip into the little nook, below twisted roots breaking free from the hillside leaving a small dirt and root covered hollow.

"What are you doing?" Rev whispers.

"Following the sprite's advice. I suggest you do the same. They said they're coming."

Tyadin crawls into the hole by me, and Rev waits. The sprites surround us both and Rev blinks when, I assume, we disappear into the darkness. "Wow," he whispers and then joins us. He shivers as the sprites cover him too.

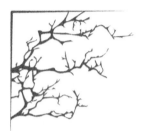

Rev

I crouch beside Tyadin in our shadow sprite-covered hiding place. This is absolutely bizarre. This shadow magic is unlike anything I've ever felt. It sings over my skin, slipping beneath my clothing and into strange places. I shiver as they tickle beneath my arms. Over my back and neck.

We're quiet, able to see out to the still forest, with those outside unable to see us.

Finally, the subtle shifting of leaves hints the approach of an enemy. Caelynn's breath shudders, and I bite my lip, resisting the urge to watch her bright eyes filled with awe, her beautiful lips curling into a subtle smile.

I turn my attention to the pathway—what's happening outside our hideaway is more important.

"Did we go through a portal?" a sharp female voice exclaims.

A bitter laugh echoes. "This is the shadow lands. They found a shortcut."

Good, they haven't yet realized the key to the arena maze. This isn't a shortcut—this was the only way to get here in a day's time.

Of course, it'd have been better if they hadn't followed us at all. Then they'd have been lost for good, but I'll take what I can get.

"But we're in an entirely different land now," Brielle says, her eyes wide as she walks forward slowly.

"We're supposed to be," Drake says. "The Black Gates, remember?"

Brielle sighs, "Yes, but I heard Kari scream. We wouldn't have heard her if she went through here."

"So?"

"So, she's back there somewhere, injured! We have to go back and find her."

"No," Drake spits. "If she lost to Caelynn or Rev, then she's lost her value. We move on without her. Besides, there was more than one reason I chose to align with Caelynn. I knew we'd spend a large amount of time in the shadow lands. The queen says it's the most like the Schorchedlands, and Caelynn knows her way around here. We need to keep close to them."

Drake certainly knew more about this trial than anyone else. How fair is that?

Brielle stops, her eyebrows pinched in concern. "You're saying we leave Kari behind, without even knowing if she's dead or alive?"

"Yes," he says.

Brielle swallows, pausing right in front of our hiding place. My muscles tense, not even daring to breathe—even though I know the sprites are very capable of silencing any noise.

"They're stronger than us now," Brielle whispers, as she begins a slow walk after him.

"Tomorrow they may be. But Caelynn used a lot of her magic, and Rev is still injured, or he wouldn't have run. We still have the upper hand, but not for long."

Her expression crumples, but she follows after Drake, sprinting through the Whisperwood and away from us.

I swallow hard, watching them disappear. "Fools," I whisper. Although that's not the right word.

"Assholes," Caelynn corrects. Yes, that's better.

They're willingly abandoning Kari. I should be most annoyed with Drake—she's his friend. His ally from the beginning. But it's my friend I'm most angry at. Brielle should have fought for Kari. Refused to follow him, and he'd have had no choice. She chose the easy route.

We sit in silence for another full minute before I dare another utterance. "What now?"

Caelynn crawls from the nook and rolls her shoulders before pulling out her compass. She chuckles darkly. "I love this game."

"What?" Tyadin asks.

Caelynn's lips flick into a wicked grin that I can't keep my eyes off of. "They assumed the portal would spit them out in the same direction they were previously heading."

I blink.

"We go that way." She points back past the portal.

"The way we came?"

She nods. "The portal turned us around. That way is north and we have to go 'backwards' to correct it."

Genius, I think but don't dare say the word aloud.

We quietly scamper back down the path away from Brielle and Drake, but Caelynn stops as we cross the stone archway. Her eyes linger on it.

"What?"

She turns back toward the forest. "Cover them?" she requests quietly to no one at all.

Shadows leap from the twisted foliage, and I jerk back. Little black mist-hands cling to my arms and legs. "What are you doing?" I say too loud.

"Stay here," she says. "The sprites will hide you if they figure it out and come back this way. There's something I need to do."

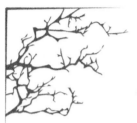

Caelynn

Black mist clings to Tyadin and Rev until they are all but invisible, even to me. I smile at their expressions as they disappear into darkness, open mouths and angry eyes.

And then I sprint through the stone archway before they can argue.

The world around me lightens, the wind blows against my skin softly and I blink in this entirely different world. Well, not literally, but it feels like a different world. The Whisperwood is something special indeed.

My heart aches at the absence of the darkness of my homeland, and for the first time, I wonder if this is a mistake.

I clench my jaw and run forward. I've already made the choice, I'm going to follow through.

A few minutes later, I turn the corner and see her. She's slumped against a tree, holding her thigh tightly. Her dark hair falls over her face, covering her dimmed eyes.

I approach slowly. Her head snaps in my direction, and I stop, hands up. Her eyes are wide and wild.

"Come to finish the job?" she says, her voice hoarse, her face pale.

"Drake isn't coming back for you. He's moving on without you," I say.

She blinks, pain clear in her eyes, but her expression betrays no other emotion. "Unsurprising."

I take a few more steps forward and then kneel in front of her.

"What are you doing?" she says, jerking away from my approaching fingers.

"Helping."

"No," she says firmly. "Why?"

"If you don't complete the challenge by sundown you'll be taken out of the competition. They'll come for you. But at this rate, you'll bleed out before that time."

A strange noise reverberates from her throat. Panic? Confusion? Shock?

"I can stop the blood loss enough that you can survive this."

Kari presses her eyes closed. "I don't understand."

I rip off a full strip of her pants to gain access to the wound at the inside of her leg. She doesn't stop me.

"I don't need any more death on my conscience."

She opens her eyes and studies me quietly as I work, but she asks no more questions.

I wrap the cloth around her thigh above the wound and tie it tightly. Bright red drips over my fingers. I drip three droplets of a healing potion onto the open wound.

Lastly, I hand her my water container. She stares at it for a long moment before closing shaking fingers around the bottle and bringing it to her lips.

"It'll be a very long night," I tell her. "But you should live."

She licks her pale lips and nods, her eyes closed again. "Thank you," she says as I stand and walk away.

"He's going to kill you, you know?" she says to my back. I stop.

"Rev," she clarifies. "I know him. He's smart, so he'll take your aid while he needs it, but it won't stop his thirst for vengeance. It's the only thing he's ever really wanted."

I swallow without turning toward her, but I nod just the same. "It would be a fitting death," I admit before continuing my march.

Her bitter chuckle echoes behind me. "You are not at all what I expected." Her soft voice is nearly lost in the breeze as I walk down the path.

I do feel a tad guilty for leaving her in this condition, but if I did more, she'd be a liability. I doubt Drake's betrayal is bad enough to make her change sides, even if we were able to recuperate her. And in order to win, I need less competition. She can't continue. This is the best I can do.

Around the bend, my stomach drops as two forms come into view.

My heart pounds wildly, hand already gripping my sword, until I realize its only Rev and Tyadin. I raise my eyebrows, forcing my body to calm—not a threat. Not yet, at least.

I keep my eyes cast low, avoiding their studying stare. How much did they see? Hear? Anything?

"It was safer to hide through the portal," Tyadin answers my unvoiced question. "Besides, those sprites tickle." He shivers.

I nod absently and walk past them, through the stone archway. The air around me buzzes and shifts until comforting shadows cover me. I pull in a long breath.

Home.

Tyadin and Rev follow silently, and when I take the southern pathway at a run, they follow.

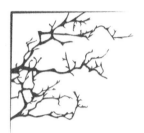

Rev

I can't keep my gaze from jumping to *her*.

Our feet pound heavily on the dirt pathway, curving through the dark forest. She takes the lead, presumably knowing where she's going—or at least pretending to.

This is her homeland, so I assume she's at least vaguely familiar, regardless of how long she's been away. At the very least, these shadow sprites are happy to help her.

I watch her hair, more silver than blond in these shadowed lands, swaying as she sprints. Her fingers curled into fists, the tension in her shoulders obvious.

I have no idea what to make of this girl. My enemy. My brother's murderer. Beautiful and powerful and... kind? She's everything I never thought she could be.

She went back to a fallen foe and... helped her. For no reason. For no gain of her own. She admitted to an enemy that dying by my hand would be a fitting death.

What in the world does that mean? I can't even imagine it.

Does she wish to die? I suppose I could understand that. She doesn't seem to be overly proud of herself, although she clearly wears indifference as a shield. Perhaps Tyadin is right, and it's all an act? Perhaps beneath her steely exterior, she's as broken as I am.

Or perhaps this kindness is an act. Maybe she knows I am still a threat and wants me to lower my guard.

But if that were true... why not kill me when she had the chance? When it was clearly in her best interest. I saw the pain in her eyes in that moment. I remember clearly the panic on her face when Drake handed her the dagger. An obsidian dagger just like the one she'd killed my brother with. Just like the one I killed her with during the orb of terrors trial. I saw the moment determination hit her eyes and knew she would turn against them before they did.

But why? Why not kill me when it could give her all the things she wants? She could still try to win the trials, and if she lost, she'd have one hell of a consolation prize—a pardon.

Now what does she have? All or nothing on winning these trials.

Killing her, I realize, is going to become harder and harder the more time I spend with her. But I am certain of one thing—I will never forgive her. Banishment is a forgiving punishment, and I wouldn't ever dream of giving her anything less.

Just the thought that my father would consider pardoning her is a bigger punch in the gut than the thought that he wants me dead. Which is really sad when I think about it.

I've always known he hated me. He doesn't think I am good enough.

He's probably the biggest reason I wasn't named heir already. If I win these trials and retrieve the cure, the queen will have basically no choice but to choose me. There would be riots in my court—if not elsewhere—if she were to spurn me again.

My father may hate me but my people don't.

I'm so lost in my own thoughts that I almost don't notice Caelynn coming to a stop up ahead, and I halt just inches from ramming into her.

My chest is so close to her back, I can feel her warmth. I can hear her rapid breathing. I freeze, every muscle tense, afraid to move.

Not wanting to move.

My breath is heavy, and I can see her silver hair dancing against it. Caelynn doesn't move, though the skin on the back of her neck grows goosebumps.

I look past her, at the sparkling black arch—a hundred times the size of the portal we passed to get here. She takes a step forward, saving me from my awkward closeness. Her steps are slow and measured, her eyes cast up to the onyx stone surrounding her.

"Have you seen it before?" I ask.

"Many times," she says, her voice soft as velvet. I swallow.

I blink and break my intense stare at her emotional reaction to the Black Gate and visually search for something out of the ordinary. At the foot of the right arch column there is a bright red stone. I approach until I'm close enough to notice a message written along the top.

"Here," I say to the others. The message is simple. "Pass through the gates. Find the caves. Answer your riddle."

"Riddle?" Tyadin says. "I hate riddles."

"It says your riddle, not the riddle," Caelynn says, her voice back to normal, her spell broken. "Do we each have our own?"

I shrug. "I guess we'll find out. Do you know of a nearby cave?" I ask her. We could spend an hour searching, assuming it's within a mile of here, but it would save precious time if we could find it quickly.

"Possibly. But the exact path..." She pauses, her golden eyes growing dimmer, then flickering back. "Well, my memories are a bit hazy."

"I can help," Ty chimes in. "Do you know the general direction?"

Caelynn nods and points past the massive black stone arches. The air between shimmers like a mirage.

I shiver because passing through the Black Gates looks simple, but I know better. Much like the Ruby Well, it's legendary. It's a Shadow Court rite of passage for adolescent fae. Had Caelynn been old enough to complete the ritual before she became a convicted murderer?

She stares at the arch, face blank but eyes wide, full of more emotion than I've seen from her. "What should we expect?" I ask her.

She pulls in a deep breath and shrugs. "I've never passed it before."

Tyadin's mouth falls open. "How? Why?"

"I was banished a few months before my ritual."

I swallow, turning away from the tears in her eyes, from the way my stomach aches. From the desire to comfort her. What the hell is up with that? *Mortal enemy, remember?* I tell myself. She deserves this pain.

"I was told you'd be shown your future," Ty says, also looking away from her.

"Nothing specific," Caelynn says. "It's said to whisper your own thoughts back to you. The things you'll think just before your death."

I swallow. "Well, that's pleasant."

"Why would they make that a rite of passage?" Ty asks.

"They say only the strongest can face their own death and continue forward. Death can be an ally like any other."

My head whips in her direction. She meets my stare, with a determined gaze.

"Are you ready to meet death?" I ask her breathlessly.

"I've been ready for a very long time."

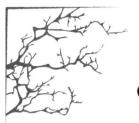

Caelynn

I clench my jaw, staring at a stolen moment of my childhood. It's a moment children fear but are also eager for because several rights are unsealed after this ritual. We are allowed to travel to the human world, for one. We are allowed to seek a mate and leave our parent's homes, though most don't for several years. We begin our trade-specific training. Our magic grows to its strongest in the years after the ritual.

I'm going to complete it now. My heart aches but warms at the thought.

It will never be like it should have been. With my parents and the Queen of the Whisperwood standing on the other side, ready to greet me. With a full celebration planned for the day after.

Had I not gone wondering on the wrong day, in the wrong place, and hid inside the wrong tunnel inside the cave of mysteries—the same cave we're heading to now. Everything would have been different. I'd have completed my ritual and been a full member of the Shadow Court.

But I still take solace that, finally, I get to pass the gates.

I am ready to face my death. Part of me is eager for it.

At the very least, I am a hell of a lot more eager for death than I am to enter the cave of mysteries again. If there was any part of these trials I may fall apart and fail, it's that. The orb tried to show me my worst fear, but it was hollow. It was nothing like what I've already faced.

And though I will very easily choose death rather than take that tunnel again, I'll be close to it. So close to the real thing. Whether that creature is still there or not—I don't know. But I will always assume he'll be there waiting for me.

I take in a shaky breath. I have to stop focusing on that. Passing through the gate will be hard enough.

I pull in a long breath and then march through the shimmering magic of the Black Gate.

A RUSH OF MAGIC WASHES over me in an instant, and I no longer remember where or who I am. There is a surprising peace, a fluttering of hope and love.

The pressure, the weight, the burden—it's gone. Why was I so burdened before this moment? I cannot remember. I cannot even fathom. But I do know that this feels good.

Death is freedom, a whisper floats through my mind, and I blink rapidly. This whisper is heavy, so much heavier than the sprites.

No, another whisper floats by. *The* right *death, is freedom. Follow the right death, Caelynn.*

I pinch my eyebrows trying to piece it together.

What does that mean? The magic shimmers over me, swirling over my skin, filling every pore. Seeping into my very soul.

And then, in a moment, the magic recedes, and I fall to my knees as the pressure, the guilt, the pain, the rage—all of it—slams back onto me. I gasp, gripping the dirt tightly.

"Are you okay?" Rev says only feet behind me, but not daring to approach—he'd have to pass through the magic first.

"Yes," I say, but the word is a struggle to pass through my lips. I'm okay—sort of. The gate was not the hard part—it's facing reality after such relief. I pull in long shaky breaths and fight the urge to cry.

Facing death is the easy part.

Facing life—that's the struggle.

Rev

Everything in my body screams for me to rush to Cae-lynn as she falls to the ground. I barely stop myself from crossing the threshold of dangerous magic in front of me.

What the hell? Why are my emotions so all over the place with her? Like every instinct is telling me...

I shake my head.

This is about me. I have to pass this magic and face the harsh reality it's sure to bear onto me. Before I can overthink it, I step into the glimmer of magic floating in the open space between the onyx stone arch, and my world falls away in an instant.

Black power rushes over me, strong as a hurricane, menacing and powerful. It pushes and pulls my body in several ways at once. I scream as my head is pulled to the west. My heart is pulled south and my body to the east. Agony pierces every thought as I'm pulled apart piece by piece in a gale of fear and magic.

If only I had known, a desperate whisper begins.

If only I had known. If only I had known. If only I had known, it continues, gaining speed, gaining urgency, gaining power. *If only I had known. If only I had known. If only I had known.*

I press my palms over my ears, and the whisper grows into a crescendo, into a roaring so painful I scream to block it out, and even that isn't enough.

If only I had known. IF ONLY I HAD KNOWN. IF ONLY I HAD KNOWN. IF ONLY I HAD KNOWN.

Suddenly, a hand grips my lapel and rips me from the pain and back to solid ground. I hardly have time to register my surroundings before Caelynn screams, pushing my body down, and hers in front of mine as a flaming arrow pierces her chest.

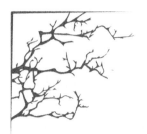

Rev

*H*oly shit, is my only thought. I leap to my feet, steadying Caelynn as blood spurts from the wound in the middle of her torso. It didn't hit her heart.

Though maybe I shouldn't be relieved by that.

We both made it through the gates. Drake and Brielle are right behind us. Where is Ty? I only have an instant to search for him, but the dwarf has disappeared. Hopefully he fled before they came. Either way, that's now my only choice.

With Caelynn injured, and Ty gone, I'm not sure I can defeat those two alone. We're dead if we don't use the advantage of having a massive and powerfully-magical obstacle between us.

I blast a circle of light around us, blinding our foes just long enough to grab Caelynn by the waist and fly off the path and into the brush. I carry her, ignoring her whimpering, and rush through the thorn bushes into a forest I don't know the first thing about.

This way, a whisper tells me.

Dammit, I've had enough magical whispering for one day! But I know these whispers are friendly sprites—well, at least friendly to Caelynn—and not the same as the whispering that nearly undid me in the magic of the Black Gates.

This way, this way, this way.

I follow the tiny whispers through the brush until I find a small pathway and follow it south, the general direction Caelynn said the caves were. In less than five hundred feet, I see a stone drop off.

This way, this way.

I follow them more slowly, hopping off the overhang to a ledge, until I see an opening I assume is a cave. Perfect.

The moment we're shaded by stone, I place Caelynn down. Surprisingly, she's able to hold her own weight, but she presses her shoulders to the cave wall behind her, arching her back, face in a grimace of pain. "*Shit.*"

I press my hand to the wound just below her breast. She groans, and I have to stop my mind from spinning, desire mingling with the panic.

Everything in my body screams at me to save her. Help her. The sprites whisper in my ears, begging me to do the same.

My magic swirls in my chest, fingers tingling with the magic needed to heal her. It's a strange thing to heal someone else. There's an intimacy to forming your own magic beneath their skin and continuing to wield it. To use it to stitch their flesh back together.

I close my eyes as I work, the power flowing easily, but the touch of her soft skin beneath my fingers, the feel of her chest rising and falling in rapid succession, is a distraction.

I rip my hand from her body as it begins to burn, as my head grows light. I've used too much magic healing my enemy. Everything about this is messed up. I press my hand up against the stone wall to brace myself from the exhaustion.

Caelynn saved my life.

I saved hers.

Aren't we supposed to be doing the opposite?

She slips to the ground slowly, head tilted back to watch me as my fingers fumble in my bag. I grip a vial, then use my teeth to pop the cork. "Drink this," I tell her.

She takes it in her shaking, blood-crusted hand and tosses it back in one big gulp while I fumble for another for myself. We're both drained and exhausted. Healing, for both parties, is extremely taxing. Particularly for the untrained.

Not for the first time, I send a silent curse to my father for not letting me train in healing magic.

I squat beside Caelynn and examine her injury. I think I did a decent job sealing the core of her injury, all vital organs are intact and functioning, but the wound isn't entirely closed.

"Let go," I tell her softly. She watches me with her dark eyes, eyebrows pulled low. She pulls her fingers away without breaking eye contact.

I tug away some of the ripped and singed fabric, exposing soft skin below the wound that was ragged open just moments ago. It's now almost entirely closed, but still bright red and inflamed and covered in blood. My forefinger brushes some of the blood away, soft and slow.

Caelynn groans. I freeze at the sound.

"Please, stop," she says breathlessly. I pull my hand back quickly, suddenly realizing how close we are, our breaths mingling.

I swallow and stand, taking a step back. My heart beats so fast, and I get the feeling that's not going to stop any time soon.

"Thank you," she says with a weak voice.

I don't respond.

"You probably should have just left me to die."

I sit on a low stone, knees nearly touching my chest. "Maybe," I say honestly. Though, in that moment, the thought did not even cross my mind. I had to save her, that's all I knew. All I felt. "But you're a pretty valuable ally right now. I wouldn't have found the cave without your sprite friends."

Her eyebrows pull down, and she looks around as if she just noticed where we are. "Tyadin?"

I shrug. "I didn't see him once the arrow hit. I'm hoping he fled."

She nods absently.

"Are we in the right caves?" I ask.

"I assume so. There's only one cave system so far as I know, but there are many tunnels and a few entrances. I'm not particularly familiar with this one, but I doubt we're far from where we need to be."

I nod.

"Just do me a favor," she says, her voice low, her breath picking up speed. "Don't go down any paths alone. This place is..."

"Dangerous?" I grin because that's obvious—everything here is dangerous—but the expression on her face gives me pause.

"You have no idea."

The Caelynn I've known has been entirely indifferent, occasionally with a hint of sadness or anger or at best nostalgia. But I've yet to see even a hint of fear in her eyes.

Until now.

Caelynn

I don't know where we are, and that is a terrifying thought. The cold growing in my veins has me shivering, and I can't tell if it's from pain or fear. Maybe both. I don't want to be here. That's the clearest thought I can come up with right now.

I don't want to be here.

He is down here somewhere. That thought has panic swirling around my head so thick I can't think past it.

"Are you okay?" Rev asks.

"No," I say desperately. It's true. I'm not. My breath picks up speed, my vision going black.

"Is it pain? Blood loss?"

"No," I say again. It's all I can get out. I'm having a dammed panic attack. I stand suddenly, but my body is woozy, and I almost lose my balance. Rev's hand is at my back, steadying me, and I have to fight the urge to fall into his arms, to cling to him like he could heal all my wounds—not just the physical ones.

"What's wrong?' he asks more firmly.

"I have to get out of here." I take a step toward the cave exit, and he helps to guide me. I focus on stepping and breathing, my throat thick and barely able to push air through.

Finally, cool air and sunlight hits my face and breathing comes easier. My teeth are chattering.

"We should find another entrance, I don't..." I shake my head. "I don't like that one."

"You're afraid," Rev says, it's not a question but there is surprise there.

"We have to be careful...."

"Something bad happened to you here."

I grip his sleeve in a tight fist and wince. I can't tell him what happened. I can't tell anyone. My chest heaves up and down, not enough air. I can't get enough air.

"Okay, calm down," he orders, gripping my upper arms tightly. "We'll go wherever you want to go. I trust you."

I swallow and focus on my breathing, calming myself.

I trust you.

I know those words aren't true, but they still soothe the ache in my chest, so I hold on to them as tightly as I've held on to anything.

"This way," I tell him and turn, taking slow but firm steps down a steep pathway toward the valley below. I vaguely recognize this. There is a large willow tree at the bottom of the valley that I know well. I use that as an anchor to reference my whereabouts. It's been so long since I've been here, and even then they are not good memories—most of them at least. Finally, I find a slope that curls off to the right that I recognize. I walk faster. *This is right.*

"Do you think this is the right place?" Rev asks gently, not wanting to trigger another panic attack. "We only have a few hours until sundown."

I chuckle. "What do you think happens if no one completes the challenge in time?"

The only other fae in the trials are certainly behind us. If we're wrong, I highly suspect they will be too. We follow a path to a new cave, one I recognize. I still don't like entering this place, but at least I know which tunnels to avoid and which should take us to the Wall of Mysteries. Where I assume the riddles will be.

"Look." Rev points to a symbol on the side of the stone wall at the mouth of the cave. A flying bird in white paint. The symbol of the High Court.

"Guess that answers that question."

We follow the main path through the cavern. I shiver at every deep shadow implying a branch-off tunnel.

"Remember." My whisper echoes through the darkness as we duck below a stone overhang and press deeper into the cave system. "No matter what happens, do not go into one of the smaller tunnels. You'd be better off facing Drake and Brielle alone than facing what may lie beyond."

Rev follows slowly, not speaking at all. The only sound our slow footsteps pounding and echoing off the walls.

The cave ceiling is suddenly hundreds of feet high, glowing stalactites hanging over us. "You won't tell me what happened to you down here, will you?"

"Never," I say firmly. "Never as long as I live."

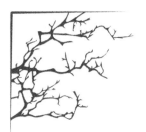

Rev

Caelynn is insanely frustrating. She has obvious trauma—although that shouldn't be surprising. Somehow, it still bothers me. I'm too empathetic for my own good. I hate seeing someone in pain.

Even though, logically, I know she deserves it. I know I'm supposed to want her pain. I'm supposed to revel in. Drink it up.

But I can't enjoy it.

Another part of me is insanely curious. What the hell is down here that has her so afraid? She showed no fear during the orb challenge. Dragons, goblins attacking while she was tied down, she rode a *Shadow-vyrn* for goodness sake. She's fearless.

But this place is causing her to shake in her boots. And that thought alone has my eyes darting over my shoulder constantly, has me jumping at every shadow, and wincing every time she jumps—which is a lot. As a member of the Luminescent Court this place is my antithesis—I should feel uncomfortable here.

And she should be in her element, but instead, she's petrified.

"Welcome," a voice booms.

Caelynn jerks so hard she nearly trips over a stone, and I find my hands at her hips steadying her. My fingers graze the skin of her stomach, where the cloth has ripped away, and I swallow. Her breathing evens.

"Champions, I am the Sphynx." I can't see any form before us, only stones and darkness. "Approach and answer your riddle."

Caelynn's breath is shaky, but she steps forward, out of my arms.

I follow behind her.

"Caelynn of the Shadow Court. You are first to find me."

She doesn't respond.

"Your riddle will appear only once, and only you may answer."

"Is there a time limit?" Caelynn asks, her voice surprisingly strong.

"Only the limit set by the trials—sun down." There are still several hours before then. "You must also answer before leaving the cave system. Otherwise, you may take as much time as you like."

"Okay, I am ready."

Against the massive flat wall in front of us, black writing appears among the stone.

Battle is my purpose, but I have no ability to fight

I am bitten again and again, enduring pain for the betterment of another

Ever diligent, I await the next attack

I may cover a wound, but it cannot heal until it sheds my protection

Caelynn reads the words aloud three times. An echoing reverberates behind me, and I jerk my head around. The sound disappears.

"Can you remember it? I'd like to get mine before someone else comes."

Caelynn nods, casting her eyes over the riddle one more time, then she steps back and allows me to approach the wall.

"Reveln of the Luminescent Court. You are the second to approach."

"Yes, please hurry, I know the rules."

"Very well." The Sphynx's voice purrs, and new words appear against the stone wall.

Every living soul searches for me
Every living soul fears me in the hands of another
Darkness hides, but I reveal
I strike without warning, and no shield can stop me
I will rip apart hearts and souls, or repair incurable wounds

I read the words slowly, carefully. At first it sounds like a weapon, which would also fit Caelynn's riddle—whose answer I suspect is "shield" or perhaps "armor."

It's fitting for her—she shields her true self so thoroughly, her wounds clearly not healing. But mine I am less certain of. What weapon reveals and cures wounds? Definitely something that can be used as a weapon in the wrong hands.

I take a step back from the wall, and the words fade away just in time to hear very clear footsteps resounding behind me. I jump out of the center of the open cavern and press Caelynn against the wall, hands at her lips.

She sucks in a breath, but I'm distracted by the swirling dark smoke at our feet. I hear only silence, but Caelynn nods as if she got some kind of message. She shifts to the right, closer to the flat wall of riddles—bad idea. But I follow anyway, trusting.

"Do you think they're here?" Brielle's whisper echoes through the cavern as if she were only feet from us, and I wince, reminding myself not to make any noise because it carries in this place.

"I don't know, don't care. I want to get the challenge finished so we can focus on the hunt once it's done."

Caelynn's back is pressed to the wall, shifting little by little, and I follow, palms burning against her hips. *Don't think about that now. Don't think about that now.*

I don't see the crevice until Caelynn steps back into a nook between two slabs of stone. The gap is maybe two feet in width but angled away from the riddle wall.

The shadow sprites chatter, and I wince. Can Brielle and Drake hear it? Shadows twist around my feet and up over my shoulder, pushing. I hadn't actually felt their strength before, more like the wisp of the wind, but they have a surprising force when they shove at my back, pushing me into the tight crevice with Caelynn. She grabs my shoulders, steadying as I slide in to face her, my back pressed tightly against the uneven stone, our chests just barely touching.

"Hi," she whispers.

I shiver at the sound of her voice, her breath tingling over my neck. I close my eyes, my chest lifting and falling dramatically. I tilt my head toward the cavern, and she somehow reads my thoughts.

"The sprites can cover noise too."

"Oh," I whisper, still too paranoid to speak any louder. Caelynn swirls her finger over the black mist by her ear, and it clears, a dim light exposed and with it, dull sound.

"Welcome, Drake of the Whirling Court. You are the third to approach me." The Sphynx's voice carries through the cavern.

Well, thanks for that, I think to the Sphynx. Now, Drake and Brielle know we've been here and are very likely nearby. I shake my head.

"We may have to stay here overnight," Caelynn says.

"Here?" I say, a smile on my lips, eyes dipping to our nearly touching bodies.

She rolls her eyes. "The caves. If they're looking for us, we can just wait it out in a nook somewhere and let the sprites aid us."

"Somewhere preferably more spacious."

A blush creeps across her cheeks, and suddenly, I feel every place our bodies touch with sharp clarity. I gaze down at her. She takes her bottom lip between her teeth, her head falls back against the wall, eyes closed, her body tense beneath mine.

She wants me.

That thought has my brain spinning. My vision blurring. My body shifting.

She gasps and squirms, but with so little space, it only pushes her hips harder against me.

"Shit," she says, gripping my forearms tightly in her fists.

Hands on either side of her head I weigh my options quickly. I could take her now—why not? She wants it. I want it. No one would ever know. No one would really care, not once she's dead. *Okay, that's a bit of a morbid thought.*

My point is, it's not like it means anything. What's wrong with indulging myself just once?

Besides, I really like the tortured expression on her face. She knows she shouldn't want me, but she does. She knows it'll only end badly, but she can't help it.

I lick my lips, playing it out in my head, unconsciously pressing my body closer to hers. Damn she feels good. Our enemies are feet away. How long will the sprites stay here to shield us? It would be some seriously kinky—and danger-ous—shit if we were to act on this attraction now. I shake my head.

Dammit, I want it. I want her. So badly it's hard to think.

But I've already admitted to myself that the more time I spend with her, the harder it will be to do what I must. I've promised up and down that I'd end her.

If I kiss her, could I still hate her? Could I still stab her through the heart?

If I give in to this feeling, what's to say I won't give in to that stupid urge to protect her? My stomach aches, a heavy feeling that spreads all the way to my chest.

"You killed my brother," I remind us both, decision made. Illusion shattered. It's the wet blanket I need to pull my body out of this spiral of need.

Her eyes are soft as she meets mine. Her sadness exposed in a way I've never seen. "Yes," she whispers.

"Are you even sorry?" I ask, mostly because the look in her eyes tells me she is. Which surprises me.

She opens her mouth to speak but then closes it and re-considers.

"Yes." She pauses, and I wait, watching the pain so obvious on her face. "If you think you hate me more than I hate myself, you're wrong."

I suck in a small breath. "Why do you hide that?" Why show the world this mask of indifference?

"Because it wouldn't change anything."

I swallow. *She killed my brother.* In cold blood. Even if he did those things to her that I saw in the last trial—he was still my *brother.*

"Why?" The harsh word slips from my lips before I can take it back. I don't know if I really want to know. I don't know if I want to have the image of my brother—strong and brave and good—shattered. And the image of Cae-lynn—cruel and calculating and manipulative—changed.

She shakes her head. "You don't want to know the answer to that question."

I sigh, knowing she's right. And I'm thankful she's wise enough to realize it too.

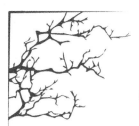

Caelynn

Holy shit, my body is on fire. I can hardly manage to keep my muscles in place, to stop my hands from roving over his sculpted body. I can feel him pressed against me. Only a few layers of clothing stand between us.

No, there are worlds between Rev and me. Physically, sure, we could remove the clothes and give our bodies what they're thirsting for, but what good would that do? I'd only want more. I'd only be giving myself false hope.

Still, the tension in his body tells me he's moments from snapping. And one move from him would have me unraveling. It's a bad idea, terrible, horrible. But if he gave me a yes, I know I couldn't stop myself.

Then he reminds us both of why we can never be together. He reminds me what I gave up all those years ago. My stomach sinks, veins going cold. Heart growing hard.

They're gone, a whisper tells me.

I take in a long breath, pulling my armor over my heart. "We can go now." Even in a whisper, my voice still breaks. He backs out first, eyes lingering on me, but I refuse to meet his.

"You're doing it now," he tells me.

My eyebrows pull down. "Doing what?"

He looks over his shoulder at the wall behind him. The wall where our riddles were written. He pulls in a long breath and looks at me meaningfully. The riddle? My riddle?

I'm doing it now. What am I doing right now? Hiding? Pretending. My riddle was a noun not a verb, I'm confident about that. So how am I *doing* it?

I think about my riddle, running the words through my mind.

Battle is my purpose, but I have no ability to fight

I am bitten again and again, enduring pain for the betterment of another

Ever diligent, I await the next attack

I may cover a wound, but it cannot heal until it sheds my protection

It cannot heal, until it sheds my protection. I close my eyes at that truth. The answer is obvious now, but I'm not sure I'm ready to expose myself to all the pain that comes with shedding my armor.

"Sphynx, my answer is Armor," I say aloud.

"Complete," the Sphynx announces. I release a breath.

Rev shrugs. "Now, I just need to figure out mine."

I smile. I know his. It's even more obvious than mine, but I wonder how much the Sphynx will allow us to help each other?

"You remember what you wished for at the Ruby Well?"

His eyebrows raise, considering for a moment. "I'm sensing a theme." His smile is more bitter than pleased, and I wonder what's happening in his mind right now.

"If only I'd known," he says quietly.

I purse my lips, *what does that mean*?

"Sphynx, my answer is Truth," he announces.

"Complete," the Sphynx responds.

Now that our task is complete, we can leave the caves while Drake and Brielle are still here pondering theirs. Of course, it's possible they completed them immediately—we were too distracted to pay attention.

Either way, the added protection of the shadow sprites is an advantage I'm not eager to give up on, so we decide to find a place to camp closer to the cave's exit and get some much-needed sleep for the both of us.

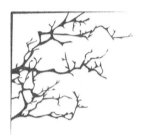

Rev

CC *Reveln."* An alluring voice rouses me from a deep sleep.

Darkness surrounds my body and soul, both. "Come here," he calls. The voice is familiar but distant.

"If you want to know the truth..." the voice rumbles, becoming clearer. "If you want to know how I died... if you want to know *why*..."

My eye fling wide, suddenly realizing why it sounds familiar.

"Reahgan?" I whisper.

"Yeeeessss."

My brain can't wrap around what's happening. Panic fills my limbs. Panic and calm, somehow at the same time. My body moves without active thought, almost without permission. But I want this, I remember. I need to know the truth.

My feet shuffle over uneven stone, moving through the darkness like they know the way even when my eyes can't focus on a thing in front of me. I wander down a thread of the caves I'm unfamiliar with, a tunnel small enough I must duck to crawl into, and the shifting of unease settles in my stomach—I'm not supposed to go here.

"Rev?" a sweet voice calls, but I barely register it.

All I know is that Reahgan is calling me, and I have to meet him. In the depths of these caves, my brother is waiting for me...

I stop suddenly as a firm hand grips my forearm. "No," she tells me, fear and determination mixing in her tone. I blink. Pausing.

"You can't take him," Caelynn says to the darkness swirling around us, her voice trembling. "I won't let you."

A voice rumbles in laughter, deep within dark cave opening before us.

"Do you want to know why Caelynn is so strong?" the voice calls, now changing into something much more sinister. I blink and shake my head. *That isn't Reahgan.*

My heart pounds in my chest as my mind clears to realize what's happening. I was under a spell. I take a step back, and Caelynn pulls me farther from the tunnel. Whatever it was, whatever dark creature is waiting down there, was baiting me. Using my own grief against me.

"She has *my* power," it calls, still laughing, but anger laces its unnatural tone. "She bargained for it. Ask her. Ask her what it cost."

I DROP MY BUTT TO THE floor beside our camp, body drained. "That's how you got this power of yours?" My throat is dry, my voice hoarse. "This creature—whatever it is. You..." I press my fist to my eyes, rubbing. "How?"

I know the creature was trying to trick me. I was his prey. But his words somehow cling to my mind and I can't let them go.

He was telling the truth. I know it. Deep down, I believe it to be true.

If only I had known. If only I had known.

My own words. A desperate plea the Black Gate so graciously illustrated. In my death, a violent, guilt-ridden death, I repeated over and over again—*if only I'd known.*

The Ruby Well tried to tell me.

The Sphynx's riddle tried to tell me.

The Black Gate tried to tell me.

I am missing something big—something I need to know, or it will end me. And as I look into Caelynn's dim eyes, once glowing bright with power no one expected her to have, I know she is the one that holds it.

"Tell me," I growl.

"No."

"Caelynn, I swear to you." I stand, hands in fists, ready to attack, ready to do whatever I can to get this information from her because everything I know, everything in me is telling me my life depends on it.

She sucks in a desperate breath, her mouth wide and eyes open in shock. I blink, confused at her reaction. What did I...

"Oh." My anger pops like a damned balloon.

I said her name.

Call me by my name before you kill me.

A wave of regret washes over me, all intensity dissolving in one instant. I drop my bottom back on the stone, unable and unwilling to hold up my own weight any longer. She doesn't speak or move. For so long, I swear the shadow sprites must be blocking our own sounds from us.

I pull in a breath. This is still important. I can't let her distract me from this.

"You bargained with that creature down there for the power you hold." That's the only truth I have so far. I could assume more, but I'd rather not. I need to know the full truth.

"Rev," she says. "I promise, you do not want to know this."

I clench my jaw. "Do you know what the Black Gate showed me?"

"You're not supposed to..."

"I don't care," I tell her. "My death must have been painful and chaotic. I don't really care about that. There were words spoken to me. My own thoughts at my death, that's what you said, right?"

She sits on her own stone, facing me, and nods slowly.

"If only I'd known." I pause, looking down at my hands. "Those were the words. That's what I thought during my death. *If only I had known.* But it wasn't just a phrase or even a quick chanting. It was repetitive and intense and... desperate. It was screaming at me. Those words. Crying them over and over. The Black Gate made it very clear that this message was important. Desperately so. So, you can tell me all you want that I don't want to know this truth, but everything within this competition has told me otherwise. The Ruby Well somehow stuck it in my head to wish for truth. The Black Gate showed me how I'd regret not knowing something in my death. Even the answer to the riddle was truth. And I am certain, more than anything else, that the truth I need most comes from you. You hold it. I know you do."

I let out a breath and suck in another.

She stares at me, unblinking. "I hold a lot of truths," she whispers. "Truths no one else in the world should know."

"Caelynn," I say.

She closes her eyes, and I wince at the serene expression that fills her face. *She likes it when I say her name.*

And there is that dizzy feeling again. No. No, there is nothing between us. We are allies until it's time to be enemies again. I will not allow anything more.

"Please," I say.

She shakes her head as a tear escapes her right eye. "What do you want to know?"

I pull in a breath, knowing I'm going to hate the answer to this question. Knowing it's going to make me hate her more than I already do—and maybe that's a good thing. Certainly, it shouldn't hurt the way it does. "What was the bargain? What was the cost of the power he gave you?"

No one in the Shadow Court has been as powerful as she is in centuries. So why now? Why her? Because she bargained for it from an evil creature. It makes sense, but now I have to know the cost.

She considers, eyes cast to the floor, at the short distance between our feet. "Banishment," she says.

I wince. "You murdered my brother," I infer for her, since she clearly doesn't want to say it aloud. "You bargained with an ancient being, and the terms were to kill Reahgan to obtain this power."

My voice breaks as I finish the sentence. I want to kill her more than I have at any single point before in my life, which is saying something. I want to strangle her, this woman who somehow thinks my brother's life was expendable. That somehow having a bit more magic was worth becoming a murderer and destroying my life in the process.

Selfish. Manipulative. Horrendous. Devious. Evil. Selfish. Awful.

Dead.

My whole body is shaking so intensely I barely hear her as she whispers, "not exactly." She stands suddenly and takes several steps away. Her rapid breathing is the only sound that fills our small camp site.

"Tell me," I demand. Before I explode. Before I react without all the information.

If only I had known.

"It's not like I went to him looking for power. He found me. He... trapped me. I was bargaining for my own life, but he likes to think himself generous, so he threw in the power as a boon. And it wasn't... well, his terms were unclear. I used that to my advantage."

"What does that mean?"

"He didn't tell me to kill Reahgan. He didn't even intend for me to kill Reahgan. He told me to kill the youngest son of Luminescent Court King."

I blink. What? "But that would've meant... me."

"Yes," she whispers.

"So, you broke the bargain? And all you got was banishment?"

"No. Banishment was my punishment for outwitting him. He'd underestimated me. If I'd done what he'd asked, no one would have ever known I was the one that killed you, he made that clear. Since I killed the 'wrong' heir but still technically completed the bargain, he made sure I was caught and suffered the consequences. He probably expected me to be put to death. It was a blessing I was still years from adulthood, even months from my first rite of passage. He had to give me the power he offered because it was part of our bargain."

"But how? How did you outwit him? And why? Why was killing Reahgan better than killing me?"

I stare at the silver hair flowing down her back. She doesn't respond, not for a long while. "I don't know if he knew it when he proposed our terms, if that was the reason he chose me as his assassin—because it would be the worst kind of torment to force me to kill my own..."

She doesn't finish the phrase, but I still leap to my feet as if she did. I should ask, to be sure what she was about to say. But I can't make my mouth form the words.

No.

I shake my head. I don't want to know that. I... can't handle facing it. I'm supposed to be seeking truth, but this one... this one might break me. So, I avoid it.

"I stalled once I found out. I learned that Reahgan was an asshole..." She shakes her head stopping herself. "And then, by another bitter blessing, I learned the one thing that could get me out of the fate he'd forced me into. Not that the alternative was all that much better—killing your brother, I knew, was still an unforgivable crime. But still, at my worst moments, I've been proud that I won. Technically. I lost, in so many ways. But I beat him."

"What was it? What was the loop hole?"

"It's probably the same reason your father wants you killed now. He doesn't want you to be his heir, because you're not actually his son."

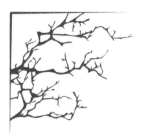

Rev

My mouth falls open.

I blink. Well, that's not what I had expected.

"That was your loophole," I say, repeating the truth back to her. "He asked you to kill the youngest son. But I am not one, so the youngest son was actually Reahgan."

She sits back on the stone. "I know you hate me, and I don't blame you."

My stomach sinks. *Shit*. How did this conversation end up with me hating her *less*? I don't know what I think or feel.

I don't even know who I am right now.

"Who is my father then?"

She shrugs. "Someone high up in the Luminescent Court. I don't know exactly."

I'm afraid to ask the next question, but I know I can't avoid it. "Why do you think... that *thing* wanted me dead?"

"He said something about your fate, but he never said exactly. That was always part of what I hated. Those questions have haunted me for years. Why? If I knew what the reason was, what it achieved, maybe I'd have felt better. Maybe I'd have less guilt. But then again, knowing this creature, he probably wants to ensure the end of the world. For all I know, he wants you dead because you're the one who will save our world from the scourge."

She bites her lips at that comment, and I narrow my eyes. "I think I've had enough truth for one day," I admit.

Caelynn lets out a barking bitter laugh. "I did warn you."

"Did you bring any alcohol with you? I could really use something to take the edge off tonight."

"Sorry," she says so softly, I almost wonder if she's talking about something else entirely. "Let's get some sleep. We still have another full day of this shit ahead of us."

I shake my head. Dammit, this challenge sucks.

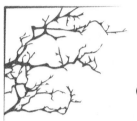

Caelynn

Rev and I don't speak the entire next day. I don't know what he thinks about everything I told him last night or the creature below the caves.

I don't know what else to say to him, so I don't. My heart's armor is back up, my face schooled into a mask of indifference. I simply focus on the task at hand. There was no clue today, but I suspect that was purposeful. We know this will be our last night of the challenge, and we still need to hit the northwest corner of the arena so that's where we go—northwest. Keeping an eye out for portals as we go.

Several hours later and no obvious portals to be found, I begin to wonder if we've missed something. We pass beyond the shadow lands and into Glistening Court. This lack of anything even hinting at the trials is disconcerting, but we keep moving without a mention of it.

Because we're too afraid to talk to each other.

We still haven't seen Tyadin. We spent the hours after our riddle hiding from Drake and Brielle deep in the caves, so it's possible he came in and completed his riddle without us knowing.

I hold out hope he's still alive, but there is no way to know.

I slow to a walk as I notice something strange. The Glistening Court is supposed to be full of lush green vegetation and twisting gorgeous fresh water streams with healing properties flowing throughout the land. But the streams here are dark, the vegetation is sparse. Did we pass through a portal without realizing it?

"We're going the right way," Rev says with a flat voice, still walking forward.

"How do you know?"

We crest a small hill, and he stops at the top. I join him and suck in a breath at the view.

"They want us to see the scourge."

I blink at the view before me. I've been to the Glistening Court many times before, as it's the closest court to my homeland. I know what this place is supposed to look like, and it is not this.

The miles before us are black and rotting.

I swallow and step forward into the broken lands. The plants beside the open pathway are dripping with black slime. Frozen in death and decay.

The smell bombards me, rotting flesh and acidic magic. I cover my nose with my hand. This is the first I've seen of the infamous plague. I knew what it was doing to our lands, I knew what it was.

But seeing it is something else entirely.

For miles, all I can see is death and decay.

"This was one of the first places it hit," Rev explains. "There will be nothing contagious here any longer, but we'll see the damage well enough."

Trees are bent and twisted, almost like they thrashed in pain before their death. Their leaves hang low with brown, putrid leaves.

The hair on my arms and neck stands up straight as we walk slowly through the damage. "What does it do to fae it affects?" I know most of the victims have been the elderly and children.

"It eats you alive," he says. "It starts with a fever, an ache in your limbs. And then wounds begin to form on your body, black spots where the disease eats away at the flesh."

I shiver.

"And this is happening to children?"

He nods. "It's taking a strange path. Instead of spreading out, it keeps its reach narrow—only a few miles wide. It moves south, then north, then east, then west, in an almost zigzag pattern, like it's searching for something. Or just teasing us. Hitting where we don't expect it, then moving on methodically."

"Like it's alive."

I bend down to examine a fern bush whose leaves have flopped onto the path, unable to keep itself up. If this was the first place it hit, it's been what? Two years? How are these plants still here?

"It's a curse," he says. "Something is controlling it, so in a way—it is."

"Who?"

"The High Court is said to know, but they haven't made it public knowledge, and my father—" He pauses, as if remembering the man he calls father is not. He swallows. "My father tells me nothing. The sorcerer responsible is likely inside the Schorchedlands."

"So, the winner of the trials will have to defeat him to stop it."

"Possibly. They say the 'cure' is there. It's possible we'll need to do both—undo the spell and kill the sorcerer so he doesn't begin a new curse."

"What's the end game? We're assuming the High Court knows what this is all about, but it would certainly be helpful to know."

"Maybe they'll tell the winner."

I raise my eyebrows. "Maybe." But if my intuition is telling me anything in this moment, it's that the High Court knows less than we think they do.

Rev

After traveling through several miles of the scourge wake, we notice blue billowing smoke in the distance. Finally, the clue we've been hoping for.

This smoke signal seems to be leading all of the champions into one place, so a battle may very well be inevitable.

"How's your magic?" I ask her.

"Fully restored."

"Your injury?"

"Healed."

I nod. That's good.

Drake and Brielle versus Caelynn and me will be a pretty even match, but I'm confident we could win it. It's strange to think Caelynn might have the most magic of all the competitors when just weeks ago I thought she had none.

She had us all so thoroughly fooled.

"You think we'll be facing Drake and Brielle again today?"

"Possibly. It's also possible they'll avoid us until the final trial." If they can ambush us out here or set a trap, they'll definitely choose that option, but otherwise, they're likely to choose to face us evenly during the hand-to-hand combat trial.

"We should be ready for anything today," Caelynn agrees. "I feel no need to pursue them, though."

"Agreed."

There is another option I could consider, though even just the thought sends an ache through my stomach. Guilt and pain a day ago I'd have slapped myself for.

Brielle turned on me because of her perception that I had some kind of relationship with Caelynn. If I were to kill Caelynn now while I have the chance and her guard is down, Brielle would likely turn against Drake and side with me again.

Then, it would be Drake against Brielle and me. I'd win these trials easily.

But guilt stirs in my stomach. Last night, things changed. I don't know what to think of Caelynn after her admission. She killed my brother to save my life. Could I return that favor with death?

It would be a fitting end.

If you think you hate me more than I hate myself, you're wrong.

We stop at the edge of a bright and glistening lake. In the middle is a small island with a blazing blue flame. Our clue.

"Do we swim?" Caelynn asks.

"Maybe. But I'd rather not if we don't have to." Who knows what's inside this lake. Bodies of water I can't see the bottom of give me the creeps. And though this water is a lovely blue, it's misty enough to veil way more than I'm comfortable with. We decide to spend some time walking along the lake bank, to get a lay of the land in hopes we'll find a way to cross without getting wet.

We walk casually, not talking, until we finally come across two small row boats.

Caelynn shrugs, and together, we pull one of the boats into the water and begin our long row out to the island. "They'll see us coming from far off, if they're already there."

I nod. "We're at full strength now. So long as we're wary, I don't see much to be concerned with."

I reach into my pocket as we sail slowly toward the smoke signal and finger the leather handle of the obsidian blade.

"Thinking of killing me?" Caelynn's voice is soft and low. Not fearful. Not accusing.

I freeze, stomach hurdling to my feet. "What?"

Her face is surprisingly blank as she continues to row. Her armor is impressively strong. "I wouldn't be mad, you know?"

I blink and then clench my jaw. I believe her. She wouldn't be surprised if I drove the dagger that killed my brother into her back. *It would be a fitting end.* "And that only makes it harder."

Call me by my name before you kill me.

She bites her lip but avoids eye contact, and I watch with more interest than I should. Then she shrugs. "I suppose that's your problem to work out. I made my choice years ago."

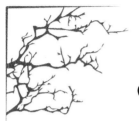

Caelynn

I don't allow myself to dwell on the conversation with Rev. I'm okay with dying. It isn't what I want, but I'd accept it. And I wouldn't blame him, not for one second, if he finally followed through on his promise. Before this trial, he didn't know me. He didn't know why I'd hurt him the way I had. Now, he does, and somehow, that makes death easier. For me, at least.

The truth is out, and he can choose with his eyes wide open.

A black owl flies overhead, screeching. Shit. That's a warning if I ever heard one. "They're waiting for us," I tell Rev.

He eyes the bird squawking above us, and I know that truth is out too. He doesn't know what she is, but Raven has exposed that she's on my side. I suspect the same will be true for my other enemies, which means Raven is in danger now too.

My heart picks up its pace.

I turn to face Rev, my eyes wide, fear obvious on my face. "I will accept death without fear or anger. I've been ready to accept that for a long time. But knowing what you do about me now, I hope I can ask one thing of you."

His eyebrows pull down.

"Take care of the bird, okay? Keep her away from *them*. Take her away from the fae realm and set her free. If you feel like you owe me anything, that would make us even, no matter the cause of my death."

His lips parts, but he doesn't speak. Finally, he nods.

Raven wisely flies off, across the rippling water to the shore, and I let out a relieved breath. She's safe, for now. So long as she doesn't do anything else stupid.

Both Rev and I pull out our weapons, and I build my magic, ready for a fight.

The island is calm, but I know better. It's only about a hundred feet in width, fifty or so in depth. The only coverage is a few clusters of trees and lush, wild bushes. A soft breeze blows gently over our skin.

I step into the comfortingly clear water, boots sinking into the sand.

My heart thumps as we march slowly to shore and toward the fire blazing in the middle of the island. For the first time, I'm wondering if this is the real clue, or if it's a distraction wrought by Brielle.

"Trees," Rev whispers as we march over the beach.

I scan what I can see of the tree branches. Still nothing obvious, but he's right—it's the only place they could be hiding. I eye a boulder hidden beneath the sand a dozen feet from the blazing fire.

Without Kari, they can't create a rock coverage to hide again, and they couldn't get themselves under this one without her, so the trees make the most sense.

Unless…

I swallow, hoping I'm wrong. Not only because it would tip the scale against us, but because I don't know if my heart can take more betrayal. It's stupid because that's what this game is all about. I guess I just didn't realize how desperate I was for friends.

"Rev," I whisper. He stops, grip tight on his blade.

I sniff the air, the gentle breeze smells of smoke, moss, and fresh water. There's the slightest tinge of metal in the air.

Dammit.

"Tyadin is here," I whisper, hoping our ambush won't hear but worth the risk if they do.

Rev's muscles go tight, his chest suddenly heaving. "Should we retreat?"

"Then what?" I say. "We need to complete the task, and they could wait here all day. We have to risk it."

He nods, eyes focusing into a determined stare.

A plan forms in my mind quickly, and my lips curve into a smile. It'll be fun at the very least. I march forward. "I can't believe how terrible of a ruler Drake would make," I say louder than before. "He couldn't even kill his enemy right in front of him with *five* allies."

Rev's eyes grow wide. "He'll blame you for betraying him," he says.

"Even once I turned, it was two against four. And he still lost." I laugh. "Will the people of his own court even want him as ruler when this is finished? He's pathetic."

"And Brielle?" Rev says, his voice growing confidence.

I keep my eyes on the boulder. Ready to be a class-A troll. If I've learned anything from the internet, it's this. "Too weak. She's only made it this far because of who she's screwed."

I almost laugh as the temperature around us rises several degrees. The bait is already working. She'll lose it in only moments.

"You're a way better kisser," Rev says with a wink.

I don't account for the rush those words send through me, but luckily our enemy's reaction is way worse.

Flames roar toward us from behind the boulder still more than twenty feet away. Two male screams reverberate over the roar of the flames, as sand and rock fly. Drake and Tyadin scramble to get away from their hiding place, where they'd burn alive with Brielle's temper tantrum. They each leap from their cover and Rev and I leap behind the closest tree. The flames recede quickly, and we each lob daggers at Brielle.

She ducks behind the boulder, missing our blades, but the magically-created barrier crumbles at her feet leaving her in the open with nowhere to hide. "Stupid dwarf!" she hollers, leaping away. "Can't you do anything?"

But Tyadin stands, shoulders back, a massive blade in his hand, the skin over his forearm is red and blistering from Brielle's fiery outburst. "Would you like to see what I can do?" he asks with a smile, just before swinging the blade in her direction.

She squeals and rolls, just missing decapitation.

Yes! Tyadin is on our side after all.

"Dammit, dwarf!" Drake yells. "Can't stay loyal for even a day?"

"You think I joined you for any reason other than survival? Stupid *fae*."

My heart leaps. If we could eliminate Brielle and Drake now, we could go into the final trials with only the three of us.

A roar of flame flies at Tyadin's head at the same time as Drake's sword. Tyadin dodges both attacks, diving away with a holler.

Tyadin is on the ground as we reach him. I just barely block Drake's killing swing, inches from Tyadin's nose. He's not fast enough for Drake.

Rev takes on Brielle, who's snarling, her blade covered in blue flame. She's faster than I'd have expected. Her rage fuels her power, making her a fair match for Rev.

Drake however, can't take me. He disarms me quickly, but I don't let that deter me in the slightest. He thinks he has the upper hand, him with a sharp sword and me with nothing. But I smile as I dodge his sword, once, twice, a third time. He screams in rage. "Die you stupid bitch!" But that comment only makes me laugh.

I keep dodging him and maneuver him away from the others. The moment he's clear, I send a blast of raging power at him. His eyes are wide in terror as his body is thrown from the island, his stupid hair flowing beautifully until he splashes into the sparkling water. At least he'd be proud of how he looked as he lost.

I turn toward Brielle and Rev. He blocks her flaming blade but doesn't take the opportunity to swing. "Stop holding back," I yell at him.

"Kill her if you have to!" Tyadin shouts.

I leap toward their fight. If he won't kill her, I will.

Magic rips from my body, and I notice Rev doing the same. Our black and white power ripples, swirling together and flying toward Brielle. She cries out as the combined magic rips into her, smashing her into the sandy beach. She stirs in only moments but we don't move.

Panting, Rev and I stop and watch as she clamors for the water, toward her ally. Not one of us moves as she swims out into the open water.

"We left them alive," I say, knowing it was stupid.

"We made a choice," Rev says.

"Did we?" I watch him as he watches Brielle and Drake swim away. We'll have to fight them again in the next trial. Was mercy worth it now? Or does he mean that he has decided my fate?

"Are you okay?" Rev asks as he approaches our dwarfish friend, still sprawled out in the sand. Rev reaches out an arm to help him up. "What happened?"

Tyadin accepts Rev's helping hand and pulls himself up to his feet. "Once I was separated from you two, they made me an offer." He wipes the white sand from his clothes. "They wanted numbers back on their side and I knew I was dead if I didn't accept. They bicker like an old married couple. It was so annoying. If I hadn't already planned to betray them the first chance I got, that would have pushed me over the edge."

Rev chuckles.

Tyadin nods. "They're idiots if they thought I'd be loyal to them."

"So, what's this task?" I ask.

He nods toward the fire. "Stare into it for a minute. It'll show you something horrific, but you can't look away. It gives you instructions for the final day of the challenge, but it's nothing we didn't already expect."

I nod and look into the blazing fire. For several seconds, all I see are dancing red flames. Then they shift and change. Shadows emerge, growing sharper until the image is as clear as a TV screen. Brielle is standing before me, a blackbird in her hands. My stomach drops, ice fills my limbs. "No," I whisper. *It's not real, it's not real. It's not real*, I chant as Brielle twists Raven's head from her body.

I cover my mouth with my hand but keep watching. Finally, the image shifts to the Flicker Court and focuses on the thorn gates. "There are no more clues. Find your way back," the flames hiss, and then the images fade. I rip my gaze from the illusion and fall to my knees, stomach clenching wildly.

She's okay, I tell myself.

I'll make sure she's okay.

"What did you see?" Rev asks.

I open my mouth but glance at Tyadin. How much can I really trust either of them? "Brielle killing a friend of mine. Someone you don't know."

"It wasn't real," Tyadin says.

"I know," I whisper. But it doesn't stop me from worrying.

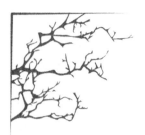

Rev

We spend our last night of the challenge on the flame island. After our fight with Drake and Brielle, we know they won't be back tonight, so it's as safe a place as we could find.

Brielle's reaction has gotten under my skin. The words I used to get to her.

I know it was all part of the plan—they were going to try to kill us. We did what we had to do to survive. But still, the look on her face, the explosion of fire. And the feeling of warmth that filled my chest at the thought of kissing Caelynn.

Have I mentioned how messed up these trials have been?

And that's not considering the task image meant to torture us even more.

My vision didn't affect me the way Caelynn's had, but even so, the image of black magic wrapping itself around my throat until my skin turns blue keeps playing in my mind.

I was watching my own death. A death very likely caused by someone from the Shadow Court. Caelynn's court.

No one said the images from the fire would be real. They're just something we fear will happen. Something that will unnerve us.

And this certainly unnerved me.

I don't sleep much this last night of the most challenging trial to date. Between nightmares and my wandering mind, I find myself barely able to close my eyes at all. Though part of me is relieved that this challenge is almost over, part of me is afraid to return home.

How can I face my father again?

My mother?

Should I confront them about the truth I uncovered?

How do I face the public, who will undoubtedly know I aligned with Caelynn, my brother's murderer?

This, here on the sand beside a blazing fire and two people I'd have never expected to call friends even just days ago, is so much simpler.

Caelynn still terrifies me. Confuses me. Allures me.

But this is preferable to what I'll face back in the Flicker Court.

The three of us plan our journey for tomorrow before we head to bed. We'll make our way back through the scourge wake, into the shadow lands, through the portal in the Whisperwood, and then through the second portal into the flicker lands. Through the desert and back to the thorn gates.

The distance is long, but the way should be easy enough.

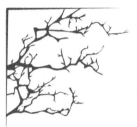

Caelynn

I spend much of the night tossing and turning in the soft sand—a much better bed than we've had in days. I must have fallen into a tentative sleep at one point because I rouse at the sound of someone walking through the sand.

"There's someone here to see you," Tyadin whispers through the darkness. I sit up immediately, panic already filling my limbs.

Tyadin nods toward the tree line where the fluttering of wings and soft chatter of a bird chirping can be heard. I clench my jaw, angry with Raven for putting herself at risk again. Tyadin lies back onto the sand, Rev's eyes are open, but he doesn't stir.

I sigh and march toward the wild brush.

The moment I see her, I flick my hand breaking the illusion. I must have put more force into it than I intended because she stumbles, her back slamming into a tree. "Ow. What the hell, Cae?"

"What the hell, to you too," I say, crossing my arms. "I told you to stay away. You're going to get yourself killed."

Raven pouts. "I thought you'd be happy to see me. I haven't talked to you in days."

I take in a long breath.

"Unless... you just don't want me around?"

The image of Brielle snapping her neck sends a shiver down my spine. "Not if it means your death. The others saw you today." My voice is sharp, unrelenting. She winces.

"I was warning you..." Her voice is high-pitched.

"It was stupid. Rash. Rev knows now. He knows you mean something to me. And even though I think... I don't think he'll hurt you to get to me, I still don't like it. Any of it. If he knows, the others might too. I don't want you here involved in my messes."

She steps closer, biting her lip. "But I want to be involved in your messes," she says sweetly. "All of it. All of *you*."

I wince. I love that about her. I love that we're broken together.

"Y-you," she says, "You won't stop me from helping you. You can't push me away anymore." She grabs my upper arms tightly, eyes so full of adoration and fear. "I love you, Caelynn."

My stomach drops. Shit. I always knew she had strong feelings for me, and in some ways I feel the same. In others...

I shake my head. I don't know what to do. What to say. Do I tell her I don't have those same feelings? Is that even true? Does it even matter? The farther away from me she is, the safer she'll be. I press my hand to my stomach. Pain and fear and confusion swirling inside like a damn hurricane.

Raven's bottom lip trembles when I don't respond. "You don't feel the same, do you?"

My eyes widen. "I—I don't know—" I don't know how I feel. I don't know how I should feel. I don't know what's best for her.

"You want this life more than you want me," she says, dropping her hands to her sides. "That's why you wouldn't leave with me. And you have feelings for him, don't you?"

My mouth falls open.

"I see a lot as a bird, you know? I see the way you look at him. The way he looks at you."

"Raven," I whisper. "I'm not leaving you. I just don't want you hurt."

"Tell me the truth," she whispers, tears in her eyes.

"The truth?" I pull in a long breath and close my eyes. "I care about you. But I should've never brought you here."

Raven gasps.

It's true, though. I do love her in some ways. I need her. But I need her safe and protected more than anything else, and I'm terrified of what will happen next. I'm so scared of Brielle figuring out the truth and taking her from me.

The sound of her neck cracking, just one quick pop, rings through my mind. I can't get it out of my head. That's Raven's fate if she stays tied to me.

Maybe that means I should pull her closer, protect her. But all I've ever known how to do is push people away. I've only ever played the part of the villain.

So, that's the part I'll play now.

"Stay away from me, Raven."

I wave my magic over her, the glistening tears over her cheeks disappear as she takes her bird form and flies off into the sky, screeching out a cry of agony.

I don't stop hearing her cries for hours.

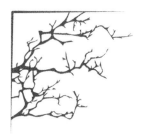

Rev

We wake with the sun and set out on our trek immediately. It's the last day of this challenge, and we're all eager to finish strong. And avoid contact with Drake and Brielle, if possible.

I never ask Caelynn about her conversation last night, but I do watch her closely. Probably closer than I should. Her shoulders are slumped, her eyes cast to the ground more often than not.

The bird doesn't appear to be anywhere nearby.

Soon, I notice Tyadin watching me as I watch her.

"What?" I spit.

He just shakes his head and continues rowing.

As soon as we're across the lake, we begin a sprint through the scourge and don't stop until we reach the shadow lands. By the time we reach the caves, my mind is clear of thoughts of Caelynn and her strange bird friend. My attention is on the competition. I need to stay focused.

We take a short break for water, but still no one talks. Then move through the forest, circling around the long way so we don't have to pass the Black Gates a second time. No one wants to relive their death more than once.

The sprites cling to us like old friends the moment we hit the Whisperwood. They urge us on and assure us no one is following. Caelynn stops as we reach the stone archway out of the Whisperwood. She closes her eyes, and tilts her head back as sprites cover her whole body.

Tyadin shakes his head, but we let her have her moment, her goodbye, and we walk through the portal together. It's only a few miles to the hidden bridge portal. This is the one we most hope Drake and Brielle remain unaware of, so we're careful no one is around, watching, as we pass through. Then, we sprint again. We're close now, only an hour or so at our current pace. The heat presses down on us as we pass into the open desert.

The thorn gates rise in the distance and my heart hammers in my chest. We're almost there. We almost made it. The gates grow larger and larger, and so do the sounds of the crowd cheering.

Just before the gates, a black orb comes into focus. Caelynn swears.

"What?" Ty says through heaving breaths.

We slow to a walk. Brielle and Drake are still nowhere to be seen. Maybe they were too injured to make it the long journey? Maybe they missed the last portal?

It doesn't really matter, not right now. Because right now, we've realized our trial is not finished. We have one more task to complete before we can pass the thorn gates. The stands of the arena are filled to the brim, and the crowd screams as they see us approaching.

"We have another task to complete," I say.

"And it's that stupid orb again." Caelynn wrinkles her nose.

"What do you think they're going to make us do this time?" Ty asks.

I shrug. "Only one way to find out."

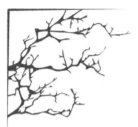

Caelynn

My skin is clammy, my stomach uneasy, as we pass into the arena. Today's journey was tiring but uneventful. Of course they'd want to screw with us one more time before it's over. One time while the crowd can watch our pain.

Wonderful.

We approach the orb slowly, ignoring the cheers and screams and boos—for me, obviously.

"Welcome champions!" a cheery pixie says, darting around the arena as her voice amplifies over the roaring crowd. "You've nearly completed your third trial. But you have one task left."

"Of course we do," I mumble. I am exhausted, both physically and emotionally. I am so ready to collapse and sleep for a week straight.

"Your final task will be to enter the orb for a second time. This time, your task will all be the same. You must prove your ability to sacrifice anything for the greater good. You must be willing to kill in order to save."

My lip curls. Kill? Who must we kill? I know the orb shows us very real illusions, somehow getting inside our minds and projecting something as we have seen it.

"The person you will face inside the orb may or may not be someone you currently know. It may be a complete stranger. Only you will be able to see their identity. Your last task of this trial is to kill your fated mate."

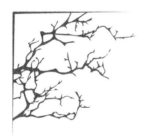

Rev

My whole world falls away as the pixie's words register. We are going to be shown who our mate is. And then we have to kill them.

My vision is blurry as panic fills me. No.

No, I don't want to know.

"You okay?" I hear Tyadin whispers to Caelynn, I glance at her pale face and my stomach sinks again.

"Nope," Caelynn says in a near squeak. My heart hammers in my chest, and I turn my eyes toward the black orb. *This is going to be the worst of anything within these trials,* that's the truth that settles over me.

I want it over with.

If only I had known.

I have to face it, I realize. That's what this entire challenge wanted to tell me. I must face the truths I've been missing. I've faced several, but there is one more left.

The worst one of all.

A truth I think I might already know, lies before me. A task that I've already completed, yet must do again. I suck in a long breath and step forward.

I hear Caelynn slide to the ground as she watches me walk forward, but I don't dare turn. I don't dare to chance I'd see the look in her eyes now.

I step through the rippling dark magic of the orb.

MY TEETH CHATTER AS I feel the magic swirl around me and clink into place, but I keep my eyes pressed closed.

Coward, I reprimand myself.

And yet, I still don't open them. *I have to face this. I have to do it.*

And I have to do it in front of everyone. My only saving grace is that they won't see what I see. They won't know who my mate is.

My stomach twists again, and I force my eyes open.

My eyelids flicker as I focus on her excruciatingly beautiful face. Her expression is sweet, adoring. She wears a soft blue, silk dress that hugs all of her curves. Her silver hair is pinned perfectly, eyes shining brightly.

God, she's beautiful.

This isn't the girl I know. She's lighter. Innocent. Happy.

She's what she would have been. What we could have been, if she had chosen differently. If she hadn't been tricked into a bargain long ago.

The Caelynn in front of me doesn't speak. I close my eyes and consider the truth before me. What does it even mean to be someone's mate? We treat the distinction as sacred. But we don't know much about what it means. Somehow, magic or fate has decided we are a good match, and the signs begin to show themselves.

Instincts draw us together, which explains my insane attraction to her and weird desires to protect her, even while wanting to kill her.

Most believe it means, together, you will have a powerful and important child. Brielle, for all she mourns, I know the child she'd have had with Reahgan is what she mourns most.

But what could have been. The future that was taken away.

I grip the dagger in my hand and walk toward the future I hadn't known was taken from me until this moment.

Caelynn

I stare at my hands in my lap, unable to watch Rev as he's faced with the truth. A truth I suspect he already knew.

"You never told me what happened to you after we were separated," Tyadin says, squatting next to me. Is he trying to distract me? Or is he seeking information? Does he suspect too?

Whatever, I'll take the distraction, whether that's his intention or not.

"I was shot by Brielle. Rev was able to get me away and lead us into the caves first. He healed me, and we answered the riddle before Drake and Brielle came. We hid in the caves and found a place to sleep there."

"I was with them for the riddle. You didn't see me at all?"

I shake my head. "We were... distracted. The shadow sprites hid our sound, and we didn't hear much ourselves."

He pauses, considering. "Rev's kiss comment?" His voice remains casual, like it's a joke. But I know it's not.

My eyes widen. I'd forgotten about that. "A lie. We were just baiting Brielle."

"I saw your reaction when he said it."

I bite my lip. Out of the corner of my eye I see Rev step forward, toward the black silhouette inside the orb. "There will never be anything between us."

Tyadin pulls in a long breath and turns to watch Rev as he shoves a blade through my heart.

"I'LL GO NEXT," I SAY. Knowing what Rev has done helps me pull my armor back on. I might lose my nerve if I don't take advantage of the numbness flowing through me now.

I stand.

"You're stronger than anyone gives you credit for, Cae," Tyadin says.

I blink.

"And I don't mean your magic."

"Thank you," I whisper. Then I approach the shimmering magic and step through.

I nearly sob when I see him there waiting for me. I could almost imagine it's really him. He was just here. I can pretend he waited for me to enter and this is the real Rev, looking at me like I'm the only thing in the world that matters to him.

My heart cracks a little more when a dagger appears in my hands.

A tear slips down my cheek. "I'm sorry," I tell him. Beautiful Rev with soft, forgiving eyes. It's the only time I'll ever see him look at me like this.

I wonder if I could stay here forever, inside this orb, where Rev loves me.

Where he doesn't know what I did. Where I am just me and he is just him, looking at me like that.

Raven suspects that I have feelings for Rev. What would she think if she knew we were fated to be together? I'd lose her for good then. Over something that will never come to fruition.

"I'm so sorry," I tell Rev again.

I step forward so that our chests are only inches apart. He looks down at me with those adoring eyes. "Want to know a secret?" I whisper to him. "If this were real, I wouldn't do it. Not now."

I pull in a shaky breath. "If I didn't know this was part of the trials, I'd sacrifice everything to save you. Even if it meant my own death."

Then, I shove the dagger into his chest.

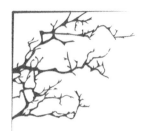

Rev

The crowd cheers as Caelynn exits the orb. I look down at my hands.

It's a strange feeling to know that inside that orb we just killed each other. Something no one else on the planet knows.

I don't look at her as she sits beside me, only inches between us. It's hard to breathe, to pull life through my body feels unnatural.

We did it. The challenge is over. Only one more trial to go. But I can't seem to allow relief or joy to enter my shredded soul. Not today. Not now.

I'm so distracted by my own misery I don't even notice that something is wrong until the crowd goes entirely quiet. Tyadin walks through the orb, a dagger still in his hand.

"Tyadin of the Crumbling Court," the pixie says, "is disqualified from the Trial of Thorns."

I stand as he approaches slowly. "Ty," I whisper. "What happened?"

He gives me a small smile. "I made a choice. I came here to make a point. To prove myself. I think I achieved that." He smiles sadly. "And I didn't want to be... I didn't..." He shakes his head.

"You didn't want to be like us," Caelynn whispers beside me, and I go rigid. Maybe we're not the only people in the world who know who we killed inside that orb.

Tyadin shrugs. "I'll be cheering you two on. If either of you win, our world will be in good hands."

Caelynn throws her arms around Ty's neck, and he chuckles softly, returning the embrace.

Tears well in my eyes as Cae releases him, and he holds out his hand to me. I take it in a firm shake. "Well, if nothing else, I know I've earned new allies during these stupid trials."

Ty smiles. "I'm glad to hear it."

I focus on something in the distance. "And a few new enemies," I say as two forms appear over the horizon beyond the desert. The crowd begins a new roar of excitement, and I take that moment to escape the arena without so much as a glance at Caelynn of the Shadow Court.

My mate and sworn enemy.

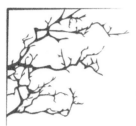

Caelynn

I wait next to the window for hours, but Raven never comes.

I bite my lip, watching the sunset and listening to the sounds of the elaborate celebration below. The Shadow Court is the liveliest of all, and I notice several of the other lesser courts joining them. But I do not.

There is not one part of me that wants to take part in a celebration. Not tonight. Not ever.

I allow myself a long bath, after which I cannot hold myself back from sleep any longer. I know Raven is mad at me. She told me something she never had before. Something that I know shouldn't have surprised me.

I love you.

They are words I haven't heard since I was a child. Words I couldn't give back to her. Not now, not like this. Not when every attachment I make puts her further at risk.

Not when my emotions about Reveln are so messed up.

But that's more reason for Raven to be mad. She doesn't know that Reveln is my mate, and I don't intend for her to find out. But she does know I have conflicting feelings for him. She knows there is tension between us that's not all bad.

All I know is that I wish she were here. I wish I hadn't told her I shouldn't have brought her here—even if it's true. Because now, more than ever, I need her comfort.

The only place she's safe is in my arms.

And now, she won't even come to me.

I pray Raven is okay and that she'll make it to me soon, but all too quickly my brain and body shut down, exhaustion winning out. For the next several hours, I am dead to the world.

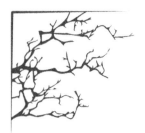

Rev

I spend the next few days sleeping, bathing, eating, and otherwise being a complete mute. My parents come to visit me when I don't join them for meals in the great hall, but I don't dare mutter more than a few words.

"What the hell happened out there?" my father asks.

"You don't know?" I accuse.

"What does that mean?" my mother says.

"Nothing. They betrayed me, that's all, and I took the only allies I could come up with."

"Well," my mother says with her head high. "Folk always look to attack their biggest threat. You should take it as a compliment."

"Even Brielle?" I ask.

My mother's eyes dart to the floor. "She won't be your bride. Her loss."

My eyebrows flick up. "I'm going to bed."

I don't care enough to check my father's expression as I turn away. Maybe he suspects I know what he did and why. Maybe he doesn't.

I don't really care.

The final trial is in a few days, and I am still not ready. Maybe I'll never be ready.

But I will win. That much I'm confident about.

Drake and Brielle aren't strong enough to beat me head-on, and I won't let *her* take anything else from me.

But then someone grabs me by the upper arm. My father's breath tickles my ear. "Tell me what happened?" he says low. I freeze. He doesn't want my mother to hear.

"I know the truth," I say simply.

He releases me with a subtle shove. "Good. You know you're not my heir. I'll find a way to disinherit you. I won't stop."

I curl my lip in a silent snarl but don't turn.

"Guess I'm just going to have to win the trials then. Won't I?" Then, I march up the steps toward my rooms.

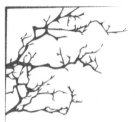

Caelynn

Rev and I still haven't spoken since the task five days ago. Today, just before the beginning of our final trial, is the first time we've been in a room together.

Our eyes meet, and I'm flooded with a mixture of electricity and pain. We haven't discussed our strategy for the final trial, but I assume we're on the same page. We'll continue to be allies until Brielle and Drake are eliminated.

We know they'll work together, so we'll be forced to as well if we want any chance to win.

I haven't slept much since that first night. Raven is still nowhere to be found.

I've searched the grounds up and down, even braving the scrutinizing public, who pry mercilessly, asking all kinds of awkward personal questions. I saw a blackbird in the tree below my window one night. Again, flying over the Black Lake in the distance. But it never gets close enough. We haven't spoken in six full days.

Is she avoiding me? Is she really that mad at me? Because of Rev? Because of what I said to her? I stare at the weapon's rack, even though I've already chosen my weapons—I'm too distracted by thoughts of Raven. I shouldn't have brought her here—I've always known that. But not for the reasons she thinks. Because I'm an idiot and spoke out of fear. Out of confusion and desperation.

Honestly, I've never made very good decisions when it comes to her, even knowing that she has feelings for me—I think I've known that for a long time, I've just avoided thinking about it. The truth is, I have feelings for her too. In a different kind of way...I think. She wants to be a couple. I want to just have her by my side for the rest of my life.

But I needed her in order to survive this. So, I brought her along to a world *she* may not survive, all to save my heart from disintegrating into nothing.

It's not what she deserves, though. She deserves a protector. Someone dedicated to her wellbeing, even when the choices are hard. Even when it means leaving her behind.

My stomach clenches at that thought.

"I'm sorry, Raven," I whisper out the window, knowing she's not near enough to hear. How do I focus on the next trial not knowing what's happened to her?

I'm a bundle of nerves, and I wonder if I can find a way to win today.

In a matter of hours, one of the four remaining fae will be the chosen savior of all of faery. In a matter of hours, I could be free of my punishment, but all I can think about is a black-haired human teenager whose heart is broken because of me.

FOR THE LAST TIME, I stand before the thorn gates, towering over us in all its brutal glory. We face the arena of cheering fae, not a boo in earshot. Not yet, at least.

The masses have come to respect me, if nothing else. They somehow learned all about how I saved Rev's life, and it has redeemed me to some. Others see it as more manipulation.

I don't really care what they think.

I stand on the end of our small line of fae warriors beside Rev. Drake and Brielle stand on his other side.

Together, enemy and ally, we step out through the thorn gates into the arena.

My newfound respect isn't enough to stop several pieces of garbage and rotten food from flying toward us. Nothing reaches within fifteen feet of our small line, but I know who it's intended for.

"Today is the day you get what you deserve," Brielle says through a tight-lipped smile.

"Looking forward to it," I tell her.

On the very bottom row of the stands, in the middle, is a section for the rejected champions. Those that survived the trials. There are two that I don't even remember, they lost during the first trial. Beside them sits Caspian, Kari, and Tyadin. That's it. We started with fifteen fae. Four are still in the trials, and out of the rest there are only five survivors.

And the trials are not yet finished.

"Good luck," a voice calls. "I'm rooting for you, Cae."

I jerk toward the row of former champions to find purple eyes pinned to me, a smile on her face.

"Me?"

"I'd be dead without you." Kari shrugs. "You didn't have to save me, but you did. And I'd love to see the look on his face when you're crowned savior." She nods towards Drake. "It was all one big political move for him. You? I'm sure you have your reasons, but there is real good in you. You're the one who should win this."

I swallow.

"Agreed," Tyadin says. "Although, you know I'd take Rev too." He shrugs.

I smile. An actual, honest smile curving my lips. No one is more surprised than me.

"Approach, champions!" a voice booms. I don't bother to see who the announcer is today. All four of us walk forward to the center of the arena until our toes touch a red line.

"Drake of the Whirling Court," the announcer shouts over the cheers.

"Brielle of the Flicker Court." Brielle waves and smiles as the crowd roars, much louder than Drake's. Home field advantage apparently.

"Reveln of the Luminescent Court." More shouts, blending into a cacophony of sound.

"Caelynn of the Shadow Court." I blink as the crowd roars even louder than Brielle's. There are definitely boos mixed in there, which probably adds to the overall noise level, but I am still shocked at the support.

"See?" Kari mouths from the sidelines. "I'm not the only one."

Did she have something to do with this? Spreading stories about me saving her life? Or is it the rebellion gaining more traction? All of the lesser courts using me as their symbolic hero? Proof they're still powerful enough to rival the ruling courts.

I don't know. I don't care.

I take what little fuel I can gather from the surprising support, and I pull my power in. Win, so I can find Raven and take her home. I'll make sure no one ever touches her.

"Today, your champion will be chosen by way of hand-to-hand combat."

The crowd roars.

"The rules will be as follows."

The edges of the arena floor begin to drop, leaving us on a rectangular island in the middle. I blink and focus on the shifting ground.

"Any weapon, any tactic, and any magic may be used against any opponent. Once a champion is deceased or falls from the platform, they are out of the competition. They will fight until only one contestant remains."

Stay on the platform. Stay alive. Got it.

"Champions, please choose a corner."

I wait, watching the others choose. Drake and Brielle march across the platform dramatically, choosing corners closest to each other. They turn to face Rev and me, still in the middle. Rev gives me one short nod before marching toward the corner opposite Drake. I take the last remaining place.

"Ready," the announcer hollers. "And FIGHT!"

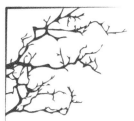

Caelynn

Brielle steps forward, eyes sharp, smile wicked.

I adjust my grip on my twin swords, fingers pressing into the worn leather, and then slip into a defensive stance. The crowd hushes, only swift whispers float around now while they wait for one of us to make the first move.

The arena is large, but the platform is only about thirty by fifty feet. Outside, there is a sharp drop into shadowed depths below. The drop should be only about twenty feet, not enough to injure us, but it's still unnerving to be able to fall into the darkness with one wrong move.

Rev is my closest opponent. Brielle and Drake on the other narrow end. Two against two.

Drake crosses his arms casually and flicks his eyebrows at Brielle. She walks forward with long, smooth steps. Confidence exudes from her.

"I've been searching up and down for a way to get my revenge," she tells me, "since the day you had the nerve to show up here."

My eyes narrow. "How's that going for you?"

"Quite well actually. Thank you for asking." Her eyes shine, her smile sickeningly sweet. "But it did take me a while. I wanted you dead—still do, if I'm totally honest." Her head tilts innocently, her auburn hair waving. "But now

I have a more appropriate revenge within my grasp. Literally." She giggles.

I blink, my eyes shifting to her hand that's within the bag strapped across her shoulder.

"You killed someone I loved—or would have loved." Her eyes turn to Rev. "Someone *he* loved."

I don't bother to turn. I don't care what Rev's reaction is. I care about what's inside her damn bag.

"So, it seems more appropriate that I kill someone you love."

She pulls her hand from the bag, and it takes a moment for my mind to register what she has within her closed fist.

A raven.

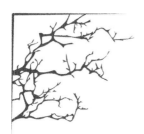

Rev

My eyes narrow at the bird in Brielle's hand. A bird.

I recall Caelynn's comment to take care of the bird if she died. I recall her strange conversation with no one at all on that island. Although wasn't that an owl? This is a raven. Either way, even despite Caelynn's words, I didn't realize how much it means to her until I see her reaction.

Caelynn is dead still. I've seen her panic. I've seen her break down. But I've never seen an expression like the one she wears now.

Caelynn, who's so good at masking every emotion, is terrified.

"A bird?" I say, crossing my arms, trying to deflect any attention from Caelynn. "You really think a bird is going to cause her enough pain to satisfy you?"

Brielle turns her attention to me. "I admit, I was surprised too. But I knew something was off when it continued to follow us. When it so clearly warned you of our planned ambush. And then, when I was able to glamour the creature, I knew."

My eyes narrow.

"This bird is certainly not *just* a bird."

I laugh. "That's not even the same bird. You're going to humiliate yourself when you kill a bird in the middle of the final trial and get no reaction whatsoever. Don't be cruel to the creature for no reason."

Her smile widens. "Perhaps you're right." She turns to Caelynn, who I'm honestly not sure is breathing. "But I'd rather find out for myself."

The bird squeaks and struggles in Brielle's grip as she reaches up with her other hand, gripping the small creature's head.

"Wait!" Caelynn screams. "I'll forfeit now. I'll let you kill me, I swear it."

Brielle's smile grows, her eyes shining red. "You see, Rev?" She pulls the bird closer to her chest, caressing its head gently. "She doesn't even love you. She loves this human. Pathetic, isn't it? And so, very, very perfect."

"I swear," Caelynn whispers again.

"I don't want you to die, Caelynn," Brielle says. Tears stream down Caelynn's cheeks, and my stomach clenches. "I want you to live with it, the way I had to live with it."

In one swift movement, Brielle snaps the bird's neck.

CAELYNN SCREAMS AND jerks forward, but it's too late. We all know it's too late.

Caelynn's scream is so palpable the crowd hushes, focusing on her agony. Feeling it with her. The voice coming from her throat fills the arena, echoing and unnatural. It's not her voice, I realize. *It's his.* It's the creature whose power she holds.

Before the blackbird's limp body even reaches the ground, a blast of power rages from Caelynn's body and slams into Brielle with utter silence.

The ground beneath us rumbles with the explosion, knocking Drake off his feet, but Brielle's body is frozen still, her arms flung open, her mouth wide in a silent scream.

The world stops in that moment.

As a dark power takes over Caelynn's body, pulling Brielle apart at the seams.

At her feet lies a slight female form with raven black hair sprawled everywhere. The girl doesn't move.

The smell of death fills the quiet arena.

Brielle remains in her frozen state of agony as Caelynn rushes to the limp child. She shakes her shoulders. "No!" she screams, and I shudder. She wails a pained sound that permeates the whole arena, and my heart aches for her.

I don't know who this girl is. Caelynn never mentioned her. But it is very clear that Brielle was right. Caelynn loves her.

Drake stands, pulling his sword from his sheath and stepping toward the mourning Caelynn. She's bent over her friend, distracted by her pain. One swing, and it would be over for her too. Brielle breaks free from her spell and scrambles away from the fight.

Oh, hell no.

Determination fills me as I sprint and leap between them to block Drake's blade just before it contacts my bleary-eyed ally.

"Fight, Cae!" I yell at her as I engage in combat with Drake.

She lifts her head, but her eyes are solid black.

I gasp, barely managing to block another blow from Drake's sword. He's ruthless. Unrelenting.

I roar in rage. For everything taken from me. Everything taken from her—the fae I hate and love at the same time. Shadows ripple from Caelynn's skin as she stands, pure rage on her inhuman expression. The darkness surrounds her, covering her so thoroughly she looks like a wraith.

Drake's eyes grow wide as another explosion of black power blasts into us, sending Drake flying one way, me the other.

I land on the far side of the arena.

This is that creature's power. Dark magic no fae should possess. Power that could bring this entire arena to the ground.

For a moment, I believe she's going to win. No one can defeat her like this.

But no, even Caelynn's magic has limits. And she's using so much of it, she'll dry out quickly. Anyone who weathers this storm will be able to defeat her easily.

I could use her emotions to my advantage. God knows that's what Drake is planning to do.

Brielle cowers before Caelynn, who's white hair ripples in dark power. Just feet from me, the nameless child remains wilted.

I crawl to her and brush the pitch-black hair from her face to find her big, beautiful eyes open—lifeless. A quiet sob escapes me for this young, innocent life ended. More useless pain.

I press my hands to her cheeks gently, and the flickering of life sparks against my palm. The girl's soul hasn't left her.

I could still stop this.

Behind me Caelynn rages, blasts of black magic thunder from her. Drake conjures a cyclone around him, blocking her magic from reaching him. His wind magic is weak, it can't protect him for long, but Cae's focus is still on Brielle, who tries everything she can to defend herself. Red flames blaze at Caelynn, but they're swallowed whole by darkness before they even get close. Caelynn doesn't so much as blink at her attempts.

Brielle's best move now would be leaping off the platform to save her skin. She can't win. Either way, Brielle has already lost. Which will leave a near magicless Caelynn, Drake, and me.

I run my fingers down the girl's cold, porcelain skin.

I could save her life. I could restore some of the light to this world. I could save Caelynn from more pain. But it would take up so much of my magic that I'd have next to nothing left to fight with.

Drake would win.

I can save her, a girl I don't know, by sacrificing any chance at being the savior. By sacrificing any chance of being the heir to the High Court and maybe even my own court. I lift my palm up, glowing with a white light.

Light footsteps sound next to me. "Do it," Drake says, his lip curling. "Do it, and I win." He smiles because he knows I've already made my choice.

I press my light to the girl's neck, summoning all of my magic into this one act and picturing Caelynn as I do it.

Pulling her soul back to the surface and healing her spine injury at the same time.

I watch as the light returns to her eyes, and she sucks in a breath.

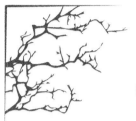

Caelynn

"Cae?" A sweet voice calls, but my focus is on my prey. The red-headed girl who will pay for what she's taken from me. She will die, slow and painful. I don't care what it costs. I don't care what happens to me after.

She's already covered in blood from the small slices I've taken. Her eyes are covered in black shadows, seeping deeper and deeper into her mind. Soon, she'll go insane. I'll watch with glee as my magic takes over her brain. The moment she lets go, I'll control her. I'll own her soul.

"Please!" she cries.

I laugh. "If I had begged for Raven's life, would you have had mercy?"

"I didn't know! Please!"

"Didn't know what?"

I slowly wrap my fingers around her throat, watching closely as her body twitches.

"She's a child," Brielle barely gets out, her body slack. She doesn't fight back.

"She's the same age I was when my life was taken. Or perhaps what you didn't know was simply that I was stronger than you?" I lift her into the air. Her throat gurgles pathetically. Legs swinging only slightly.

I smile, even though I know she can't see it.

Behind me the sound of blade striking blade alerts me that my other opponents are fighting again. It's time for me to end this, so I can finish them all.

"Cae!" the sweet voice calls again.

I turn, ever so slightly to see a flash of blue-black hair, and my stomach drops. My hand slackens, and Brielle falls, crumpling into a ball at my feet.

My vision clears, eyes focusing on the entire scene before me.

The arena with slack-jawed spectators.

Raven is on her knees in the very corner of the platform, eyes wide in fear. Only feet from her, Rev and Drake twist and turn, blades swinging.

"Raven?" I say, all my rage dissipating, and with it, the fuel for my magic. She scrambles to me, and I meet her halfway, bringing her into my arms. I sob into her hair as she clings tightly to me.

My hands pat her back and neck, uncertain she's even real.

"Get her out of here, Caelynn!" Rev screams to me.

I pull back. "Go," I tell Raven, still unsure exactly what happened. I consider going with her, just so I don't have to release my desperate grip, but no, I still have unfinished business here. "Hop off the edge," I instruct her. "It's not a long drop. I'll be with you soon."

She nods quickly, her teeth chattering. "He saved me," she mumbles. "He saved me."

I kiss her cheek and guide her to edge. She crouches and then hops with a slight squeal, I send a quick black of magic to cushion her fall.

The courts won't be happy I brought her here or disguised her as a bird, but they also won't hurt her. It'll be me who's punished.

The moment Raven is clear of the platform I turn toward the battle. Brielle is on her hands and knees, the black magic still clinging to her eyes. I don't know where her mind is, but I don't care. She's blind, and she'll stay that way for a very long time.

Maybe forever.

I rush to retrieve my twin swords before approaching my final opponents. Drake conjures a gust of wind so strong it knocks Rev off his feet. Why isn't he using magic?

He saved me. I swear, realization hitting me. He drained his magic saving Raven. One more way I'll owe him.

He leaps up and begins their dance anew.

I find my second sword and grip it tightly, all the while watching as the males twist and swing. Block and shift. The clang of metal against metal and the patter of shifting feet like a beat to which I could create a symphony.

I make haste to join the fray, but Drake sees me coming, and before I reach them, the beat changes. Drake's wind rushes into Rev's feet, knocking him off balance. Rev nearly misses blocking Drake's flying blade. The clang reverberates through the arena, sharp blade inches from his nose.

"Rev!" I shout. Drake double downs and his hilt slams into Rev's temple.

I swear. Rev crumples on the edge of the platform, inches from falling into the trenches below.

Before Drake can serve the killing blow, I leap between them, creating a new rhythm. Quicker. Sharper.

I take the aggressive stance and maneuver him away from Rev.

"Brielle!" Drake calls between swings. "Brielle."

"She's not coming," I snap.

"Worthless," he spits, glancing at the still heaving Brielle clawing at the black ink covering her face. With renewed vigor—or perhaps desperation—Drake leaps at me, his wind twisting and pulling at me, but his magic is weak. He used too much of it defending himself against my attack on Brielle.

I smile. I can beat him, even with little magic left.

His strength was in manipulation. He can fight, but it's not his strength, and he's already tiring. We cross the arena, my twin blades flying, striking swift and true. Drake's face is red with fury.

A tingle of magic swirls in my chest. It's small, just an inkling of what I had minutes ago. But he thinks I'm drained entirely. Another wind gust blasts me from behind, but I watch his eyes and duck just before he swings at my head.

"Dammit!" he screams.

Our dance approaches Brielle, sobbing into the stone as she scoots from the skirmish, only stopping when she reaches the edge. She has nowhere else to go, but she's too petrified to fight.

I leap back, close to the edge, readying my moment. Brielle is just at his back.

"Out of the way!" he yells at Brielle, turning away from me. He shoves his boot into her side, and she topples over the edge with a pathetic scream.

"She wasn't even a threat," I yell. She's my enemy, and I still wouldn't have treated her that way unnecessarily.

"But she still had to go over."

I shake my head. What a damned fool.

I leap at him, flying back into the pattern of our fight. I step and move, let him think he has control. Let him think I have nothing left to give.

His blade slices into my thigh just before I move away. I cry out but keep fighting. The wound is shallow but the sight of bright red blood seems to fuel him. Anger fills me again, and I throw it into my swings. He smiles, his eyes lighting.

He thinks he's won.

"Think again," I tell him just before releasing my very last blast of magic, my last shot at this. His eyes grow wide as the inky black magic slams into his chest and sends him flying toward the edge—right where Brielle had just been.

Maybe she'd have stopped him from toppling over, had he not already pushed her off.

He screams, scrambling for a grip on the edge of the platform, his fingers dig into the loose dirt, but he can't hold his whole weight. He slides off the edge of the platform and out of the Trial of Thorns.

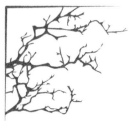

Caelynn

My chest heaves, air struggling to enter my lungs. Holy crap.

I beat Drake. I destroyed Brielle.

The crowd rumbles around me but nothing changes. There's no announcement. No shift in the arena.

I roll my shoulders and realize it's not over yet.

There is still one opponent left.

Rev.

With a long deep breath, I find him on his knees on the far end of the arena. His face is pale, his arm twisted awkwardly, his magic drained. His presence in the arena is a technicality. The crowd is already celebrating my win.

A roar of boos and a symphony of cheers compete around me. They love me. They hate me.

Rev's eyes are dim as he meets my stare. "You did it," he says with a sad smile. "You won."

I swallow. "Did I?"

His eyebrows pull down in confusion.

"You saved her."

He nods slowly.

"You used all of your magic to save Raven's life." I shake my head, still trying to understand. "You don't even know who she is."

He shrugs. "She was a human girl. Young. Innocent. And you love her. What else did I need to know?"

My knees buckle, and I slide to the ground, muscles losing their will to fight. "You gave it up, all of it. For me."

He looks down at his hands. "I made a choice."

My teeth chatter. "So have I."

My resolve firms in my mind, and I force strength back into my legs, enough to stand, jaw tight as I face the crowd that has quieted to a dull cheer and scattered chattering—they're wondering what we're saying.

"Attention courts!" I scream. "Today, someone has proven themselves your rightful champion!"

The crowd screams.

"Today, a terrible crime was committed before you all. An innocent life taken for no reason but petty revenge. But luckily for all of us, there was a hero here."

I pause, taking in long breaths. "Brielle of the Flicker Court took an innocent child's life right in front of you. And Reveln of the Luminescent Court saved that child's life at great cost to himself—with you all as witnesses. He used all of his magic to bring her back." *For me*, I leave out.

"Isn't that what a champion is?" I cry louder than before. Tears sting my eyes. I believe what I'm saying. I believe it with everything inside of me.

The crowd hushes at that.

"Caelynn," Rev warns. "What are you doing? You won."

"Isn't that what a savior is?" I scream again, emotion breaking my voice. I take in another deep breath. "To all the courts—ruling and non—I tell you today that your world is in good hands." I pause for a quiet sob before focusing every ounce of strength I have left. "I give you the winner of the Trial of Thorns!" I scream. "I give you Reveln of the Luminescent Court—your savior."

I meet Rev's gaze one more time, then hop off the platform, leaving him alone with the raging crowd.

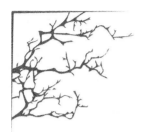

Rev

My mouth falls open as Caelynn leaps out of the arena, forfeiting her chance to be the champion.

She tore apart Brielle's mind while I fought Drake—and lost. And she beat him.

But then she gave the victory to me.

The crowd thunders around me, so loud I can barely think. She could have just pushed me over. Shit, she could have just told me to jump—I would have. I almost did before she started shouting to the crowd. The victory belonged to her.

Will the High Court even accept this result? A contestant choosing to let me win?

Based on the crowd's response, they're happy with the result. I was the favorite to win from the start. Many hope and expect me to be their next ruler, so they're pleased to see me crowned as champion.

But am I even deserving? Is Caelynn right?

She knew I'd given up the chance to win to save the girl, and she found a way to give it back to me.

The ground shudders beneath me as the outsides of the arena raise back into place. I'm alone in the massive arena for several minutes while the crowd continues their cheering. They chant my name over and over.

"Courts!" a voice booms over the crowd, magically amplified. "I give you your savior—Reveln of the Luminescent Court!"

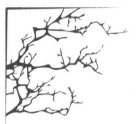

Caelynn

Raven trembles in my arms as I listen to the crowd chanting Rev's name. As the queen announces him as the winner.

Good, they accepted my speech then.

"What happens now?" she whispers to me.

"We go home," I say, hoping it's the truth.

I don't know how the High Court will react to Raven or treat me now that I gave up my chance to be their champion and hand it over to Reveln. No one dares come near me in the moments after the trials. The worker fae scuttle around me but move out of the way as I guide Raven from the arena.

No one stops me as I take her all the way up to my room and close the door. I hold her tightly, exhausted beyond all reason.

"I'm so sorry, Raven. I love you. I do. I want you with me always, but I swear, I'm going to do what's best for you from now on. I don't care what it costs me. I don't care if it hurts you."

"I know," she says soothingly. "I know."

Together, we fall into bed, curled up in each other's arms and fall into a deep sleep.

Caelynn

A soft knock on my door rouses me from a fitful sleep.
I groan and shift but Raven pulls me closer. "No,"
she begs, grabbing my upper arms in a tight grip.

I kiss her forehead and chuckle. "Someone is at the door.
We should probably get it."

She sits up as I crawl out of bed and cross the room. Her
eyes are wide in fear.

"I'll protect you," I whisper, then open the door.

A centaur stands there, his head and eyebrows high.
"Miss Caelynn. Your presence has been requested by the
High Queen."

I swallow. That's not unexpected but unnerving all the
same.

He looks down at my ragged clothing. I'm still wearing
my fighting leathers from the trials last night. "Do you wish
to change?"

I look down at the ripped and frayed clothing. "No. I'm
fine."

"Very well. Come along."

I begin to follow him, but he pauses. "Bring the girl."

My eyes grow wide. "Why?"

"This pertains to her as well."

I purse my lips but I nod. Nothing I can do about it. They'll find her eventually. "Raven?" I hold my hand out to her.

She scrambles out of bed and grips my hand tightly in hers. Together, we follow the centaur hand in hand.

We reach the great hall, where I assume the queen is waiting. The double doors open wide for Raven and I to step through. I keep my head high, but Raven dips hers, nearly cowering.

We stand at the top of the stairs beside the centaur. "Your Highness, may I present Caelynn of the Shadow Court and her raven," he calls.

"Come down," the queen says.

I pull Raven along, down the stairs to a table where the queen and several court officials sit. Including Rev's father. I stop, looking over the fae in front of me. They're all at least a hundred years old and powerful—in more ways than one. This is the current ruling generation, the heads of each ruling court.

We stand before them and wait.

The queen stands, her harsh eyes direct and commanding. "Miss Caelynn, you've caused quite the stir."

"Did you expect anything less?" I ask. To my surprise several chuckles break the tension.

"No, I did not." She smiles. "But I did not expect you to bring a human child into our courts. Or into the trials for that matter. You do realize how reckless that was, don't you?"

"If she didn't before," Reveln's father says, his eyes dark, his hair a light shade of brown, "she certainly does now."

I ignore his comment. "Yes."

"Then, tell me. Why did you?"

I swallow. "It was a selfish choice, I realize. I did it... because I didn't want to be alone."

"And neither did I," Raven adds in a whisper, pulling me closer, her hand tight over mine.

"You have no one in your own world?" a fae female beside the queen asks.

Raven shakes her head. "My parents are drug addicts. They haven't been around for a long time."

"I see," the queen says. "The matter of the girl is quite simple, miss Caelynn. She will return home and never be allowed in our realm again."

My eyes widen in surprise. Usually, humans who make their way to the fae realm are never allowed to leave. She's ruling the opposite.

"She is not nor will she ever be safe here. You can understand that, yes?"

I take in a long breath. "Yes, ma'am."

Raven has proven herself important to me, everyone will know about her now. Even if I'd won, I would still be hated. There will still be those that seek to hurt me. She'll be a target if she stays here, even among the humans.

"You on the other hand—" she begins.

"I won't be banished?" I interrupt. I assumed losing the trials meant I'd immediately return to my former punishment.

"You have already been banished," Rev's father spits.

The queen eyes him, and he sits back, crossing his arms in open annoyance, but his jaw clamps shut.

"Your previous punishment has not been revoked, Cae-lynn. However, as runner up to the trials... you do still hold importance."

"Runner up?"

"Yes. This task will not be easy, and it is very possible that Reveln will not survive his time beyond the walls of the Schorchedlands."

My stomach twists.

"As you know, only one can return from that dark place. But more than one can go, but we will choose one at a time so we don't forfeit our most powerful fae uselessly. It was important we give the honor to the right person. The right court. It was important that everyone had a fair chance. Rev will have his chance."

"So you'll send me, if..."

"If Rev dies, yes."

I bite my lip. I don't like how she says *if he dies*, like she expects him to. Reveln has been the target for assassins since he was an adolescent. I tap my finger on my thigh.

"And if you do not survive, Drake will be sent. Then Brielle. You get the idea."

I nod.

"Until the cure is retrieved, I'd like to allow the tempo-rary suspension of your banishment to remain."

I blink rapidly. "I can stay?"

"For now."

Rev's father slams his hands on the table and stands. "That's ludicrous," he hollers. Again, the queen shoots him an angry stare. Just one look is all it takes. He sits and puffs out his chest, composing himself. "She won't be safe here. Do you know how many people still desire her death?"

"Like you?" I spit.

He narrows his eyes at me but doesn't respond.

"He is correct, you may not always be safe in the fae realm. But I suspect you will do well inside the shadow lands. What do you think, Caelynn?"

My mouth falls open. "I can go back to the shadow lands?"

"They will take care of you, I am sure."

This is not at all what I'd expected. Raven squeezes my hand suddenly, and I realize the problem with this offer. "That is... very generous of you. I am honored, truly." I turn my attention to Raven. "But I don't think I can leave her alone. Not right now."

"If you had won? Would you have left her then? Or would you have brought her into the Schorchedlands with you?"

"Of course not! If I'd won, I would have done my duty. We'd talked about that already." Raven nods somberly at my words. "But I didn't. I don't get the rewards; I shouldn't also get the punishment."

"Well said. You may go home with your human, if that is your wish. But you may also enter the fae realm as you wish until otherwise declared. I will announce your protection under my name until the time the cure is found. However, even my reach is not powerful enough to keep all enemies from you. You will do well to keep our Lord of the Luminescent Court's warning in mind. You may have made an ally of the Luminescent heir— "

Rev's father coughs and curls his lip in disgust.

"But you still have enemies," the queen continues. "Enemies who may deem the consequences worth the reward of your death."

I nod.

"You may leave, Caelynn of the Shadow Court."

I bow my head and then pull Raven back up the stairs and out of the hall.

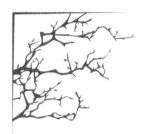

Rev

Caelynn comes rushing from the banquet hall, the human girl tucked under her arm protectively.

She freezes the moment she sees me, waiting just outside the doors. "Rev." Her voice is soft.

"That was quite a scene you created yesterday." I shake my head, unable to meet her eyes. Am I still supposed to hate her? I don't know.

"You saved me," the human squeaks in my direction.

I nod.

"Thank you."

"That debt has been repaid," I say, eyes on Caelynn whose cheeks turn red. "I'm still not sure what to make of it. That wasn't the victory I'd imagined."

"I suppose not," Caelynn says smoothly, "but you're still beloved. And once you retrieve the cure, no one will doubt you."

I pull in a long breath. Yes, the cure. The whole thing I competed for—the chance to torture myself to save the world. *Right.*

I can do it, I remind myself.

"When do you go?"

I blink. "Soon. They want to make sure I am fully prepared and my health restored. I heard you're allowed to stay."

I smile, not mentioning the fact that it was my idea. And that my father doesn't know I made the suggestion. He already nearly disowned me the first moment he laid eyes on me after the trial's conclusion.

He wasn't happy I'd aligned with Caelynn but he seemed even more enraged once I won. My mother tells me he hates *how* I won.

I suspect he hates that I won at all.

Now, he can't disown me without making his personal information public. He's just going to have to hope I die in the Schorchedlands. I know he's not the only one.

I also don't plan to tell Caelynn about my dream last night—that creature from the caves whispering threats. Telling me I will perish inside the walls of the Schorchedlands. Laughing at me. At us, for thinking we can beat him.

I swallow and shake the thoughts from my mind. It was just paranoia, nothing more.

"Yes, they allowed me to stay. But..." Her eyes turn to the black-haired girl under her arm.

"You're going back to the human world... with her?" I ask, my stomach squeezing uncomfortably. I don't know why that bothers me. It's not like she could stay in the Flicker Court or travel to the Luminescent Court. She wouldn't be safe in either.

"Yes."

"But she'll be back," the girl adds.

Caelynn's eyebrows pull down.

Raven smiles. "I know you want to be here."

Caelynn shakes her head absently. "We'll talk about it later."

"Well," I say, awkwardly. "I suppose, I'll see you. Maybe."
Hopefully.

"Thank you for everything, Rev. I know..." she shakes her head. "I know this was complicated and painful, but our... alliance means a lot to me."

I take in a breath. "Friendship," I amend.

Another blush crosses her cheeks, and I find that I quite like it.

"Friends?" she asks sheepishly.

I nod. "Just don't tell my father."

"One more secret to add to the bunch." She laughs. "If you need anything, ever. Schorchedlands or not. I'll come."

Her smile is small and sad but real. I watch my brother's murderer walk away and soak in the irony of how much I hate to see her leave.

The ache in my gut tells me this isn't over.

This is only beginning.

KEEP READING FOR A sneak peek at next book of the Wicked Fae series, Curse of Thorns!

Acknowledgements

First, thank you to my husband, Sean. Indie publishing is so much more of a commitment than what we've been used to (because I had to do nearly EVERYTHING myself). Thank you for supporting this dream of mine.

Thank you to Lisa Murray Kroger and Madeline Dyer for your awesome feedback! Karen Meeus and Claudia Frazer for assisting in proofreading!

Thank you to my beta readers Kelley York for the lovely cover and Cait Marie at Functionally Fiction for copy editing!

All my newsletter and everyone at Stacey's Page Turners members for helping me to name characters and overall being supporting and amazing people! I couldn't do this without you!!!

All the awesome indie author Facebook groups, especially Author POD of Awesomeness. Can't wait to read all of your fae books!!!

Night Bringer

Read Caelynn's prequel story, available on my website now! www.StaceyTrombley.com

Even the most evil monsters can be outwitted

Caelynn adores her homelands in the Shadow Court, but as the one of the poorest and weakest courts in the realm there's little opportunity for a talented fae like her.

When she overhears her parents deciding to send her away to a different court she runs away—straight to the Cave of Mysteries to jump start her initiation into the court she loves. She'll become a shadow fae or die trying.

But there are monsters in those deep tunnels. The Night Bringer is waiting for her. And once she's in his clutches there is only one way out.

Outwit him.

Curse of Thorns
Rev

The door to the banquet hall slams open and the monotone voices of the Luminescent Court royals are hushed in an instant. Some stop mid bite to watch the intruder, wide-eyed. The whole court is frozen, even myself, as a blond fae in skinny jeans and thick black boots—our sworn enemy— stomps down the aisle towards the ruling family. Towards me.

Admittedly, Rev of six months ago would have stood, sword in hand, eager for the chance to remove her beautiful head from her beautiful body. Today...I still don't know what to feel. A desire to kill her is the only thing I *don't* feel.

Excitement. Intrigue. Amusement. Fear. Pride. Concern.

I can't help but glance at my father's expression—it's a moment I suspect I'll cherish the rest of my life. His face is red, eyes dark but wide. He's shocked—and pissed—to see her here. I hold the image in my mind for just long enough to memorize it, then I turn back.

As she marches forward, past fae shrinking back in fear, murmuring begins and I'm reminded of her homeland. Whispers that bounce through the dark leaves of the shade maples. Of the expression on Caelynn's face as she stood in the Whisper Wood for the first time in a decade. For the first time since killing my brother.

My stomach sinks.

And it sinks a second time as she draws close enough for me to see what's in her hand.

A head.

She carries the head of a fae swinging by its white hair, crimson blood dripping onto the marble floor of our banquet hall. Caelynn's face is impassive, her eyes harsh but glowing with golden light. Her ability to hide the brightness of her eyes is a talent I've not run across before. She uses emotional pain to hide her power when she desires.

Right now, she has no desire to hide the massive amounts of magic flowing through her veins.

She's killed another fae from my court. Jasper, I recognize. He's been a guard since I was a child. She stares straight ahead at my father, her signature indifferent expression on her face. My mother and I on either side of him.

Guards charge in, feet stomping loudly—a bit delayed, I'll admit—but my father holds up his hand, his eyes never leaving Caelynn's. The guards freeze, swords still held at the ready.

She reaches our table, and drops the dismembered head on my father's still full plate. I flinch at the squishing sound it makes as flesh meets his dinner plate. Blood pools, dripping onto his fork. His hooded gaze regards her, his features much more controlled than mine are. How does he block out that putrid smell?

Caelynn leans in, her long neck stretching over the table, her blond hair dropping into the bloody mess tinging the tips of the strands in red. "Next time you send an assassin for me, make it a better one." She smiles, eyes alight with wickedness. "Oh, that's right, you sent two." Her head tilts innocently.

Sick amusement fills my belly and I have to hold back a smirk at the spectacle. One glance down at the grey skin of the dead face on my father's plate is sobering enough to keep my wits about me.

My father's eyes narrow but he doesn't respond. He doesn't so much as flinch—is he breathing?

"Don't underestimate me again," Caelynn says, leaning back and folding her hands behind her back casually. "Or I'll be tempted to send the next head to the High Queen and let her know of what you think of her ordinances."

Caelynn was banished from the fae realm a decade ago, but it was temporarily rescinded while the queen searched for a savior, someone designated to travel into fae-hell to fetch the cure for a terrible plague. As runner up, Caelynn is currently under the queen's protection. Once the cure is secured, her banishment will be reinstated.

If my father were to send assassins to the human world to kill Caelynn once this is all over with, no one would bat an eyelash but right now? While the queen herself has declared Caelynn to be under her protection?... it wouldn't go well for him.

My father wrinkles his nose but otherwise doesn't speak. His eyes flit down to the head on the table for the first time.

"Yes, the other is alive." Caelynn says, as if answering the question, he didn't voice. "You'll find him on edge of your boundary, strung up in a tree."

Caelynn turns on her heel and my stomach sinks for a third time. Not because of what she did or who she is, but because while she was here, she never, not once, looked in my direction.

WE WATCH IN AWE AS Caelynn leaves the banquet hall. I quickly grab a napkin and use magic to scrawl a quick note. Then I hand it to the wide-eyed and tense guard standing behind me. "Be sure our visitor gets this before she leaves."

The guard blinks but then nods proudly and marches from the room, apparently relived at his new orders. In-action tends to be a difficult task.

The moment the door shuts behind Caelynn the room breaks into chaos with whispers and shouts. There are close to fifty royal Luminescent courtiers here for our weekend banquet. This was a larger show than I suspect Caelynn expected. Every Friday night, we invite every Lumi-fae of rank to join us for a meal. It's a weekly tradition. It's a bit pompous and annoying, most of the time but at least here, my father must keep his sharp tongue to himself.

Luckily for us, despite the number of fae that witnessed Caelynn's show, the people in this room are privy to many court secrets and it's unlikely for this one to get out.

"How did she get in here?" my father says loudly. The captain of the guard scurries to stand before my father.

"It's unclear, sir. She snuck by several on duty guards. We'll conduct a thorough investigation immediately."

"I want those guards banished," my father announces.

The captain winces.

"Without trial?" my mother whispers.

"Caelynn is a shadow walker, father," I say. "I imagine it would be quite easy for her to get around even our most astute guards."

"That is no excuse! She is our enemy!"

"Clearly," I mumble and my father shoots me a glare that could cut through ice. I raise my eyebrows but then sit back in my chair casually. I have more power now than ever before. More than my father is used to just yet. I won the Trials, which makes me quite influential and, though the queen hasn't announced it officially, a shoo-win for the high court—if I can survive the Schorchedlands.

My father must accept my voice, particularly in front of the entire court. "Conduct the investigation," I tell the guard. "We will discuss their punishment in the meantime. However, you can be sure there will be no grace given if it happens a second time. Learn what you can about shadow walkers and how to use our natural abilities against shadow magic. Caelynn is particularly resourceful and powerful. Learn from this mistake—all of us—and do not underestimate her again."

My father purses his lips, something he does when he's considering being impressed. He nods his acceptance of my command to the captain of the guard. The captain nods sharply, his shoulders less tense than only moments before. Then he marches from the hall.

Now, the whispers are settled my father announces than everyone in the room is duty bound never to mention what they saw today. Together, we will defeat this "great enemy."

I, however, am eager to be done with dinner, so I can talk to this *great enemy* before she leaves forever.

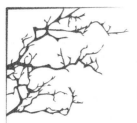

Caelynn

The guards allow me exit through the mains gates with no more than a few sneers. I simply wink and smile, while also realizing with hidden sympathy that they may have known the fae I just presented to the king is an incredibly brutal manner.

If I could go back, I'd have found a more private way to make my point. Like maybe his bedroom in the middle of the night. I'd have loved to make him pee his sheets. My smile grows wider.

One guard rushes towards me, and I shift into a defensive stance but he simply hands me a piece of paper. Wait, no, that's a napkin.

My eyebrows pull down as I examine the napkin and unfold it.

I hope you don't intend to leave
without paying your old ally a visit.

My eyebrows rise and then my lips curl into a surprising smile. It seems the prince wants to see me before I leave. It's also a relief that he doesn't seem to be angry with my actions. I did kill a fae from his court, after all.

I pause to consider. I doubt I'd be welcomed to just walk into the palace for a chat with the prince, even if he'd invited me.

"Thank you," I tell the guard then turn and continue my slow walk. I'd had other plans but now, I suppose I'll have to alter those slightly. The Queen of The Whisperwood can wait one more day, I suppose.

GETTING THROUGH THE gates of the Luminescent Court was surprisingly easy the second time. I don't suspect they considered I'd leave, just to turn back and hop back through their defenses a moment later. The guards are still reeling from the first "invasion" as I heard them call it and hardly looked up to consider a return trip.

I cover myself in shadow and slip over the white grass, sparkling like glitter was dumped everywhere, then past the crystal pond, and a maze made of bright white hedges. Everything here is white, reflecting sunlight everywhere. The palace itself is made of white marble and the damn thing reflects so much light it hurts my eyes.

It's beautiful, in a typical sort of way. It's just...not really my style.

I slip into a pantry window, and down the hall, up a set of spiral stairs and to Rev's bedroom door in only moments. I know my way around this place fairly well. I spent three full days hiding out here when I was a teenager.

The Night Bringer, an ancient being that tricked me into a terrible bargain, sent me to this court during a ball all so I could assassinate a prince.

I could have completed my end of the bargain before the ball ended and no one would have known I was the culprit.

I was promised magic stronger than any Shadow Court fae in a hundred generations, and influence. I could pull my poor, mistreated court out of obscurity with one stab of an obsidian dagger. I only had to steal one life.

I was guaranteed to get away with my crime and go on to live the life I'd always dreamed of. And most importantly—I would be free of the curse I was trapped in the day that monster caught me in his clutches.

If I failed my mission, I'd be his slave for eternity.

I had no choice but to comply. Except, when I'd met my mark, the fae I was sent to kill— I couldn't do it. So I went to that ball, and danced in that same banquet hall I just presented the dismembered head of a fae assassin to the king, only hours ago. I'd danced with the youngest heir of the Luminescent Court not realizing who he was.

The king's second son. The youngest heir of the Luminescent Court King. The fae I was ordered to kill.

And he was incredible. Kind and sweet and handsome. And for those few minutes while I spun in circles beneath their glittering lights, held in his arms—I forgot my pain. My fear. My confusion. My doubt.

For those moments I was simply a young fae dancing with a handsome boy who made me feel beautiful. Until I realized he was my mark.

The Night Bringer would give me everything I wanted, all I had to do was kill an innocent and good male fae. All I had to do was to kill my fated mate.

It's too bad I was so good at secrets. Maybe, if I hadn't been so clever I wouldn't have figured out at Rev was my mate and I would have been able to do the deed.

Instead, I hid.

I couldn't leave the palace or the Night Bringer would find me and declare I'd failed. I had to keep trying. So I stayed hidden in the shadows of his palace for three days, searching for some escape.

I was alone and freaked out, hiding from my fate.

So yes, I know more about this place than any outsider should.

I tap on the door.

It swings open quickly, revealing a very shocked Rev.

"Caelynn." He blinks. "How did you—"

"Never underestimate a Shadow Court fae." I wink.

He knows I killed his brother in this palace. He doesn't know how much time I spent here. He doesn't know that I spied on him too, while desperately searching for a way to save him.

I did. I found a loophole that could save his life and keep me from the Night Bringer's clutches. But it meant killing his brother.

His brother was a sadistic arrogant fool that deserved his fate. I am not sorry for shoving a dagger through his chest, because of how he treated me and others. Because of what he threatened to do to me. Because the realm is better off without him as their king. And because by killing him I out witted the Night Bringer and saved Rev.

I'm proud of that kill and no matter how much Rev loved his brother, I can't stop that from being true. I hate myself for many things and one of them is that feeling, that sick joy swirling around inside makes me a bad person.

And that's the reason Rev and I can never be together.

I won the game, but I lost Rev. We lost our life together. Because I'm his brother's murderer, and that will never go away.

Rev lets me into his room. I shift awkwardly, crossing my arms gently as I glance around his bedroom. It's mostly the same as a decade ago—I don't think he even knows I've been here.

The desk in the corner is larger than before, more ornate. Dark mahogany instead of white, a nice contrast. There's a huge quadruple set of shelves covering the far wall full of books and a few knick knacks. I cross the room, eyes pinned to a shoe wedged between two sets of leather-bound books.

A female's lovely black heeled boot. My breath comes out shaky as I stare at it. Had he had it back then? I didn't notice.

I clear my throat and turn back to him. "So, how's the plans to save the world coming?" I ask him casually, trying not to show any more emotion than is necessary. This place brings up memories, good and bad. Memories better left buried.

My breathing is just a tad too shallow, heart pounding too fast.

He watches me closely. His hair has grown since the end of the trials. Black locks swept to the side so they don't fall into his eyes. He's wearing a casual tunic, the sleeves rolled to his elbows exposing his intricate black thorn tattoos. His eyes are bright, brighter than I've seen them. The trials were a source of pain and fear and exhaustion which dimmed the true color of his silver eyes.

"Not as well as I'd have hoped." His eyes darken.

My eyebrows rise but I shrug. "You're not dead yet. Can't be all that bad." I smirk but it fades as I notice his expression. Something is wrong.

"It's... not good, I'll tell you that."

I purse my lips. "What is it?"

"You can't tell anyone. No mention of it. Not even to my father."

I laugh. "Your father? You're joking right." With any luck I'll never even be in the same room with that man.

He shrugs. "You could assume he knows and let something slip in passing. He doesn't, he doesn't know."

"Well, I'm very good with secrets." I walk past the white cushioned bench, and sit on the window sill that overlooks a small copse of white leaved trees in the courtyard below.

"I was supposed to enter the Schorchedlands three weeks ago."

I open my mouth but stop and snap it back closed. Rev stares at the ground intensively, his expression grim.

"Why haven't you?" I say casually, but anxiety curls in my stomach. This mission is everything. To him and the realm.

He sits on edge of silver sheets of his massive four poster bed that I have very purposefully not glanced towards. His hands fall into his lap and he stares at them. "In order to enter the Schorchedlands," he begins slowly, "You must pass through the wall of thorns. It is impenetrable for a physical body—only bodiless souls can pass."

I nod absently. It's called "fae hell" for a reason. It is the permanent home for souls too wicked to find peace in the afterlife.

"The only exception is the Wicked Gate. The Wicked Gate will allow one being to enter and return with their body intact every ten years."

"Yes," I prompt him to go on.

"Well the gate refused to allow me to pass."

Rev meets my eye, the color dimming. My stomach sinks.

"Why?" I breathe. "Someone else has already passed?"

He shakes his head.

"Then what?"

"I went three weeks ago. The queen wanted to keep the journey quiet as long as possible, knowing my time inside may be longer than the people expect and they will get nervous. So, I went without out anyone knowing. I approached the gate, slit my palm and pressed the blood against the door. Nothing happened."

"Nothing at all?"

"It whispered to me. A message. It said, *the one who enters must belong*. And then it flung me backwards onto my damn butt." He sighs. "I tried three times. It stopped whispering to me and wouldn't even let me approach any longer."

I blink several times, trying to wrap my mind around it. We fought, fifteen of the strongest fae, one from each court in a brutal competition. The winner was chosen to enter the Schorchedlands in order to save us all. Inside those walls, among the souls of evil fae, is a cure to the curse plaguing our lands. But the one who won the games... cannot enter.

That's... interesting. And potentially bad. Really, really bad.

If all of this was for nothing, if there's no hope for us to retrieve the cure—our world is doomed. And for Rev personally...

He needed to win the trails to prove his place in his own court, or risk being outed as a bastard. His father has quietly looked for ways to get him out of the way without his dirty business –i.e. his queen's apparent affair—coming to light. For many years he's worked to undermine his ability to rule, spread rumors and belittled him in front of his people. Now that he won the trials, there's no hope such small actions could turn the people against their beloved prince.

Now, his only hope is killing him. Unless..

"Do you think your father could be behind it?" I ask.

Rev blinks. "How? Why?"

"He hates that you won. He wants you to look the fool...He wants to find any reason to disinherit you." Or excuse that fact that you never were an heir to begin with.

Worse than losing the trials and his princely status, if he were to fail in his *responsibility* to save the realm... his father would have all the ammo he needs. If he cannot enter the Schorchedlands, he will be considered a failure. Everyone will blame him. Thousands of deaths will be on his hands.

He considers this, face crumpled in concentration. It's adorable, actually. "But would be really put the entire realm at risk in order to achieve it?"

I bite my lip. "Maybe he'll wait for your failure to be exposed, then orchestrate a solution—I don't know, let Drake get through so he'll be the savior instead of you. It would by-pass me as the runner up too."

Rev shakes his head dumbfoundedly. "That's quite a conspiracy."

I chuckle. It is. Any yet I wouldn't put it past these wicked men. But I nod, "You're right, there are probably more realistic options to consider first."

I first wonder if the gate does not recognize Rev as the winner of the trials. It was a fairly...controversial ending. I beat our opposition and then gave the win to the magically drained Reveln because he'd sacrificed his chance to win to save Raven's life.

Perhaps, to the gate, I am the rightful savior.

That would imply some kind of magical bargain the High Court made with the gate itself, and I'm unsure if that's even possible let alone likely. Does the gate actually care who won?

It seems to care who enters.

My next thought is that Rev is too...pure. Too good for that place. It is hell, after all. The message was *the one who enters must belong*. My translation: the soul of the being allowed to pass must belong in that wicked place.

Rev isn't exactly a saint, though, so even that seems outlandish.

These two theories are still problematic because even if someone else could enter and retrieve the cure... Rev would still be considered a failure. He'd be the fae who should have saved the realm, and left them to die, forcing another to save them.

"So, now what?" I say softly.

"I'm working with the queen for a solution and well, stalling."

"Do you have any theories?"

"Some. None I like."

I bite my lip and nod. I look out the window, to the lands beyond this one. I came come straight here from the human world because I wanted to give the king of the Luminescent Court a message but I do have something quite important I want to do before my banishment is reinstated.

I haven't been free in the fae realm in a decade. Allowed to travel anywhere.

As a child I had one goal. One wish. All I wanted, truly wanted, was to be a full member of the Shadow Court.

I was trapped into the Night Bringer's web before I reached even my first rite of passage. If I completed those two, I'd be invited to the Shadow Castle to meet the Queen of the Whisper Wood. The castle is ancient and massive, a relic of the time our court was powerful, rather than poverty ridden.

I'd be invited now, if only I could make my way across the realm. I could fuel it with my magic—a gift from the very creature that destroyed my life. My pain could give the court I love life, for a little while at least.

I sniff. Ironically enough, those rites of passage I was barred from as a child were two of the tasks we completed during the trials. Now all that's left is being welcomed by the queen inside her throne room.

I've met my queen, a few times now, but never in our own court. And I still have never set foot inside my own court's palace. I long, more than anything else, to go there.

To see it for myself. The history of our people. The remnants of our pride, our power that was taken from us so long ago.

I could have this one thing. It's small, and maybe even pointless. But it's something I always wanted, something I mourned during my time in the human world.

And I could have it now. All I'd have to do is leave here and go take it.

All I'd have to do is abandon Rev in his time of need.

Maybe if I'd thought it through, I wouldn't have given the win to Rev. Because if I'd won the trials, I would have been free and able to use my magic to help my poor kingdom, lift them out of obscurity and give them hope.

But I'm not sorry. I've always picked him over me. And I'm going to do it again.

I sigh, knowing I won't be travelling to the Shadow Court any time soon. I won't enter those palace walls like I've dreamed about so many times.

Because right now, Rev needs my help. And I won't fail him.

Printed in Great Britain
by Amazon

16101971R00226